Readers are ~~falling in~~ love wi~~th~~

with this kiss

'This book was everything I didn't know I needed. A story of love, friendship, knowing yourself . . . and a big dose of hope'

'A delight to read . . . Captured me from the start'

'I have loved all of Carrie's books and this was no exception. Highly recommended'

'A five-star read . . . I was completely absorbed in this story'

'A love story with a difference . . . excellent'

'An original idea, with great characters . . . Escapism at its best. Loved it'

'A charming book that I read in one sitting'

More praise for
with this kiss

'*With This Kiss* was a complete joy to read, and once I'd started, I genuinely couldn't stop . . . I was entranced and beguiled from start to finish by this beautiful story'

Jill Mansell

'Spellbinding and enchanting . . . guaranteed to sweep you off your feet . . . Captivating and beautifully written, this is a story about not giving up on true love'

Holly Miller, author of *The Sight Of You*

'Spellbindingly romantic . . . A feat of magical and mystical storytelling'

Laura Jane Williams, author of *Our Stop*

'I loved the original premise to this magical story . . . the sweet, slow-burning romance with Grayson was written beautifully . . . you'll be rooting for [Lorelai] to find her happily-ever-after'

My Weekly

'Carrie Hope Fletcher is not afraid to tackle big themes in this ambitious story, and the emotional pay-off cuts deep'

Heat, Book of the Week

'A timeless romance that will pull on your heartstrings'

New!

Carrie Hope Fletcher is an actress, singer, author and vlogger. Carrie's first book, *All I Know Now*, was a number one *Sunday Times* bestseller and her debut novel, *On the Other Side*, also went straight to number one. She has written several more novels for adults and children, including the magical love story, *With This Kiss*, which was a *Sunday Times* bestseller.

Carrie played the role of Éponine in *Les Misérables* at the Queen's Theatre in London's West End for almost three years. She has since starred in and received awards for a number of productions including *The War of the Worlds*, *The Addams Family*, *Heathers: The Musical*, and Andrew Lloyd Webber's *Cinderella*, in which she played the lead role.

Carrie loves to connect with readers on social media. Find her on:

🐦 @CarrieHFletcher

📷 @CarrieHopeFletcher

📷 @PrattleAndPages

Also by Carrie Hope Fletcher

In the Time We Lost
When the Curtain Falls
All That She Can See
Winter's Snow (novella)
On the Other Side

Non-Fiction:
All I Know Now

Children's Fiction:
Into the Spotlight
The Double Trouble Society

Carrie Hope Fletcher

with this kiss

HQ

ONE PLACE. MANY STORIES

HQ
An imprint of HarperCollins*Publishers* Ltd
1 London Bridge Street
London SE1 9GF

www.harpercollins.co.uk

HarperCollins*Publishers*
Macken House, 39/40 Mayor Street Upper,
Dublin 1, D01 C9W8, Ireland

This edition 2023

1

First published in Great Britain by
HQ, an imprint of HarperCollins*Publishers* Ltd 2022

MIX
Paper | Supporting
responsible forestry
FSC™ C007454

This book is produced from independently certified FSC™ paper
to ensure responsible forest management.

For more information visit: www.harpercollins.co.uk/green

This book is set in 11.1/15.5 pt. Bembo by Type-it AS, Norway

Printed and Bound in the UK using 100% Renewable Electricity at
CPI Group (UK) Ltd, Croydon, CR0 4YY

This book is dedicated to all the 'Joanies' in my life.
You know who you are.
I don't know where I'd be without you.
Thank you.

xxx

PART ONE

The
Bad
Beginning

Prologue

How often does death cross your mind? Is it once a year, when you hear of a tragedy that sends you spiralling into an existential crisis? A scare that can only be escaped by vowing to live every day as if it were your last? Do you wake up each week in a cold sweat after dreaming a loved one passed away unexpectedly and, as soon as morning hits, you call to let them know they're loved? Or is it daily, when something as simple as the prospect of a kiss sends you reeling into the abyss? If you knew the lightness of your lips created such darkness, would you ever kiss me again? If you were me, would you press your mouth against another's, knowing the nightmare that awaits you? Or would you be done with it? Done with love and its embellishments and frivolities? So tell me, can you really call it living when all you do is run from death? Because if there's one thing I know with certainty it's that death will meet us all.

One

Lorelai wondered what it was about the small hours of the morning that made her mind so much clearer. Maybe it was the initial clarity that came once the fog lifted from yet another bad dream or maybe it was that Joanie, her best friend, was still fast asleep and therefore quiet. Either way, five o'clock in the morning seemed to be her sweet spot. Long enough after a nightmare for the gruesome details to subside yet soon enough after waking that she didn't slip back into tiredness. She had started leaving her notebook and her favourite pen out on the kitchen table each evening. This way, a rough night was sweetened with the prospect of doing what she loved the most as soon as she awoke – writing.

Lorelai crept into the kitchen to put the kettle on, and then tiptoed into the living room to browse her pride and joy: her books. Each book sat next to its movie or television version. Lorelai was fascinated by the differences between the book and its adaptation. How did screenwriters choose which scenes to cut, which characters to change and which lines of dialogue were so integral that they had to be kept? It fascinated her so much that she had adapted forty-three books herself and yet not one of them had ever been sent to anyone other than her grandmother, Sylvia, her biggest champion right up until the day she had died. Lorelai plucked *The Catcher in the Rye* from its place on the shelf and went back to the kitchen. It wasn't one of her favourites but it was one of the very few books she owned that hadn't already been adapted for the screen. She wasn't doing it for anyone but herself, although the dream of seeing at least one of them make it to the screen one day was particularly palpable at this time of the day. So much so she moved slowly out of fear that she might disturb the air and scare that almost tangible feeling of possibility away. A feeling that often made her shudder but when it came to writing she welcomed it with open arms.

'One day.'

Lorelai sighed to herself as she made her tea, sat at the table and opened her notebook. Two words she had said to herself maybe more so than any others. Two words that gave her so much hope and yet also kept her in a perpetual state of longing for a dream she was making no move towards achieving. She swept her long, tangled, dark hair into a scrappy bun on her head. She took a sip of her tea then took the lid off her pen and savoured the moment just before the tip of it hit the page, knowing once it made connection she wouldn't come up for air until Joanie was up and forced her to pay her some attention. It was the kind of blissful trance that only came with doing something you truly loved. Her job at The Duchess, a cinema that showed old movies from eras gone by, brought her joy, yes, but it didn't come close to touching these moments.

'It's like that feeling you get when you're reading a good book,' Lorelai had tried to explain to Joanie one day. 'It almost hurts to stop reading, and then, when you do have to put it down, all you can think about is reading it. As if living your life is just getting in the way of the time you could be spending in the world someone else has created.' Joanie had nodded slowly but Lorelai knew she'd zoned out at the first mention of reading.

'What ungodly hour were you up this time?' Joanie yawned from the doorway, rubbing yesterday's make-up further into her eyes, before stumbling towards the coffee machine. Joanie's nightwear was all black and dark grey. Lorelai often joked they matched her black heart but despite her wicked sense of humour and her often blunt delivery, Joanie was the kindest person Lorelai knew. They had met at The Duchess, and their friendship had been instant. It had only taken a few months before they decided becoming flatmates was a good idea and they had swiftly found a place to share in Bromley. They were complete opposites, but they just worked. Where Lorelai was quiet, Joanie was loud. Where Joanie was a little naive, Lorelai had more life experience. They both loved nights out, cats, and agreed wholeheartedly that pineapple did not belong on a pizza. It was a match made in heaven.

Lorelai blinked, realising only now just how sore her eyes were from staring at her notebook so intently. She turned to check the time on the kitchen clock. It was almost seven.

'Not that long ago,' she lied. She nodded towards the coffee machine. 'I'll have one if you're making.'

'You ever gonna let anyone read this one?' Joanie asked over her shoulder, pushing a piece of thick, white bread down into the toaster.

'Maybe,' Lorelai mumbled. Joanie had attempted to have this

conversation with her a million times before, but Lorelai wasn't ready to share her writing with anyone – not even her mother. Lorelai had become an expert in swivelling her mother's attempts at conversations away from herself a long time ago.

'Someone as talented as you should not be stuck sweeping up popcorn for the rest of her life.'

'I like sweeping up popcorn!' Lorelai said with complete conviction. It was corny, probably the writer in her, but she felt that the spilled popcorn was proof that people had had a good time and that's what she loved.

'Is it what you want to do forever though?' Joanie asked.

'No. But I'm only twenty-five! I have plenty of time to hone my craft and *then* send my work to film studios. It'll happen for me one day, I swear.' Lorelai crossed her heart with the end of her pen.

'As long as it actually happens *one day*, I'm happy.' Joanie sipped her coffee but then sniffed the air. 'Bollocks!' She jumped over to the toaster just as her bread was in danger of becoming charcoal. Lorelai took the moment to rest her head on her arms, the weight of her lost sleep finally catching up with her and pressing against her temples.

'Was it a bad one?' Joanie asked gently, scraping the blackened crispy bits into the bin.

Lorelai shrugged. She had always slept fitfully. Getting to sleep was never the issue – it was the nightmares. Brutal, twisted, terrorising nightmares that would wake her up, soaked in sweat and in floods of tears. Joanie was always nearby for some comfort and a cup of hot milk (or whisky if Joanie had her way) when they got bad enough that Lorelai needed company, someone to talk her down, but most of the time she dealt with the aftermath alone. Once awake, she stayed awake, not daring to close her eyes again and be consumed by the waves of terror once more. It had led her to her love of writing all those years ago, but now the nightmares were getting worse. More vivid. More frequent.

'Do you think it means something?' Joanie asked, her voice still soft and kind. 'That they're suddenly getting worse now, when they've been manageable before?'

Lorelai shrugged again, but she knew in her gut it wasn't a coincidence. How could it be? For years, nightmares had plagued her but the details faded almost instantly once she was awake. Now, all of sudden, not only could she remember everything, but the images were beginning to resurface when she was fully awake. The hairs on Lorelai's arms stood on end as the memory of the most recent nightmare forced its way out, front and centre. Dreams were easy to ignore when they were just that. Dreams. Non-existent, make-believe concoctions from your subconscious that never came true. Lorelai's nightmares were not the same.

Because they were formed from things she had seen long ago. Things that had, in fact, come true.

◆

First kisses aren't always as blissful and romantic as we make them out to be. Sometimes they can be quite traumatic. Some people butt teeth; It can be awkward for both people, or you make the wrong choice of kissing partner, but Lorelai's first kiss was traumatic in a different way.

She was thirteen years old and he was her first crush. He snuck a note into her pencil case that said he'd be waiting for her behind the giant hedge after school. The hedge lined the wall of the playground but there was a small break in the branches you could crawl through. Most people only went in there to retrieve missing footballs but there were rumours that it was also the location of many a surreptitious kiss.

Excitedly, Lorelai snuck away when no one was looking and crawled through the gap. There she found Arthur Trent, clutching the straps of his rucksack with sweaty hands. He had almost-black hair and skin so pale it was translucent. It couldn't have been more perfect. Lorelai vividly remembered how tentative they both were, the sweet anticipation of it all.

When their lips finally touched, Lorelai heard the crunch of bones in her ears. She tried to open her eyes but it was as if they were glued shut. Images were flashing through her mind at lightning speed.

An airbag. Shattered glass. Mangled metal. And the cold, lifeless, hauntingly familiar blue eyes of a boy she knew, but older, closer to the age of twenty.

Arthur finally pulled away and Lorelai's eyes shot open, meeting Arthur's wide-eyed gaze. She'd noticed his eyes a million times before. She'd stolen thousands of glances in class and quickly looked away, blushing, when he'd caught her staring. But now she had seen those same eyes dead, lifeless. Gone. Lorelai had no idea what she'd just seen, but she knew it had terrified her. And so she turned and ran as fast as she could. They never spoke again after that day, because how could she explain what happened during their kiss, when she didn't understand it herself?

✦

TWO

Situated just off Piccadilly Circus, surrounded by competitive, big-chain cinemas, The Duchess, although small, had its own unique selling point to set it apart. While the big cinemas showed the latest releases, The Duchess showed movies that had long disappeared from the big screen. Black-and-white romances, wild westerns, niche cult movies and even films from the last decade that had been quickly replaced by the next blockbusting, box office smash. The Duchess could provide something nowhere else could – the nostalgia of a past that was familiar and comforting. They held singalongs, quotealongs and all-night movie marathons, but their most popular promotion was the one night a month they showed *The Cellar*, dubbed as 'The world's best worst movie'.

'People love love,' Wesley, the owner, would say with a smug grin as he cashed up each month, 'but they sure do love to hate!'

Wesley was sweet but he ran a tight ship. He was approaching seventy and although incredibly sprightly and nimble, he was hoping to hand the business over to his son, Riggs, someday soon and retire somewhere quiet by the sea. The only problem was that, frankly, Riggs was a buffoon. Lorelai often wondered how The Duchess hadn't imploded under Riggs's lack of care, and then would watch Joanie manage everything perfectly and understand exactly what was going on. Joanie worked part-time, splitting her week between the cinema and a fifties-themed burger place down the road where she was forced to wear a baby-pink wig and roller skates. Yet she still managed to keep the cinema running smoothly, and in half the time Riggs did. Riggs was more interested in eyeing Joanie up than doing a good job. Unfortunately for him, he wasn't Joanie's type on account of him being a man.

They were a motley crew, but they made it work. While Joanie focused on the day-to-day, and Riggs did nothing at all, Lorelai was always thinking of ways to bring in more customers. During the day, she realised it was better to throw herself into her work than leave spare time to replay any previous nightmares in her mind. Especially now that they were becoming more vivid and cruel. And her most recent idea to entice a new audience into The Duchess was a welcome distraction – her Page to Screen club.

'But what exactly is it?' Riggs asked. Again.

Lorelai sighed. 'Every month, we'll pick a book and read it—'

'So it's a book club?' Riggs interrupted, pouring himself a large free drink of 7Up.

'No,' Lorelai said tightly, the muscles in her jaw clenching, 'I haven't got to its USP yet.'

'What's an usp?' Riggs said it phonetically, and Joanie rolled her eyes.

'A Unique Selling Point, you idiot.' Joanie clipped him round the back of the head but even a sharp smack didn't stop Riggs making doe-eyes at her.

'I think the book club is a great idea.' Joanie swept a hand through the short dark-brown curls that sat in a tangled quiff on top of her head.

'It's not just a book club. It's a book club *with a twist*,' Lorelai said, bouncing with excitement.

'And the twist is...?' Riggs asked, slurping from his drink again.

'We only read books that have been adapted into movies. On the last day of the month, we watch the movie adaptation, and then afterwards we discuss the differences and similarities between the film and the book. The first meeting will be an introduction to the club. A 'get-to-know-each-other' type of thing.' Lorelai paused, suddenly nervous. 'So... what do you think?'

Riggs shrugged. 'Sounds dull.'

'Thanks, Riggs. Constructive as ever.' Lorelai lifted his bottle and wiped away the sticky ring it had left behind. *I dread to think what his bedroom looks like,* she thought.

'Don't listen to someone who considers *FHM* a heavy read,' Joanie said, ignoring the way Riggs was staring at her.

'People will come, won't they?' Lorelai asked, suddenly unsure.

'They will! I'm sure of it.' Joanie smiled – and she was right. The sign-up sheet filled up quickly and all the spots were soon taken. All serious applicants, too, except for Riggs who had written 'Mickey Mouse'. Lorelai wanted to start with something fun and easy-going so she opted for *The Wizard of Oz*.

'A kid's book?' Riggs said, poking her copy with a finger.

'It's a book, Riggs, it's not going to bite. Pick it up and read a bit. You might learn a thing or two.' She swatted him with it and he took it from her, a smirk on his face.

'From Aslan?' he said, pointing to the lion linking arms with Dorothy on the cover.

'Aslan is from *The Lion, The Witch and...* never mind.' His eyes had already glazed over. 'Wesley is letting me use the function room, so do not disturb us please.'

Lorelai was determined that the first book club would be a success. She wanted this to become a permanent part of The Duchess's programme. She bought custard creams and bourbons, as well as two travel kettles so everyone could make fresh tea in the function room during their discussions. She had just finished pinning up the WELCOME sign she'd made herself when the first sign-ups arrived.

Lorelai wasn't entirely sure what she was expecting but it certainly wasn't the ragtag group that arrived. There were the Shaws, a couple in their mid-thirties who brought their own wine (two bottles for an hour-long meeting) and plastic cups. Next there was Mrs Blenheim, who only answered questions with a nod or a shake of the head, both of which usually brought on a hacking smoker's cough. Nadia, Shanice, Sue and Meera, all mid- to late-twenties and friends from high school, had signed up together and were using the Page to Screen club as a reason to meet up once a month. As Lorelai mingled she met Joy, a trans woman, and her boyfriend James whose last name, she enjoyed learning, was Love, and insisted on being called as such. Their hands were constantly entwined. The final person had yet to arrive and it was already quarter past six. She couldn't wait any longer.

'I think we had best begin. Please take your seats, ladies and gentle…' Lorelai flushed when she spotted Joy and Love giving each other a sideways glance. 'Oh no! I'm so sorry.' Her heart dropped into her stomach. *Not the best start,* she thought, and wished the ground would swallow her whole. She was usually more mindful.

Joy batted her hand through the air. 'I'm still saying stuff like that myself! It takes a while to get used to.'

Lorelai was touched by Joy's kindness, yet still couldn't help but feel ignorant. 'I'll do better next time,' she promised.

'That's all we ask, sweetie,' Joy said.

Mrs Shaw, Sarah, was already halfway through her second glass of rosé. She frowned and raised her hand. 'I don't understand what's going on?'

'Ladies and gentlemen implies that those are the only two options,' Love explained gently. 'Although our personal pronouns are he/him and she/her, there are those who don't identify as either and so prefer they/them. So terms like ladies and gentlemen reinforce the idea that gender is binary, which it isn't.' It was a perfect, well-rehearsed response. Lorelai wondered how many times Love had had to say those words, not only to those who didn't understand, but also to those who *refused* to.

'Riiiiiggghhhttt,' Barnaby Shaw nodded slowly, clearly not following. His eyes were a little red and Lorelai could see he was getting drunk quite quickly. Neither he nor his wife would be able to follow this conversation if the pace at which they were getting through their wine was any indication. She caught Joy's eye and they silently agreed this might be a lesson for another time and Lorelai made a mental note to make sure the list of books and movies for the club was truly inclusive.

The function room's door burst open and a man almost fell through the door. He righted himself and hurried towards Lorelai.

'Glad you could join us, Mr...' She snatched up her list and found his name, 'Mr Brady.'

'Just Grayson is fine. I'm sorry I'm late.' He had the grace to look sheepish.

Lorelai took a beat to assess the new arrival. He wore simple black trousers and a black shirt, open at the collar. His brown skin glistened in the fluorescent strip lighting. A singular bead of sweat was making its way down his strong jawline, the dark stubble on his chin halting its progress. It was proof, at least, that he'd run some of the way there in an attempt to not be as late as he'd ended up.

'Take a seat, Mr Brady,' Lorelai said pointedly. He held her gaze and although she was irked he'd turned up so late, she couldn't stop the corners of her lips curling upwards. *Stop it,* she warned herself. *You don't do this.* Lorelai had learned long ago how to immediately push down feelings of attraction, no matter how big or small. She looked away and cleared her throat, trying to ignore the sound of her racing heartbeat.

'Welcome... everyone!' she said (too) brightly. 'I've worked at this cinema for three years and The Duchess has never had anything like this club before. My boss is convinced the sign-up sheet was filled with names I made up, so he's thrilled you're not figments of my imagination.' They laughed politely. A good start. 'We're beginning with *The Wizard of Oz*. An indisputable classic when it comes to kids' books, and its musical adaptation has gone down in cinematic history. Not to mention *Wicked* by

Gregory Maguire with its long-running show on Broadway, and in the West End, *The Wiz* starring Diana Ross, and the Disney sequel, *Return to Oz*.'

'Yes, about that.' Barnaby sat forward, his elbows on his knees and his glass of wine teetering precariously between his fingers. His tone immediately put Lorelai on edge and she braced herself for what was coming next. 'Neither Sarah or myself know anything about *The Wizard of Oz*.' He rolled his eyes ever so gently as he said it that Lorelai almost missed it. He trailed off with a, 'So...' and a shrug, as if his unwillingness to participate was Lorelai's problem.

'This is the perfect chance to get to know the story. We'll all read the book over the next few weeks and then watch the film together at the end of the month.' Lorelai felt her fake smile drop a little, and knew her tone was sharper than before.

'Where do we get our copies from?' Sarah mumbled into her glass.

Lorelai dug her nails into her hand. 'Most bookshops will stock copies of classics such as *The Wizard of Oz*. Or you can order it online. Waterstones will be able to get you a copy, I'm sure.'

'You mean we have to *buy* our own copies? It's not included in the ticket price?' Barnaby howled.

Nadia, Shanice, Sue and Meera shared a glance before pulling their copies from their bags. All brand new except for Shanice's, which was dog-eared, its spine broken. Clearly well-loved from her childhood.

'There are always libraries,' Joy said.

'Didn't all the libraries close?' Sarah drained the last of the rosé into her glass, shaking it to make sure every last drop was out of the bottle.

'No, there are still lots of libraries,' Lorelai said. This was frustrating – she wanted to get on with the club.

'Oh, but they're just for *poor people*,' Barnaby whispered the words and waved his hand dismissively. Everyone shifted uncomfortably in their seats.

'No, they are not. They're for everyone.' Lorelai wondered if he always made such invidious statements in public, and so thoughtlessly.

'How about we read a book for *adults*?' Sarah squinted at Lorelai with such condescension it made her blood boil. She took a deep breath. 'I'm sick of reading kids' books to my little ones at home and I came here for something a bit more grown-up.'

'Most books written for a younger demographic still appeal to a wide age range. Take Harry Potter, for instance.' *Why are you still having this conversation?*

'I can't get away from that bloody wizard. Harry Potter this, Hermione Granger that. I'd happily *Avada Kedavra* the bloody lot of those books and be done with it,' Barnaby said, slugging down the rest of his wine.

'I'm just not sure reading is really our thing,' Sarah slurred, waving her glass at Lorelai.

'Then why did you come to a *book* club?' Grayson laughed incredulously.

'Oh, no one takes these things *that* seriously, do they?' Sarah said.

'How about a show of hands? Who here planned to actually read the books?' Lorelai raised her own hand and felt foolish when no one immediately followed suit. What were the chances every-one aside from Tweedledee and Tweedledumb-arse had signed up with serious creative and educational intentions? Thankfully everyone slowly began to raise their hands. Lorelai realised it may just have been to spite the Shaws but she was grateful nonetheless. She was pretty sure Barnaby mumbled, '*Liars*.'

'Right. Well, I'm not sure this is the right club for you then.' Lorelai stood so abruptly that Sarah missed her mouth by approximately five inches and the last of her wine dribbled down her clean, baby blue, crease-free blouse. Lorelai fished two ten-pound notes from the cash box. 'I hereby revoke your club membership.'

'You can't be serious?' Sarah snorted.

'This... this...' Barnaby's face quickly became slick with sweat and a vein on his meaty neck began to pulse. 'This is discrimination!'

'Sorry, but did you really think you could come to a book club just to drink? And not read a single word?' Joy asked far more gently than they deserved. Neither of them answered.

'Sarah, Barnaby, you're not in Kansas anymore.' Lorelai smiled, feeling mischievous. 'You're somewhere over the rainbow but it seems Oz has no place for you.' She ushered them up from their chairs and towards the door. 'Please follow the yellow brick road back from whence you came and don't let the Munchkins bite your ankles on the way out.' The door slammed with a satisfying thud and the remaining members of the group expressed their gratitude with a small round of applause.

After a quick gossip, the group settled down and Lorelai was happy with how the rest of the meeting went. Everyone was taking the club seriously, wanted to do the reading and enjoy the company of other people who also loved reading. They had discussed their favourite novels and favourite movies, and Lorelai had been pleased to find that everyone had brought their own copy of *The Wizard of Oz* by L Frank Baum. Everyone except Grayson.

'I had planned to pop to Waterstones after work but it closes far earlier than I had anticipated,' he explained to Lorelai at the end of the club. Everyone else had left but he remained seated, tea in hand, showing no signs of leaving.

'So what's it like working front of house at a cinema?' he asked, leaning back in his plastic chair.

'It's fine.' Lorelai laughed nervously. His lack of punctuality aside, Grayson appeared genuinely interested in the club and showed an eagerness not only to return next month but to actively participate. And he was always smiling *that* smile.

'Sorry. That's was an odd question. It's just that I work front of house at a theatre nearby so I was trying to find common ground, I suppose.' His smile had settled into an inconspicuous sort of curve but it was still doing things to her insides. He needed to *go*.

'Then you know how dull it can be. Nothing much of interest to report.' She began to pack away the tea bags, sugar and the very few leftover biscuits in the hope that he would take the hint.

'I *love* working at the theatre. Dealing with enraged customers and shouting, "*Souvenir brochures for sale! Only ten pounds!*" can get tedious pretty quickly but when the show starts, I get to watch it on the big TV monitor in the foyer. The lights dim, the orchestra starts up, the players take their positions… it's magic.' Grayson was no longer looking at Lorelai but into the middle distance. She could almost see the theatrics come to life in his eyes.

'Ten pounds for a programme? No wonder your customers are enraged.' She softened, returning his smile with a small one of her own while she continued to clear up half full cups of tea. Grayson stood, grabbed the roll of bin bags, unravelled one and followed her around the tiny room, holding it open for her.

'Tell me about it. We could do with someone like you when front of house gets heated. The way you dealt with those two was…' He kissed his fingers like a chef tasting his own exquisite dish.

'Weren't they just a treat?' She laughed, and then caught herself. She shouldn't be enjoying his company this much.

Lorelai disposed of the last of the rubbish and took the bin bag from him, their hands brushing slightly. A rush of warmth exploded through her body. She turned her face away so he wouldn't see the blush creeping along her cheeks. She must look like Violet Beauregarde from *Willy Wonka & the Chocolate Factory* after she turned into a blueberry.

'I guess that when I meet intelligent, open-minded people like you, it restores my faith in humanity so it's easy to forget how ignorant people can be,' Grayson said, oblivious.

Lorelai could feel herself yielding to the pull of the conversation and a bubble of panic rose from the pit of her stomach.

'I need to close up this room or my boss is going to have a fit.' She snatched the bag from him and opened the door.

'OK. No need to ask me twice,' he said, laughing.

Why is he laughing?, Lorelai thought while enjoying the way the corners of his eyes crinkled.

'But I'll be back next week.'

'Oh, sorry but there isn't a meeting next week. The next time we meet is at the end of the month.' Lorelai had begun to close the door so was now speaking to him through a two-inch gap but she still clocked the slight falter in his smile.

'Actually' – he rubbed the back of his head, and Lorelai tried to ignore how his bicep flexed, his jacket sleeve tightening around it – 'I do the matinee at work and get the evening off on Saturdays, so I've been coming here every weekend for a while. That's why I was able to make today's meeting so if you could always arrange them on a Saturday, I'd appreciate that.' He flashed her a smile, but it wasn't charming or suave. It was simply natural and genuine, and Lorelai felt something light up inside her.

'*Barely* made today's meeting, you mean,' she corrected, quickly snuffing out whatever had lit up. 'You're a *Lord of the Rings* fan, then?'

'I am.' Instinctively, he stood slightly taller. Clearly a *proud* fan.

'And you're coming for the extended director's cut trilogy marathon next weekend?'

'That's the one.'

'Isn't that, like… twelve hours? That's quite a lot of orcs and elves in one sitting.' Lorelai thought of the usual crowd that attended these showings. They often came dressed as the characters from the movie and she just couldn't picture Grayson spending hours creating the perfect costume and then wearing it for the best part of a day.

'This will actually be my second attempt at this marathon. I came two years ago and fell asleep long before they reached Mordor.'

'Spoilers!' Lorelai cried out.

Grayson's mouth fell open. 'Are you telling me you've never seen *The Lord of the Rings*?! None of them?'

'I'm not much of a fantasy fan.' She held up her hands.

'Umm...' He pointed to her beaten-up copy of *The Wizard of Oz*, sitting on a chair behind her.

'That's not the same!' Her voice rose in protest.

'It's totally the same.' Grayson pursed his lips, unimpressed.

Lorelai realised she was staring at his lips and mentally shook herself. *Get it together.*

'I'll have to watch it one day.' She began to close the door gently.

'You could always get the evening off and come with me? I know a date at your own place of work is a little—'

'A date?'

'Doesn't have to be,' he said hurriedly. 'We could just go as friends.' He shrugged, all his confidence suddenly gone.

'We're friends?' She raised an eyebrow. 'We've just met. Pretty fast friendship.'

'I don't tell just anybody I'm a giant *Lord of the Rings* fan!'

Lorelai laughed, and decided to give him a break. He was being quite sweet. 'It's probably too short notice to get the night off but maybe I'll be able to sneak in the back,' she said politely. Grayson paused for a second and then bobbed his head.

'OK. Another time. Maybe.'

'I'll set aside a bucket of popcorn for you. On the house.' *Why am I trying to make him feel better?* she thought. *He's a big boy. He can deal with being told 'no'.*

'On the house or under it?' He raised his eyebrows at her as if he were saying 'get it?' But she didn't. 'Sorry. That was a really bad *Wizard of Oz* joke.'

'Ah, I see. Huh… that was actually quite clever.'

'I'll keep practising until I don't have to explain why my jokes are clever.' He smiled a goodbye, walked backwards a few steps, holding her gaze and her attention and then disappeared up the stairs.

Lorelai closed the door, leaned back against it and let out a sigh of relief and frustration. She didn't know this guy at all. They had just met but she couldn't ignore the way her pulse was beating faster. Meeting a beautiful stranger with a love of fantasy would be the ideal scenario for most people. A meet-cute. Something that only happened in books and movies. But Lorelai was not most people and Grayson would run a mile if he knew her secret.

◆

Lorelai had run all the way home after kissing Arthur. After kissing him and watching him die. Because that's what it had been, hadn't it? Tears streamed down her cheeks as she ran. Her lungs burned. She'd never felt so scared. The muscles in her legs were screaming for her to stop but she couldn't until she was safely home. As though the images in her head wouldn't be able to cross the threshold of her house.

'Lorelai? What's wrong?' Her father, David, said as she fell through the front door. Her mother, Lila, caught her in her arms. Lorelai tried to pull away, but her mother held her firm and eventually she gave in to her warmth and gentle hushing. Lila stroked her daughter's hair until her whimpers died down.

'Darling, what happened?' Lila tried to prise her daughter from her torso but Lorelai's arms were wrapped so tightly around her, her face buried in her stomach, she was immovable.

As she steadied her breathing, Lorelai tried to find the right words to explain why she was in such a state. *I just kissed Arthur Trent behind the bushes at school and I saw him die. No, he's not actually dead. I just saw how he's going to die. In the future. In my mind.* Her mother wouldn't believe it. If someone had said that to her she wouldn't have believed it. It sounded crazy. Maybe she *was* crazy. Because it couldn't be true. Could it? But she couldn't shake the images from her mind.

She was only thirteen. A child. Lorelai had enough self-awareness to know that adults didn't take thirteen-year-olds that seriously. Especially when what this thirteen-year-old had to say was so completely impossible. Lorelai loved her mother and she knew her mother loved her very much but did she love her enough to believe something she couldn't even believe herself? Was her mother's love so unconditional that she wouldn't instantly think that there was something wrong with her daughter and that she needed help?

Maybe I do need help, she thought. Had she really just seen Arthur die? Could it have been her brain playing tricks on her because she had just kissed someone for the first time? No one was going to believe her if she told them... what? That she had *magical powers*? And they certainly wouldn't believe her without proof. And what proof did she have except the memory of the life leaving Arthur's eyes?

'I'm fine. I'm OK.' She finally pulled away from her mother but didn't meet her eyes. There was a part of Lorelai that wanted her mother to push her. To pester and insist she tell her what was wrong. To reassure her that no matter what, even if Lorelai had killed Arthur herself, she was her mother and she would try to help her in whatever way she could.

Instead, her mother nodded and said, 'OK. Dinner will be ready soon so why don't you go and clean yourself up and come down in a little while.' She gave her daughter's face a squeeze between her soft hands. 'Oh, Lorelai. I hate seeing you so sad. Tell you what, how about Viennetta for dessert? I know it's your favourite. Your dad can pop by the shops, can't you, David?

'On my way!' Lorelai's father grabbed his coat and was out the door before Lila could say thank you.

Lorelai's heart sank. She realised then that she'd inadvertently set her mother a test and she had failed. She wanted her mother to make her tell what was wrong, and to kiss it all away, tell Lorelai not to worry and that everything was going to be OK. If her mother didn't care enough to push her to tell her the truth, to confide in her, then she wouldn't tell her. She didn't know how to anyway – she didn't have the words to explain the unexplainable.

And so began, at age thirteen, Lorelai's new life of secrecy and loneliness.

◆

Three

Lorelai worked full time at The Duchess and by the time her day off rolled around, the one day of the week The Duchess was closed, she was exhausted. Mondays consisted of books, Netflix and desperate, fruitless attempts to cuddle Nora, Joanie's biting, hissing satanic fur-ball of hate disguised as a cat. Lorelai loved cats and was overjoyed to find out Joanie was bringing hers with her when they originally moved in together. But Nora turned out to be the most vicious creature known to mankind. While Lorelai spent her day off mooching on the sofa, Joanie, on the other hand, successfully juggled two jobs, a thriving blog and would, at least once a week, also drive to visit her girlfriend, Cassie, who was training to be a nurse in Croydon. Just watching Joanie live her life exhausted Lorelai.

'The only way I can justify my own lack of motivation,' Lorelai said from the depths of her dressing gown hood, 'is to pretend you're just not human. I can't compete with you if you're not of this world. It's not a fair fight. If you were human that means I'd have to admit that I am, in fact, lazy.'

'You're not lazy.' Joanie kissed her on the forehead, as she raced past where Lorelai was sat on the stairs. 'You have a full-time job and you do it well!' she said, slipping on her boots without untying the laces.

'But you have *two* jobs and there's all the other crap you do on top of it all. How is anyone meant to keep up?' Lorelai looked up at Joanie. Her curls were freshly washed and bouncy and she had a pretty dress on. She looked lovely but she definitely wasn't dressed for the autumn chill that awaited her outside.

'Alright, you've got me.' Joanie sighed, pausing at the door. 'I am god of gods, ruler of all, specifically sent to Earth to piss you off.'

'I knew it,' Lorelai whispered. 'Now I can go back to bed for the next twelve hours, guilt-free. Thank you and goodnight.'

'Just save me some gin and some chocolate from the stash I know you have hidden in your wardrobe. And I don't care how you spend your *day off*. Honestly, Lollie' – a nickname reserved for Joanie and Joanie alone – 'who else has to be talked into having a day off without feeling terrible about it?'

'Erm, you?'

'Don't be silly. I don't have days off.' Joanie planted another kiss on Lorelai's forehead. 'See you tonight!' The door closed and Joanie was gone.

Lorelai sighed. She'd usually pick up a book to while away the hours but today she was too preoccupied. There was only one thing on her mind: Grayson Brady. She kept thinking about the way his hand had grazed hers, the looks that had lasted a moment too long, and the curve of his smile. Lorelai wasn't much of an Instagram stalker but, as the day wore on, she found she couldn't help herself.

'Just one harmless search,' she mumbled to herself later that afternoon. 'Everyone stalks everyone. It doesn't mean anything at all.' She settled back and hit the search button. There were a few different results matching with 'Grayson' and 'Brady' but only one matched the two names together. His username was @GraysonStage and his profile picture looked like a professional shot. 'Ahh, so you're an actor...'

As Lorelai scrolled through his feed, she saw photos of him with a woman and a younger-looking man, who turned out to be his mum and brother, and another lady who might be an aunt, she guessed. There were photos of Grayson in his front-of-house theatre uniform posing next to packets of sweets, fanning himself with several souvenir brochures. There were even a couple of photos in the seats of The Duchess, waiting for a movie to start. In the background of one, Lorelai spotted the blurred face of Riggs. She rolled her eyes. Lorelai had no idea how long she surrendered herself to scrolling through Grayson's Instagram but for a while she revelled in the tingling sensation of a crush beginning to brew, allowing herself a little time to feel *normal*. It was only when the doorbell rang that she quickly closed Instagram and threw her phone down like it had suddenly caught fire.

'What am I doing?' The warm fuzzy feeling had turned into a nauseating concoction of panic, disappointment and shame. *Why am I even entertaining the idea of him? One handsome guy looks my way and that changes everything?* But it wasn't as simple as that. Lorelai knew how to walk away from attention that would only lead to those horrific images, but Grayson had stirred something in her. Why was he different?

A noise at the door to the flat pulled Lorelai from her thoughts. She quickly shoved all thoughts of Grayson to the back of her mind, and opened the door assuming it was a parcel delivery. But instead she found Joanie, her shoulders slumped and her head bowed. Joanie gently pushed her way inside and closed the door behind her. She put her rucksack on the floor, crouched beside it and busied herself searching for something at the bottom.

'Everything alright?' Lorelai asked. She could sense something was wrong. Joanie sniffed and raised her tear-stained face. Lorelai sat next to her on the floor. 'Oh, honey. What happened?'

Joanie briefly put her head in her hands and let herself sink into pity. Lorelai waited, knowing Joanie would speak when she was ready. Joanie rarely showed this kind of vulnerability, so Lorelai sat there, silently, giving Joanie the space to cry without judgement.

'Cassie says she's too busy and too stressed to continue our relationship,' Joanie said eventually.

Lorelai blinked at her in disbelief. She wrapped her arms around Joanie and pulled her closer. 'What? No!' Lorelai rocked her back and forth. 'What did you say?'

Joanie shrugged, hopelessly. 'I said we could still make it work. I could give her more space so she could focus on her training. I even suggested just taking a bit of a break but—' a sob escaped '—she'd already made up her mind. I think she'd been rehearsing it for weeks. She just shut down on me; I couldn't get through to her.'

Lorelai's heart broke for her friend. She had assumed Joanie and Cassie were one of those couples who'd end up growing old together. One of those couples that made everyone else believe that the perfect, fairy-tale, happy-ever-after relationship could really happen because they were the proof. It killed her to see Joanie this devastated.

'I'm so sorry, Joanie. Do you think you could try talking to her again in a few days?'

Joanie shook her head. 'She wouldn't even look at me when I left. It's over.'

Lorelai hugged Joanie tighter. 'Tell me what you need. Your wish is my command!'

'Well' – Joanie swallowed hard – 'she's asked that I don't contact her for a while, so I propose I get very drunk tonight and call in sick tomorrow. Wallow in self-pity for a day or two. And then…' Joanie's face crumpled, and more tears ran down her cheeks.

'And then,' Lorelai continued, 'then you give yourself a stern talking to.' She pulled back and looked down at her friend. She knew Joanie needed one of her pep talks. Lorelai had given her many over their friendship and they always seemed to do the trick. They geed her up and gave her fuel to keep going. Joanie wasn't the type who responded to mollycoddling. 'Joanie. You, my dear friend, are amazing.'

'Here we go.' Joanie rolled her eyes, but she was smiling.

'I mean it! You're intelligent, funny, not to mention drop-dead gorgeous… Cassie was unbelievably lucky to have you. She didn't appreciate you as much as you deserved.'

'I didn't realise you thought that,' Joanie said, surprised.

'I'm just able to be a little more objective than you can be right now. You're currently only remembering the good and it's my job, as your best friend, to remind you that your relationship wasn't perfect. Yes, you've lost all the lovely stuff, but you don't have to worry about all the other crap. You've broken up because something was obviously broken. But it wasn't you. You are not broken and this break-up will not break you.' Lorelai punctuated her lecture with a nod. 'Thank you for coming to my TED Talk.'

'Can it ever be fixed?' Joanie's lower lip began to wobble again.

'Maybe. One day. But not right now. Right now you need to focus on yourself.'

'You know, for someone who "doesn't do relationships", you know an awful lot about how they work.'

'Ha, that's because I have a lot more time to watch telly than you do. Everything I just said to you is thanks to Oprah, Ellen, *Love Island*, *Married At First Sight* and *The Bachelor*.' Joanie smiled and a little sparkle returned to her eyes. Lorelai heaved her off the floor and put on her best cheesy American TV presenter's voice. 'In tonight's episode, we have Ben and Jerry on the show who are going to teach us how to drown our sorrows in pints of ice cream. Later on, we'll also learn how a vat of margaritas can make life look infinitely better.'

◆

The word 'hangover' didn't quite cut it. Lorelai and Joanie weren't strangers to a night of drinking but there was something about drinking while feeling sad that intensified the 'morning after the night before' feeling. Lorelai came to, bleary-eyed, to the sound of the shower running. The only good thing about falling asleep when intoxicated was that the night was often dreamless, with no nightmares to shake her awake from her drunken stupor.

'Urghhhh,' she groaned loudly.

'Urghhhh,' Joanie groaned in response from the bathroom.

Lorelai peeled herself off her sweaty bed sheets and clung to the walls as she made her way to the bathroom. The door was ajar and Joanie was sat on the floor of the shower, under the jets of steaming water, still wearing her floral pyjamas.

'You're ruining your pyjamas,' Lorelai said, running her dry, fuzzy tongue over her equally fuzzy teeth. Her voice was deep and husky, and her stale breath wafted up from her mouth, sending a wave of nausea through her. Lorelai sat on the closed toilet seat and took a few deep breaths.

'By the time I realised, I was already wet.' Joanie shrugged, and tucked her head between her knees, massaging her temples. 'I genuinely feel like something in here is about to explode.'

'Good night, though,' Lorelai said, smiling.

'Which bit? The bit where I laughed until I cried, or the bit where you laughed so hard you farted?' They both giggled, before groaning again and clutching their aching heads.

'Don't make me laugh,' Lorelai begged.

'No more impersonations then?' Joanie tipped her head back and let the water wash over her. Lorelai was pleased to see a playful smile on her face.

'Not until my head has stopped banging.'

'As much as it cheered me up, your Alan Rickman's gotten worse. Much worse.'

'That's worrying. That's the best one I've got.' Lorelai gently shook her head and closed her eyes for a moment. 'Turn to page three hundred and ninety-four…' she said in a voice very much unlike Alan Rickman's.

'Your Christopher Walken is better.'

'I'm gonna have to come up with a few more, just for you.'

'Can't wait.' Joanie looked over at Lorelai. 'Don't suppose you called the cinema? We're meant to be at work.'

'Oh no.' Lorelai couldn't believe she hadn't clocked the time. 'Wesley is going to kill us.'

'We could say it's a stomach bug?'

'Better off saying it's food poisoning from a bad takeaway. Riggs will just have to pull his finger out and cover for us for a change.'

'Fat chance.' Joanie rubbed her eyes, smudging yesterday's mascara.

'He's not got a choice.'

'Bagsy not calling Wesley.'

'That's fair. You're the one with a broken heart.' Lorelai stood up slowly, hoping the room would stop spinning soon, and then realised what she'd said. 'Oh god. Sorry, Joanie, I didn't mean to bring it all up again.'

'That's alright. It's not as though I'd forgotten. I'll just have a little weep while you call Wesley.'

'I thought I'd cheered you up!'

'You have! If it wasn't for you, my little weep would be hours of wailing.' Joanie gave her a half smile, which was enough for Lorelai to feel comfortable leaving her alone for a bit.

'That's more like it. I'll make some dry toast.' She made her way into the hallway and then yelled, 'Take your pyjamas off, dickhead.'

Wesley was less than pleased. Lorelai knew, though, that this was less about them not being there and more because Riggs would have to take over for the day. Riggs always managed to screw up even the simplest of tasks. Lorelai had wondered if it was a tactic, some kind of masterplan to ensure he was never entrusted with any significant responsibility, but then she'd come to the conclusion that he was just a bit useless. Lorelai knew she was condemning Wesley to a stressful day but they had no big events planned so it should be a quiet shift.

An hour or so later, Lorelai and Joanie were on the sofa, freshly showered, and Joanie was in a new, clean, and dry pair of pyjamas. 'I forgot to ask, how did the book club go?' Joanie said as she handed Lorelai a pint glass of water and two paracetamol.

Instantly, memories of Grayson flooded Lorelai's mind. She gulped down the water, enjoying the icy tingle as the liquid made its way down her fiery throat, buying some time. She exhaled loudly, trying to knock away thoughts of his warm skin and soft eyes. 'I did have to kick two people out within the first half an hour for not really buying into the point of the club, and everyone gave me a round of applause so…' Lorelai held up two thumbs and Joanie did the same. 'There *was* this one guy though.'

Joanie's ears pricked up and she was on high alert. She swung herself forwards. 'A *guy*? Tell me!'

'Yeeees…' Lorelai said slowly.

'As in a man? A male human being who has caught your attention enough for you to mention him to me in casual conversation.'

'Let's not read too much into it, shall we?' Lorelai sighed, already regretting mentioning Grayson. Joanie was going to turn this into a huge deal, she could feel it.

'Er, *sure, OK.*' Joanie's voice was heavy with sarcasm. 'Lollie. My dearest Lorelai. You're twenty-five and you haven't kissed anyone since you were eighteen. And this is the first time I've heard you mention a man since we've been living together.'

'No it isn't!' *Surely that's not right?*

'It is! You haven't mentioned anyone. Not even once. And moaning about Riggs or talking about your dad's allotment doesn't count. I mean a romantic prospect. Someone who you go to sleep thinking of—'

'This isn't that,' Lorelai protested weakly.

Joanie's voice became gentle. 'It's me, Lollie. I know about your... situation.'

Joanie was the only person that knew about her reasons for not letting anyone get close to her. Not even her parents had been trusted with the knowledge, despite their worrying. The only reason Joanie knew was because she had painted her into a corner on a morning much like this one, and the only way to make her incessant questions stop was to answer them. It had taken a surprisingly small amount of convincing to make Joanie believe what Lorelai was telling her. She smiled at the memory, grateful that she was able to be honest with at least one person. Would Grayson react in the same way, or would he push her away? *Why am I even thinking that?!*

'I totally understand that things are different for you but... are you sure there's no one out there for you? There's no one worth the inconvenience?'

'It's a bit more than an inconvenience, Joanie.'

'I know, I know. I didn't mean to belittle your, erm...'

'My condition.' This was the word Lorelai used to describe her secret.

'I just worry that you're condemning yourself to a life of

loneliness when there might be someone out there who's willing to understand. To battle through it with you. If you just took a leap of faith and trusted someone.' Joanie's eyes became soft and sad. Lorelai had to look away.

Lorelai often thought about the life she was creating for herself. A life with no one by her side, a life lacking intimacy and passion. She told herself she was OK with it, because she had to be, and most of the time she really was fine. But there were other times when she wanted nothing more than someone to come home to, to share her life with, but the idea of opening herself up to someone so completely terrified her. It was better for her to be alone.

'Trusting someone isn't on the cards for me,' Lorelai said. 'You know that.'

'And you're certain there's not one single person who's worth it? This guy from your club seems to have turned your head. No one's ever done that before. That's pretty significant, if you ask me.' Joanie raised an eyebrow.

'I've only met him once.' Lorelai couldn't stop her smile, and she felt her cheeks begin to flush.

'And yet here we are talking about him,' Joanie said matter-of-factly. She took a sip of her water and gave Lorelai the side-eye.

'This could hardly be called talking about him. I've not even told you his name.'

'And aren't you just *dying* to tell me?' Joanie said, nudging Lorelai with her foot.

'Nope, not at all. Anyway, I'll probably never see him again. I made a terrible impression and he probably thought I was a total bitch. I was really rude, and why would he give me a second chance—'

'A second chance!' Joanie exclaimed. 'You *do* like him! Lollie has a crush! Lollie has a crush!'

'Lollie's gonna be sick…'

Lorelai bolted to the bathroom, making it just in time to throw up the water and the remnants of last night's alcohol. *It's the booze that made me vomit*, Lorelai reassured herself. *That's all.*

'So even the mere thought of getting close to someone sends you hurtling to the toilet bowl?' Joanie appeared in the doorway, arms folded.

Lorelai groaned. 'It was the booze.'

'No it wasn't.' Joanie's voice was firm.

'This can't happen, Joanie. Just let it be the booze. Please.'

'As much as you want to fight your feelings, you aren't wired that way. It's part of being human.'

'Asexual people exist, Joanie. I can be one of them,' Lorelai said feebly.

'Of course they do… but you aren't one of them. And that's OK.' Joanie knelt down next to her and pushed Lorelai's dark hair away from her face. This simple gesture of friendship was enough to undo Lorelai.

'It's not. It's not OK,' Lorelai wept, the tears coming thick and fast. 'I don't know what I'm going to do.'

Joanie pulled her closer, stroking her hair. 'You're not going to do anything. Whatever happens, happens. There's no point in worrying about it until it does. But I really think it's time to rethink your I'm-going-to-be-alone-forever life plan.'

'I can't. It's too much.'

'I didn't say it'd be easy. Or fun for that matter. But I've known you a long time and I've never seen you light up at the mention of a guy before. Up until now, your plan of celibacy has been fine because the best option you've had is Riggs. But this guy from your book club, whoever he is, seems to have made an impression and I think that's a sign.'

'A sign of what, weakness?'

'Will you stop it? To love someone, let someone in, it takes strength. Especially when you do so despite the thousands of reasons not to.'

'There are a *million* reasons not to.'

'Well, then, you'll be a million times stronger when he asks you on a date and you say yes.'

And with that Lorelai vomited once more.

Lorelai didn't kiss anyone again until she was eighteen. Eventually, she convinced herself that she'd made the whole thing up. She had always had a vivid imagination so the most horrifying experience of her life must have been nothing more than a confusing childish fantasy borne from an over-active mind. Over time, she'd turned the experience into something worse than it had been. And so, when, drunk at a house party, Thomas Schumer kissed her, she let him.

But no.

She screamed into Thomas's mouth when she saw the knife plunge into his stomach. He was standing on a street, outside some kind of bar. He was only a few years older than he was now, and that scared Lorelai more than anything. Both Thomas and Arthur were closer to death than they realised. Sobbing, Lorelai tore out of the party, leaving a stunned and speechless Thomas in her wake.

The following morning, all Lorelai wanted to do was stay in bed and block out the world, but her grandmother was coming over and no one could make her feel better like her grandmother could. Sylvia, her mother's mum, was a confident woman who was unashamedly herself. She wore floor-length silk robes, covered in a kaleidoscope of patterns, that gave the impression she was gliding rather than walking. After Lorelai's grandfather passed away, Sylvia had never remarried and instead she lived her life boldly and brightly, surrounded by her friends. She was getting slower as the years went on, but she still got the train down and visited twice a month, bringing a delicious bake in a mint-green tin that usually took all three of them to twist open.

On this particular Saturday, Lila had put together an afternoon tea for them all. Her father would have loved to have joined them, but Lila had shooed him out of the house. 'A girls' lunch,' she'd called it. Lorelai kept stuffing finger sandwiches in her mouth to avoid making conversation but as soon as Lila left to get more jam and cream for the scones, her grandmother quickly took hold of Lorelai's wrist.

'Something's wrong, sweetheart. What is it? Tell me now before your mother comes back.' She was gazing at Lorelai with such intensity, Lorelai had to look away.

'Nothing's wrong!' Lorelai shoved a piece of quiche in her mouth and pulled her hand back.

Sylvia took her granddaughter's chin between her fingers and turned Lorelai's head from side to side. 'You've not been this quiet since the day you were born and there's something different about your eyes... They look older.'

'Geez. Thanks Gran!' Lorelai pulled away.

'Well?' Sylvia looked her dead in the eyes. A stare she couldn't easily escape from. She could feel the confession forming on her tongue, ready to burst out in one great sob. If anyone was going to understand the absurdity of her story, it was her grandmother, and here she was, giving her a chance to unburden herself of the great weight she'd been carrying around for the last five years.

'Cream first? Or jam? That is the question!' Lila chirped as she returned to the garden.

'Don't be silly, darling. Only monsters put the cream on first,' Sylvia said, her tone light again. She reached for the jam. Before she knew what she was doing, Lorelai reached for the clotted cream, tore off the lid and smeared it over her scone. She looked pointedly at her grandmother, desperately hoping she'd understand. Praying she would realise this was a way of communicating that she was not OK without alarming her mother.

Sylvia watched her granddaughter closely during the rest of the afternoon, but there wasn't another chance for the two of them to be alone until it was time for her to catch her train.

'Lila, would you fill my water bottle for me please? I get ever so thirsty on the train home,' Sylvia asked as she was getting to ready to leave. Lila disappeared, leaving grandmother and granddaughter alone. Lorelai's heart was racing.

'I'm going to say this once and only once.' Sylvia took Lorelai by the shoulders and turned her to face her square on. 'Whatever is troubling you, do not keep it in or it will eat you alive. Are you listening to me, Lorelai? Secrets eat you up from the inside until there is nothing left. It's a dangerous game to play and one you won't ever win.' Lorelai bit her lip. 'Whatever it is, you must tell someone. You can trust me, my darling. And trust me when I say this, there are people out there who may understand what you're going through much better than you might think.'

Lorelai lifted her head to look at her grandmother then and, for a split second, she saw a look flash across her face. It was a look she knew well – the look of someone who was keeping a secret, carrying a burden they wanted rid of.

'Here we are!' Lila wiped down the water bottle with a tea towel and handed it back to Sylvia. She glanced between her mother and her daughter, noticing their serious expressions. 'Everything alright?'

'Fine!' Lorelai smiled.

'I love you both. Very much,' Sylvia said and, after promising to call when she got home, she was gone.

◆

Four

'I trust you two are feeling better?' Wesley asked, arms folded, as they shuffled through the doors the next morning. The place was still standing but Riggs was nowhere to be seen. They nodded sheepishly, eyes averted, but Wesley's accusatory gaze couldn't be avoided for too long. 'Yes, well, let's make today a good day to make up for it, shall we?'

'In other words, fix all of Riggs' mistakes from yesterday?' Joanie asked, rolling her eyes behind her giant sunglasses.

'As much as it pains me to say it, yes. He hasn't even shown up this morning. Probably because I kept snapping at him yesterday. He really should know where everything goes and how everything works by now.' Wesley threw up his hands and stalked off, muttering to himself.

'When's your next club, Lorelai?' Joanie asked, hanging up her coat and scarf in the tiny mop closet behind the main counter.

'Last Saturday of every month so we've got ages yet, why? You gonna come?'

'Looks like lover boy has turned up early.' Joanie gestured towards the door where Grayson was stood outside, browsing the cinema times for that month. His scarf was pulled up high over his chin and under his ears but there was no mistaking that it was him. As he looked up from the schedule, Lorelai ducked down behind the counter, almost hitting her chin on the way down.

'I knew showing you his Instagram was a mistake,' Lorelai hissed.

'I don't think crawling around on the floor will make a better impression than your first one.'

'I'm just… counting the cups for today.' Lorelai's voice jumped a couple of octaves and Joanie snorted with laughter.

'Come on in! We're open!' she called, waving through the door.

Whether Grayson had seen Lorelai duck for cover or not, remerging from her hiding place was bound to be an awkward moment. She dropped onto her hands and knees and began to crawl towards the door that led off the main foyer. Underestimating the amount of space she had, her hips knocked over the precariously balanced box of paper cups. Riggs hadn't stored them properly and had left them in the perfect place to foil Lorelai's getaway.

'Everything alright down there?' His voice was smoother than Lorelai remembered. Suddenly, very aware that she had her arse in the air and both Grayson and Joanie were getting the full view of it, she hopped up and quickly brushed herself down.

'Yes! Yes. Just, um…'

'Counting cups?' Joanie bit her lip, ready to burst with laughter.

'Yes, actually. I'll erm… pick those up later.' Lorelai shuffled through the cup confetti on the floor. 'What can I do for you?'

'I've just come to pick up my tickets for this weekend. The *Lord of the Rings* marathon.'

'Said without an ounce of embarrassment,' Joanie teased.

'Absolutely not! I'm a man who knows what he likes.'

Lorelai could feel his pointed gaze in her direction, and she busied herself tapping his name into the computer system to find his tickets.

'You're a member here?' Lorelai asked, looking at his file.

'Yes. When I started coming every Saturday it just made sense.'

'Can I see your card?'

'Oh, Lorelai.' Joanie gently pushed her aside. 'She doesn't need to see your card. We're going to take your word for it. Lorelai is also going to let you use her discount on top of the membership discount because she's very much looking forward to seeing you again and wants you to keep coming back.'

Lorelai gaped at her friend. What was she *doing*?

'Is this ventriloquy at its finest or are you just bailing out your actually quite disinterested friend?' Grayson asked, smiling and yet there was a nervous tremor in his voice, insecurity bubbling to the surface. Lorelai felt a pull in her chest. Did he have to be cute, smart *and* sweet? She needed to put a stop to this.

'I've been Lorelai's ventriloquist for years. She never answers the phone if it's a number she doesn't know, will only order the same food I order in a restaurant so she doesn't have to speak to the waiter and clearly I'm now the intermediary between her and her romantic prospects.'

'Joanie…' Lorelai warned, elbowing her sharply in the ribs.

Joanie ignored her, and handed Grayson's tickets over with a flourish.

'Two tickets?' she queried.

'Yeah, my younger brother always comes with me if it's anything to do with *The Lord of the Rings*, Marvel or *Star Wars*.'

'Good-looking *and* generous.' Joanie looked at Lorelai pointedly.

'Nah, I make him pay for this own ticket.' Grayson rubbed the back of his head, clearly feeling awkward.

'In that case, good-looking and a responsible adult teaching his siblings the value of money.'

'Something like that.' Grayson was talking to Joanie, but he kept looking over at Lorelai and she wished he wouldn't. Everything in Lorelai's being was telling her to shut this down, to leave no room for interpretation, make it clear she wasn't interested. And yet… she couldn't ignore the pleading look in his eyes.

'We'll see you on Saturday,' she managed, finally.

'Thanks. Wish me luck. Staying awake through these marathons isn't my forte and my brother tends to draw obscenities on my face if I'm the first to fall asleep.'

'I'll have a Red Bull waiting,' Joanie said.

'And a Sharpie for your brother,' Lorelai said before she could stop herself. Grayson's face lit up in surprise, and there was that smile again. He gave her a small wave and was sucked back out onto the streets of Soho, a very definite spring in his step.

'God, Lorelai! Next time can you let me get a word in! And maybe turn down the volume a bit? You're just so loud!' Joanie stuck her finger in her ear and winced.

'I just cannot believe you.' Lorelai picked up a stack of paper cups and one by one began to pelt them at her annoying friend.

'Yes, you can.' Joanie picked up a popcorn bucket and tried

to catch the cups as they flew through the air. 'I've always been like this. It's your fault for hanging around me!'

'I'm still furious!'

'I know, I'm just the worst! Thanks to me, we know the guy you like is clearly into you.'

'Clearly?' Lorelai hoped the intense frustration in her voice masked her need to know the exact details of how Joanie knew for sure that Grayson liked her.

'Lorelai. It's nine a.m. The cinema has been open all of twenty seconds. He could have just printed out his tickets at home or shown them on his phone on the day.'

'Maybe his printer's not working or… or maybe his phone's broken,' Lorelai huffed. She began picking up the cups she'd thrown, knowing Wesley would be furious if he saw them.

'You're ridiculous,' Joanie said, ruffling her hair as she walked past her into the storage room in the back. 'Umm… Lorelai?' Joanie called a few moments later.

Lorelai followed her voice to the storage room, and spotted Joanie standing, arms folded, looking through the open door, an incredulous look on her face. Before Lorelai could say anything, the sound of thunderous snoring hit her ears.

'Is that…?'

'The laziest man in the universe? Yes, it is.'

Lorelai followed Joanie's gaze to where Riggs was sleeping on the floor, propped up by a bucket and a mop, headphones clamped over his ears, his black puffer jacket laid over him to keep him warm. Joanie looked at Lorelai, eyes wide in disbelief.

'Joanie, be gentle with him…' Lorelai warned but Joanie was already stomping towards Riggs.

'Oi!' Joanie nudged the sole of Riggs's combat boot.

Riggs jolted awake with a giant snort, and dribble escaping his mouth. He squinted up at Joanie, the harsh strip lighting too much for him to take. It took him a while, but eventually his expression cleared, his vision adjusted and he took in Joanie looming over him. He began to babble.

'Erm, er, um...' Riggs scrambled to his feet as quickly as he could, knocking over the mop.

'Riggs!' Joanie yelled. 'Are you kidding me? We've been open for all of ten minutes and you're already taking a nap?' Joanie was so cross that she'd failed to notice an open rucksack on the floor. A rucksack in which Lorelai could see a toiletry bag sticking out.

'Riggs, have you been sleeping here?' Lorelai asked quietly.

Joanie halted mid-rant and followed Lorelai's gaze to the open bag on the floor.

'What? No!' Riggs said, a defensive tone creeping into his voice.

'Riggs...' Lorelai gestured to the bag, which Riggs quickly tried to kick out of the way. His foot caught in one of the straps and he would have fallen over had Lorelai not caught him and kept him upright. With sympathy clear on her face, Riggs hung his head, defeated, and began to sob.

'Sorry...' he mumbled, keeping his face down, unable to look them in the eye.

Lorelai looked at Joanie over his head. Her expression had softened, but it was clear she was still suspicious, Riggs's history of laziness playing on her mind. Lorelai on the other hand just felt awful and she looked at Joanie with tears in her eyes. Joanie pulled her to the side.

'Stop that right now,' Joanie said. 'We don't know what's going on here.'

'He *needs* us,' Lorelai pleaded.

'He needs *everyone*.' Joanie's face was set, but Lorelai could see she also looked uncertain. It did look like Riggs was living in the cinema.

'Thanks for whispering for my benefit.' Riggs took a step back. 'I don't *need* anyone. I can look after myself.'

'Riggs, does your dad know you've been sleeping here?' Lorelai asked. Riggs didn't respond – his silence spoke volumes. 'Where does he think you've been?'

Joanie's shoulders relaxed, finally believing that this situation was more serious than she'd initially thought. She gestured to his mess scattered about the floor. 'You're not exactly being subtle about staying here.'

'Dad kicked me out of the house a couple of months ago,' Riggs said quietly. 'Made a big speech about standing on my own two feet, start becoming responsible. He thought I'd found a flat share in Bow. And I had, except it didn't work out for too long.'

'How come?' Lorelai asked.

'I didn't do anything!' Riggs exclaimed.

'Relax,' Joanie said. Only Joanie could sound sympathetic and stern at the same time. 'Lorelai never said you did anything. Just tell us what happened.'

'The flat turned out to be right next door to a crack den so I didn't want to stay. But then they wouldn't give me my deposit back and so I couldn't afford to look for anywhere else.'

'How long have you been sleeping here?' Joanie asked.

'A few weeks,' Riggs mumbled.

'A few weeks? Why didn't you say anything?' Lorelai reached out and rubbed his arm but he tensed under her fingers so she awkwardly withdrew.

'Why would I? What could you have done?'

'Well—'

'Lorelai!' Joanie interrupted. She knew her friend well enough to know what was coming, but there was no stopping Lorelai. She couldn't ignore Riggs's misfortune.

'We have a sofa…' Lorelai smiled kindly at Riggs.

'No.' Joanie shook her head.

'…that you could stay on.' Lorelai took Riggs' hand.

'Nope.' Joanie rubbed her temples.

'Just until you get back on your feet.'

'Have you lost your mind?' Joanie exclaimed.

Lorelai nodded towards Riggs, who looked so bereft, even Joanie couldn't deny him this kindness. Joanie sighed.

'One week.' Joanie held up her index finger and pointed at Riggs. 'You can stay with us for one week, and that's it.'

Lorelai leaned towards Riggs and whispered, 'You can crash for as long as you need.'

'Thanks, Lorelai. That means a lot. It won't be for long, I promise.'

◆

Lorelai was nineteen when Sylvia became sick. The tumour was discovered too late, and it felt as though Sylvia went from being so full of life to bedridden overnight. Lorelai had always known the day would come when she would have to say goodbye to her grandmother, but her grandmother had seemed so invincible that that day had always felt years, if not decades, away. Now, all of a sudden, Lorelai was faced with the reality that her grandmother had merely days left.

Sylvia had kept a gentle pressure on Lorelai since that afternoon a year ago, quietly suggesting that Lorelai should unburden herself of whatever she was holding onto. Lorelai knew telling her mother was not an option. She had distanced herself from both of her parents since she had kissed Thomas. At first she hadn't realised she was doing it, and, although her mother had put up a little more of a fight to stay in Lorelai's life, she had eventually given up and let Lorelai slip further and further away from them. Her mother stopped prying and Lorelai took that as a sign that her mother didn't care enough to want to know what was going on, so she simply continued to keep her secret to herself, and the walls around her grew more impenetrable every day. It wasn't until she had to face her grandmother's mortality that Lorelai felt this might be the only chance she'd have to share the weight of her secret.

'Now, I don't want Gran to see any of us crying,' Lila said from the driver's seat. Lorelai's father nodded solemnly.

'Why not?' Lorelai asked. 'She's dying. It's sad.'

'Of course, it's sad. Don't you think I know that?' Lila snapped. She took a deep breath. Silence. 'I just don't think that's what your gran would want. This might be the last time we all get to see her together. The last thing she'll want is tears and wailing. So we should all try and be happy. For Gran.'

Lorelai could understand what her mother was trying to do, fill Sylvia's final moments with happy memories, but she couldn't help but feel it would just end up being fake. But none of it mattered because as soon as Lila saw her mother in the hospital bed, frail and grey, she immediately burst into tears and ran to her side.

'Sweetheart.' Sylvia smiled weakly, her eyes closed. 'None of that. Come on, now.'

'I thought you were all for letting things out, Gran?' Lorelai walked round to the other side of the bed and took her grandmother's hand.

'I am. But if I'm not sad then you don't need to be.' She coughed and struggled to sit up enough to clear her throat. Lila helped as best she could. 'I've had quite the life but even the best books come to an end.'

The visit felt too short. Lorelai would have given anything to be back in the garden with her gran at that afternoon tea. She wouldn't fight or hide this time. She would tell Sylvia everything. Now, the only hope she had was the letter she had written and hidden in her coat pocket. She just needed to find the perfect moment to give it to her gran without raising her mother's suspicions. Lorelai knew if her mother saw it she'd want to know what it said.

They spent the day sharing stories and trying to make Sylvia as comfortable as possible, yet all the while Lorelai couldn't get rid of the feeling that time was running out. But for whom? Sylvia? Or herself?

When the time came to finally leave, Lorelai pretended she'd left her phone by Sylvia's bedside. 'I'll be back in a moment.' Before her parents could object, Lorelai quickly darted back into the room.

She took the letter from her coat pocket and pressed it into her gran's hands. 'You were right. I can't keep it in. We're back tomorrow. We'll talk then?' Lorelai kissed her gran's cheek and suddenly found that no more words could slip past the lump in her throat. She wanted to say she loved her, that she wished she'd opened up to her sooner but it was suddenly all too much.

Sylvia held the letter to her heart. 'Oh, darling,' she said with a smile and glistening eyes. 'I'm so proud of you.'

Lorelai left that day with hope, knowing she wouldn't be alone for much longer. But that was not to be. 'I'm so proud of you,' were the last words Lorelai heard her grandmother say. Sylvia passed away quietly in her sleep that night and Lorelai lost the only person she'd trusted with her secret thus far, not knowing if she lived long enough to find out what that secret was.

◆

Five

Piccadilly Circus station was hot and heaving. Joanie had headed off to Liberty, her favourite nightclub, determined to regain a bit of control and have some fun now that she was suddenly single again, leaving Lorelai to battle the central London crowds alone. Streams of people, many coming from one of the various theatres on Shaftesbury Avenue, were starting their journeys home at Piccadilly Circus. Lorelai joined the back of the hordes slowly filtering through the ticket barriers, one by one, flipping her Oyster card over and over in her hand. Everyone was crammed together and conversations bled into each other, contributing to the sound that was the orchestra of London at night-time.

When Lorelai finally reached the barrier, she swiped her blue card against the grimy fading yellow circle. It beeped embarrassingly loudly. She stepped back slightly, nudging the person who was so close she was practically giving him a piggyback ride. She swiped again but it just beeped once more.

'God, I'm sorry. I'm so sorry, let me just try once more,' she pleaded with the man behind her whose face was beginning to turn purple.

'It's alright!' a voice called out and an Oyster card appeared on the reader next to her and the gates swung open with a clunk. Lorelai quickly stepped through before they crashed shut and turned around to see who had helped her out.

'Hi.' Grayson smiled at her as he switched his Oyster card for his phone and used it to let himself through the gates.

Of all the people…

'Hello! Thank you!' Lorelai's voice was too bright, and she cringed. 'What are you doing here?' She tried to keep her expression neutral but her smile had a will of its own.

'I work round the corner,' he explained as they stepped onto the escalator.

'I remember you saying. I just meant… it's weird how we're both here at the same time, I guess.'

He was on the step in front of her which meant they were now both the same height. Her breath caught at the proximity of their faces. It was too late for her to move to the step above as someone was already behind her.

He's so close. I could just reach out my hand and—

'You sound like you're about to say it's a sign.' Grayson's smile twitched mischievously.

Lorelai laughed, embarrassed at herself. 'Do you believe in stuff like that?'

Does my breath smell? Do I look OK? Do I have popcorn stuck to my face? Why do I care so much? You're not meant to care this much!

'Signs? And fate and destiny? That kind of thing?' Grayson shrugged. 'I think we make our own luck.'

'Is that code for you saying it's not a coincidence you're here? Did you follow me to the station from work or something?' she joked.

Why do I kind of wish he had? You're losing it, Lorelai.

'Of course not! But I did figure out our shifts must end around the same time so I kind of hoped I'd bump into you on the way home at some point.'

The end of the escalator was nearing and Lorelai found herself hoping that they would be travelling the same way but as they stepped off the silver steps he edged left towards the Piccadilly line, and she needed to go right.

'I'm headed this way.' She nodded towards the old, paint-chipped sign of an arrow. How many thousands of people had said goodbye and parted ways in this exact spot?

'Ah, OK.' Grayson's shoulders deflated slightly. 'Will you be alright getting home?' he asked, his gaze heavy on her face.

'I'll be fine,' she said, frowning.

'What is it?'

'I've just… I dunno. Never had anyone ask me that, I guess.'

'Well, now you have. See you soon?'

Grayson put a hand on her shoulder, leaned in and kissed her cheek softly. It was only a polite peck, his lips a momentary pressure on her skin, but the warmth of him pressed into her entire being and Lorelai felt weak under his touch. The people around them melted away. Her heartbeat pounded loudly in her ears, and she was painfully aware that his lips were mere inches away from hers.

And just like that he pulled back, and was waving goodbye as he walked away.

'See you soon!' she called. She watched him get smaller until he was swept away by the crowds. When he was out of sight, Lorelai touched her cheek, closed her eyes, and wished she didn't feel what she so clearly felt.

Six

The nightmares were getting worse. Lorelai splashed her face with water and looked at her reflection in the bathroom mirror. Tonight's was inexplicable, full of confusing images of Thomas and Arthur, but Grayson too. It made no sense. Wearily, she made her way to the kitchen, hoping some writing would help calm her mind, but she was surprised to see the kitchen light already ablaze.

'What do you think you're doing?' Lorelai demanded.

After a nightmare, Lorelai found peace at the kitchen table where she would be undisturbed and could focus on something to help push away the disturbing images in her head. To find Riggs in the kitchen interrupting her quiet time instantly put her on edge again but seeing him thumbing through her notebook made her downright mad.

Riggs dropped her notebook onto the table as if it had suddenly burst into flames. 'Nothing! Just a bit of reading. It's very good!' He was babbling, wrong-footed.

'Give me that.' Lorelai snatched her notebook up and hugged it tightly to her chest, feeling suddenly exposed.

'Sorry, I didn't mean to…' Riggs's voice faded away.

'You're here as a guest. You shouldn't be looking through my private things.'

'You're right. I'm sorry,' Riggs said sheepishly. 'But in my defence, it was just lying there on the table. I didn't know what it was until I started reading it. And then I couldn't put it down. You weren't meant to know I'd read it.'

'So, you're just sorry you got caught?' Lorelai snapped. She needed to distract herself so she started making coffee.

'I'd be way sorrier if what I'd read was terrible. But I liked it. You're actually a pretty good writer.' When Lorelai didn't say anything, Riggs tried again. 'Look, I promise I wasn't snooping. Forgive me?'

Lorelai felt herself thawing. She *had* left the notebook out, and she couldn't deny she'd felt a jolt of pride when Riggs had said he'd enjoyed her writing. She retrieved two mugs from the cupboard, and poured them both a coffee, her silent acceptance of Riggs's apology.

'Why're you even up, anyway?'

'Why are *you* up?' Riggs countered.

Violent images flashed through her mind. Names screamed in terror. Blood. The crunch of metal. Lorelai swallowed and smiled brightly.

'I asked first,' she said.

'Never been one for a late night. Much prefer to be in bed early and up early rather than the other way around.'

Lorelai was surprised. She'd just assumed Riggs would be a late riser, not an early one. And he'd reached for something to read when he'd woken up? Maybe she should give him more credit.

'Five o'clock is a little extreme though, isn't it?'

'I've had at least six hours of sleep. That's enough for me. So come on. Why are you up?'

Lorelai shrugged. She finally settled on, 'I just never tend to sleep well.'

'Insomnia?'

'Something like that.'

They sat there for a while, wordlessly sipping coffee. When the silence became unbearable, Lorelai said, 'So…'

'So…' Riggs repeated.

Lorelai didn't really know Riggs. They had worked together for three years but they had never had a conversation about anything other than the cinema. She knew he was twenty-eight and that he'd grown up in London but she had no idea what qualifications he had, if any. His likes or dislikes. She'd never met any of his friends or romantic interests. She didn't know if he even wanted to take over his father's business or if he had other aspirations of his own.

'What do you want to do when you're older?' Lorelai blurted out.

'When I'm older?' He laughed. 'How young do you think I am?'

'Sorry.' She massaged her forehead, trying to kickstart the rational part of her brain. 'What I meant was… the cinema. Is that what you want to do with your life? When Wesley decides he's ready to hand over the keys? Or is that *his* dream?'

'Who wants to work at a cinema their whole life?' Riggs scoffed but then said quickly, 'Sorry, I mean… is that what you want to do with your life?'

'No, clearly not' – she gestured to her notebook – 'but I don't hate it as much as you seem to.'

'I don't hate working at the cinema,' Riggs said in a small, hurt voice.

'Really?' Lorelai couldn't hide her expression. She felt her face twist into one that said, *I don't believe you.*

'OK, OK, I don't love it,' he said, holding up his hands, 'but that's not the same as hating it.'

'You *act* like you hate it.'

'It's not my dream job, no. I didn't realise it was that obvious,' he said, wincing.

'So what *is* your dream job?'

Riggs looked as though he was about to say something and then stopped himself.

'Go on,' Lorelai encouraged.

'Well, the thing is, I don't really know,' Riggs admitted.

'What do you mean *you don't know?*' Lorelai fought hard not to roll her eyes.

'I don't know! Dad always wanted me to take over at the cinema so I left school when I was sixteen, after my GCSEs and I've been working there ever since.'

Lorelai wasn't used to hearing Riggs call Wesley 'Dad' and it always took her by surprise when he did, mostly because they looked so different that it was easy to forget they were father and son. Wesley was short, his skin weathered, wrinkled and pale from being cooped up in the cinema for days on end. Riggs was at least six foot with a ruddy complexion. Riggs had a youthful bounce to the way he walked and talked that made him seem far younger than he was. Lorelai wondered if this was why she viewed him as so incompetent. Neither she, Joanie nor Wesley trusted him with any of the bigger responsibilities, but was he actually more professional than they gave him credit for? Then she remembered when he had been entrusted with locking up at the end of the day and he had completely forgotten to set the burglar alarm. They had been robbed and the burglars had vandalised the place too. Did those errors in judgement come from not feeling pride in his work?

'Have you ever thought of quitting? Trying something else?'

Riggs narrowed his eyes at her. 'Don't be silly. My dad would never forgive me!'

'I actually think you'd be doing him a favour. Can I ask why he kicked you out?' Lorelai asked.

'It's obvious, isn't it? I'm twenty-eight and I've never taken responsibility for myself. I could easily have moved out years ago, but I just like having my washing done and having my meals cooked for me. I know I need to grow up.' His voice became small as he finished speaking, and he looked into the distance, looking every bit the scared little boy.

'At least you're honest,' Lorelai said, trying to lighten the mood.

'Dad got fed up of Mum doting on me and after a while she started to feel the same. I was officially a burden.' Riggs's eyes glistened with tears.

'Look on the bright side. When you go and visit, the food will taste twice as good.' Lorelai smiled kindly and was grateful when he smiled back. She decided to change tack. 'So have you ever had any ambitions, outside of The Duchess?'

'Not really. I think it was always just a given that the

cinema was my future. For as long as I can remember. That's just the way it was.' He shrugged.

Lorelai wondered what that must feel like, to feel your entire future was mapped out for you, whether that's what you wanted or not. With a start, she realised she knew exactly what that felt like. Sometimes there was security and stability in knowing exactly where your life was headed. Other times, it was suffocating.

'Nothing at school ever pique your interest?'

Riggs laughed. 'I was rubbish at school. I was usually trying to get off with girls behind the bike sheds.'

'Right.' *That sounds more like the Riggs I thought I knew,* Lorelai thought. 'So no other hobbies or interests?'

He just shrugged. 'Why?'

'Just… curious. There must be something that interests you, excites you?'

'Well, there isn't,' Riggs snapped. 'I'm what everyone says I am – unmotivated and useless.'

'Riggs, I didn't mean—'

'Forget it.' His face shut down, and Lorelai sensed he wouldn't be pressed any further.

'I'm sorry,' she said. 'I didn't mean to upset you.'

'You didn't. Anyway—' he suddenly smiled at her, the happy mask back in place '—what about *you*?'

'What about me?'

'I know you like working at The Duchess, but surely it's not your life's dream, right?'

'No.' Lorelai took a long sip from her mug, hoping he would take the hint and stop prodding. This was getting too intense.

'So, what's the grand plan for your future, then?'

'That's a bit of a big question, isn't it?'

'That's what you just asked me.'

Lorelai sighed, knowing he wouldn't let up until she gave him an answer. Why not tell him the truth? He'd shared something personal with her.

'Alright.' She got up from her seat and walked through to the living room, leaving her coffee behind. Riggs took a large gulp of his coffee before abandoning it and following obediently. Around the television, mounted on the wall, were her bookshelves filled with books and the DVDs of their adaptations. Lorelai was suddenly nervous about explaining this to Riggs.

'Joanie once asked me what one possession I would save if the flat was on fire and my mind zipped straight here. I spent ages wondering how many I could feasibly carry from a burning building.' She looked at the bursting shelves, and felt her heart swell.

'So... what exactly is the dream, then?' Riggs probed.

'Someone has to sit and turn the book into a script when it's adapted for the screen,' Lorelai said feebly and shrugged.

'That's the job you want?'

She nodded, looking up at her collection.

Riggs just nodded, no look of scepticism on his face. 'Been writing long?'

'Years. That's how I know I love it and that I wouldn't be terrible at it. I've written so many of my own scripts.'

'Which books have you adapted?'

Lorelai hated that she'd started down this road. Her dream was safest when it was just her own. Sharing it with someone else made it seem so *real*. She felt like a four-year-old who'd just told her teacher she wanted to be an astronaut. It felt just as ridiculous and impossible.

'I can't remember them all off the top of my head.'

'Tell me.'

'I think I'm up to… forty-three, now?' She knew it was definitely forty-three but for some reason she just couldn't find any conviction.

Riggs's mouth dropped open. 'You've adapted forty-three books into scripts for movies. Blimey. Who have you sent them to?' Riggs pulled out her copy of *The Bridge on the River Kwai* and thumbed through it.

'Oh god, no one,' she said, running her fingertips across the spines.

'Wait, what? You've not sent your scripts to anyone. Like, no one at all?'

'No.' She'd had this conversation with Joanie many times before. She never thought she'd be having it with Riggs of all people.

'Why not? Isn't that the aim?'

'Sending it to someone would mean risking someone hating it and telling me I'm not good enough.' She knew it was stupid but this was the reason and she wanted to be honest about it.

'Riiiight.'

'I'm just not ready to be told all my hard work has been for nothing.' Lorelai felt this was valid and so when Riggs replied with a sing-song, 'Suuuure,' she bristled.

'If you've got something to say just say it,' she demanded.

'I just think it's a waste!' He threw his hands in the air. 'No one's ever ready for rejection. It always sucks and it always stings but that shouldn't stop you from trying. What if you send it to someone and they end up loving it and hiring you on the spot? Isn't it worth the risk?'

'Riggs…' She turned away from him but either Riggs was not very good at picking up on hints or was very good at ignoring them.

'Surely after forty-odd attempts you'd be confident enough to send your work to a small studio?'

'Maybe. One day.' Another bog-standard phrase.

'It'll always be one day though, Lorelai, won't it? What if one day never comes?' Riggs's tone was suddenly serious.

'Why are you pushing this?' Lorelai laughed, trying to regain control of the conversation.

'I just think it's a bit rich for you to push me so hard about having a "dream" or whatever when you've got one and you won't even chase it!' Riggs said, his voice rising.

Lorelai felt something snap. She was only trying to be kind and now he was throwing it back in her face?

'Well, I'm definitely not going to take any advice from someone who's throwing their life away! Where's your drive? Your ambition?'

'Ouch,' Riggs said quietly, with a sad laugh.

She hadn't meant to say it. But it didn't matter. It was out there now. Lorelai realised that it was better to have an unfulfilled dream, than no dream at all. Riggs looked beaten.

'Riggs—'

'Thanks for the coffee.' He was hurt and stung and needed to retreat as quickly as possible. Which was why when he grabbed his jacket and left the flat, Lorelai didn't try to stop him.

◆

Despite the lingering trauma of her first teenage kisses, Lorelai did end up attending university. She had put it off for a year while she wrestled with the practicalities of being in that environment with her particular set of circumstances. But after Sylvia died, she retreated even further into herself, and had needed to put some physical, as well as emotional, distance between her and her parents. Starting university had been the obvious choice and surprisingly, it wasn't as challenging as she had expected. Fresher's week is usually a time that's rife with social events and meeting new people. A time that might lead to your first few drunken mistakes, and those in turn lead to avoiding certain people for the rest of your time at university. Lorelai had assumed that sex would prove pretty difficult if she was to avoid kissing anyone on the lips. Turns out it wasn't as hard as she had first thought.

If you're drunk enough, there are certain people out there who won't question the fact you turn your face away each time they lean in for the kiss. They would, though, find her behaviour strange so Lorelai never repeated the situation twice with the same person, but she did what she had to do in order to have the experiences she wanted to have, while also following the rules she had set for herself.

It just meant she gained the reputation of being the girl who never kissed the people she slept with. When asked why, she would simply say, 'It's too personal,' like Vivian in *Pretty Woman*.

She thought it was a good line that might make her a little mysterious. She had hoped it would surround her with intrigue, drawing people closer to her to find out more. Instead, her peers gave her a wider berth than they had before. She realised now that her grandmother had been her only hope of sharing her burden. The one person she was sure would understand and accept her regardless and yet the one person she could no longer tell.

◆

Seven

Lorelai needed to say sorry. She had a perfectly worded speech prepared that she'd practised under her breath on the way to work. However, when she arrived at The Duchess, Riggs was nowhere to be seen. It was Saturday and *The Lord of the Rings* marathon was taking place that evening, which meant there was a long night of work ahead of them all, but Lorelai would make sure she found time to talk with Riggs at some point.

'Are you looking forward to seeing *lover boy*?' Joanie asked, startling Lorelai.

Lorelai had been so focused on her apology to Riggs that for a while, Grayson hadn't been the only thing on her mind. Now, all thoughts of him thundered forward and her stomach was in knots. Was she looking forward to seeing him? She felt like a ticking time bomb of emotion, ready to explode at any moment. But what else? Her face grew warm when she thought about seeing him again. Yes, she was looking forward to him, and the thought terrified her.

'It's OK,' Joanie said, dropping her teasing tone. 'It's OK to want to see him again.'

Before Lorelai could respond, Wesley strode past, towards

the doors, where a queue of *Lord of the Rings* fans were patiently waiting. Lorelai looked around. Still no Riggs. Where was he?

'OK, Duchess team. Are we ready?' Wesley asked, his hands gripping each door handle, ready to swing them open. Joanie waved her popcorn scoop and Lorelai straightened up the countertop. 'Where the bloody hell is that boy?' he grumbled.

'I'm here.' Riggs emerged from the door behind the counter and tried to slip past quickly. Lorelai reached out and gently touched his arm.

'Hey, before the craziness begins I just wanted to say—'

'Lorelai, you really don't have to do this. It's fine.' Riggs didn't look at her.

'No, it's not fine. I'm sorry I said what I said. You're right, I am being a coward when it comes to my future but it wasn't fair to take it out on you. We all move through life at different speeds and you trusted me with some' – Lorelai dropped her voice further – 'personal things and it was unfair of me to throw it back in your face. I was a dick. And I'm sorry.'

'It's fine,' Riggs repeated, still not looking at her.

Lorelai ground her teeth, frustrated with herself for not getting this right. 'Let's find some time later to talk,' she said. 'Please?'

'Riggs!' Wesley clicked his fingers, summoning him. He jogged over to his father, and stood next to him. Riggs was on the door all night, checking tickets and collecting the stubs. It was going to be impossible for Lorelai to speak to him until everyone was seated.

'I officially declare that the marathon has… BEGUN!' Wesley swung the doors open and almost knocked out Riggs in one fell swoop. A cheer erupted from the crowd and creatures from Middle Earth quickly filled the foyer.

About half an hour later, as Lorelai was ringing up what felt like her hundredth drinks and snacks order, Joanie nudged her in the ribs.

'Joanie! That hurt!'

'Would you look over there!' Joanie hissed.

Lorelai looked towards the door, where Joanie was pointing, and saw two figures approaching, dressed in full hobbit costume. Their capes were held together with matching leaf-shaped brooches and their hairy feet looked alarmingly real.

Lorelai felt her whole face lift into a smile. *I'm excited to see him*, she thought. And then the memories crashed into her.

Cries of pain.

Dripping blood.

Crunching metal.

Bones breaking.

With considerable effort, Lorelai pushed the nightmares away and forced herself to smile. 'Merry and Pippin, I'm pleased you could make it.'

'I thought you said you weren't a fan of the movies.' Grayson leaned against the counter, ducking his head so they were almost at eye level.

'I can still know who all the characters are! So who's who?'

'I'm Pippin,' said the hobbit who must've been Grayson's younger brother, adjusting his strawberry-blond wig.

Grayson's brother looked to be about nineteen, but standing next to Grayson, with Grayson's height and width, he seemed even younger still. Even so, there was a strong family resemblance and Lorelai wondered if Grayson had ever been this fresh-faced and innocent-looking.

'And the costumes were...' Joanie reached over and tugged at a corner of Grayson's forest-green cloak.

'My idea, of course,' Grayson said.

'Yes but *my* handiwork!' Grayson's brother interjected with a proud grin.

'Sorry, I haven't introduced you. This is Aden. My younger brother.'

'I'm the handsome one,' Aden declared.

'You wish,' Grayson said good-naturedly. 'And be nice. Remember who bought the tickets.'

Lorelai laughed. 'Nice to meet you, Aden. I'm—'

'Lorelai, right?' Aden interrupted. Grayson elbowed him in the side. 'Oi! What was that for?' Grayson glared at his brother, a blush creeping along his cheeks. 'Oh. Sorry, Gray.' Aden looked sheepish.

'You're a pain in the arse,' Grayson said, trying to cover up his embarrassment. He caught Lorelai's eye and that brief look sent a wave of emotion rippling through her. *Get a grip,* she scolded herself.

'*You're* the pain in the arse, *lover boy*,' Aden said.

Joanie snorted with laughter, amused to hear her name for Grayson come out of his brother's mouth. Grayson quickly grabbed the ends of his brother's cloak and pulled him into a headlock. Aden was half laughing, half yelling expletives while fighting for breath. Lorelai knew she should move them along; the line behind them was getting longer, but this display of brotherly play-fighting did something to Lorelai's insides and she wasn't ready to let that feeling go. She glanced up and saw that Riggs had begun to pay a keen interest in Grayson and Aden from his position at the doors, and he didn't look happy. Finally, Grayson let Aden go.

'You're such a bastard!' Aden growled. 'It took me ages to get this wig perfect!'

'Mate, no one in here is going to mistake you for the real Pippin so I wouldn't worry too much.' Grayson put his arm around his brother's shoulders and ruffled the wig, messing it up further.

'Are you not freezing?' Lorelai asked, glancing down at their bare legs.

'Nah, all the fake hair on these feet keeps my toes toasty.' Grayson lifted a hobbit foot and wiggled it about.

'OK, you two,' Joanie said, waving her scoop, 'serious question: sweet or salty?'

'Salty,' they both said in unison. Lorelai grimaced.

'Are you judging my popcorn choices, Miss Lorelai?' Grayson said, arching an eyebrow.

Her name on his lips…

'Of course not. I mean, I think anyone who likes salty popcorn is a psychopath but no, no judgement.' She arched an eyebrow right back at him.

'Surely you don't actually like sweet popcorn?' Grayson asked.

'And if I do?'

'Then I might have to rethink this whole thing.'

'And what "whole thing" would that be?'

The air was suddenly heavy around them. Lorelai knew that Joanie and Aden were probably exchanging a knowing look, but she couldn't tear her eyes away from Grayson. Despite all of her misgivings, she couldn't stop herself, and now things had taken a turn and this seemed like much more than an innocent conversation about popcorn. Grayson looked at her intently, his expression unreadable.

'The "whole thing" that is me and you,' Grayson said finally. 'But I think you could bring me round to your *sweet* ways. If you wanted to. Away from here. Or somewhere else. Whatever you like. Just somewhere we can talk. Or not. You can't really talk at the cinema, can you? Unless you don't want to talk?' He'd been so close to being somewhat suave but as soon as he began bumbling over his words, Lorelai suddenly found him even more attractive.

Aden groaned. 'You are *so* cheesy. Where do you get this stuff from?! You have zero game.'

'Don't worry,' Joanie said, her eyes dancing mischievously. 'Lorelai's game isn't much better.'

They were all so preoccupied that none of them had noticed Riggs approach them.

'Is everything OK over here?' he demanded. His voice was deeper than usual, and he was holding himself up to his full height.

'Yeah. Of course. Why?' Lorelai shot a glance at Joanie who was also looking confused.

'I can easily ask these two to leave if they're bothering you.' Riggs was staring at Lorelai so intently she had to look away. His jaw was clenched, and his whole body was tightly coiled, just waiting to spring into action.

'Riggs, they're not bothering us.' Joanie's voice was firm but not firm enough to dissuade Riggs. He leaned a little closer to Lorelai.

'It's just that I heard him ask you out.'

'Yeah… So?' Lorelai almost laughed in Riggs's face. Is that what constituted being asked out these days?

'Not exactly professional, is it?' Riggs said, raising his voice, his eyes darting to Grayson.

'He doesn't have to be professional,' Joanie shot back. 'He doesn't work here.'

'Mate—' Grayson stepped towards them both and Riggs straightened up again '—yeah, I asked her out, well, sort of, but Lorelai was nothing but professional.'

'So you *were* bothering one of our staff at work, then?'

'Riggs, stop it,' Lorelai said. A thought struck her. 'Is this about earlier?'

'Earlier? What happened earlier?' Joanie looked between Lorelai and Riggs.

'Because if it is, I apologised. There's no need to embarrass me like this. I said I was sorry.'

But Riggs was on a mission. He rolled up his shirt sleeves and turned to Grayson and Aden. 'Right, I think it's best you both leave.'

'We haven't done anything,' Aden said indignantly.

'I'll happily apologise to Lorelai and Joanie…' Grayson offered.

'Really, there's no need,' Lorelai said quickly. 'Riggs, come on, everything is fine. They're our friends.' Lorelai needed to shut this down before it got out of hand, but Riggs wasn't paying attention to her anymore. He didn't appear to have heard a word she'd said. He was too busy glaring at Grayson.

'Just take your free popcorn and your free drink and go!' Riggs picked up Grayson's bucket and cup from the counter and shoved them at him. Grayson instinctively held up his hands and caught Riggs's wrists, who then tried to yank himself out of Grayson's grip. Grayson let go of Riggs's wrists but Riggs was already pulling away hard, expecting resistance. The popcorn bucket and the contents of the cup flew over his shoulder, showering Lorelai in a cloud of kernels and a tsunami wave of Diet Coke.

'What the *fuck*, Riggs?!' Lorelai shrieked. *Men.*

Riggs stepped back and surveyed the result of his toxic masculinity masquerading as a defence of Lorelai's honour. His mouth flapped open and closed in an attempt to catch an explanation, an excuse, anything to make sense of what he'd just done, but he clearly came up short.

Lorelai glanced over at Grayson, hoping by some miracle he'd somehow been distracted and missed this highly embarrassing moment, but no. Eyes wide, the corners of his lips twitching, not knowing whether to be shocked or to laugh, Grayson had seen it all.

'Have you lost your mind?' Joanie clipped Riggs around the head.

Riggs clutched his head, looking down at the floor contritely, before mumbling, 'I just… I thought…'

'What did you think, Riggs? I'm desperate to hear this,' Joanie said, her hands on her hips.

'I thought you… needed a hand!'

'But Lorelai told you they were our friends,' Joanie said sternly. 'We were just having a laugh! Look at her!'

'I'm sorry! *God,*' he huffed, 'I was only trying to help!'

'Umm… want to help me now?' Lorelai wrung out the ends of her sopping sleeves. Riggs picked a single piece of popcorn out of her hair. Lorelai shooed him away and grabbed a handful of napkins. 'What's got into you? This sort of testosterone display is so unlike you. You completely ignored what I said.' Lorelai shook her head at Riggs who was staring at the wet patch on the carpet.

'Lorelai! What on earth…?' Wesley appeared, eyes wide as he took in Lorelai's appearance. 'What happened?'

'It was an accident,' Riggs began.

'An accident?!' Joanie was incredulous. 'It was classic caveman behaviour, you thinking you know best.'

'Will someone tell me what's going on?' Wesley demanded.

'Riggs just soaked Lorelai with a Diet Coke – a large one, might I add – after trying to throw these two gentlemen out for absolutely no reason,' Joanie explained.

'I got the wrong end of the stick!' Desperation crept into Riggs's voice and, despite her soaking, sticky clothes and hair, Lorelai felt a pang of sympathy. Things really weren't going Riggs's way at the moment.

'My office. Now,' Wesley said, glaring at Riggs.

'But Dad—'

'NOW!'

'I think an apology is in order first, don't you?' Joanie folded her arms.

'He hasn't apologised yet?!' Wesley yelped.

'I have!' Riggs said, pleading.

'Not to me,' Lorelai said gently, before Joanie could stick the boot in again. She gestured to where Grayson and Aden were standing. 'To them.'

Riggs shoved his hands into the pocket of his apron and turned to Grayson. 'I'm sorry, mate. I didn't know you knew

Lorelai and I thought you were coming on to her...' He cleared his throat and added, 'and Joanie. Obviously, I was wrong.'

'You were. But no hard feelings, OK. Easy mistake to make.' Grayson held out his hand. Riggs stared at it in surprise.

'Shake it, you idiot!' Joanie cried.

Riggs, startled, shook Grayson's hand, not quite able to meet his eye.

'My office,' Wesley instructed and Riggs walked away, head bowed. 'Grayson, was it? I can't apologise enough. My son is... well, he's not exactly employee of the month. I would like to offer you a refund on your tickets for tonight for you and your friend.'

'I'm his brother,' Aden said, stepping forward and putting a hand on Grayson's shoulder.

'We'd love for you to stay and enjoy the marathon if you feel like your night hasn't been entirely ruined. Joanie and Lorelai will make sure your bucket and cups are never empty, courtesy of the cinema. Now if you'll excuse me, I have something to take care of.' With that, Wesley deftly took his exit, through to the back where Riggs was waiting.

'Are you OK?' Joanie grabbed a handful of napkins and attempted to help Lorelai dry off.

'I'll be fine. It's only a bit of fizzy drink. I think it's Riggs who isn't OK.' Lorelai glanced in the direction of Wesley's office.

'Do you have any idea what that was? What got into him?' Joanie asked.

'You mean he's not usually like that?' Grayson asked.

Joanie shook her head. 'He's annoying and lazy, but harmless.'

Lorelai stayed silent. She was almost certain their conversation that morning had been the catalyst for Riggs's behaviour, that he felt he had something to prove, but she couldn't say that to anyone. It was too personal.

'Maybe we should go,' Aden said to Grayson.

'No! Don't go. I'd…' Lorelai took a deep breath. 'I'd like you to stay. But obviously I get it if you're not feeling it.'

'It's not that,' Grayson said, struggling to find the right words. 'That guy… he seemed pretty intense. About you.'

'We had a bit of row this morning,' Lorelai said quietly so Joanie wouldn't overhear. 'I think it put him on edge. And it's Joanie he's got the crush on, not me.'

'Good to know,' Grayson said, holding her gaze again.

How can this man be a bumbling wreck one second, and then hold me completely captive the next? Lorelai frantically searched for more popcorn kernels in her hair, anything to keep her distracted, no matter how mad it made her look.

'So that guy said free popcorn, right?' Aden craned his neck to look at the popcorn machine that was popping away, fluffy goodness spewing out of the central silver canister and spilling down into the glass case.

'*And* a full refund *and* free fizzy drinks,' Lorelai added.

'What d'ya say? We'd be fools not to stay and take full advantage, right?' Aden put his arm around his brother's shoulders.

'Right,' Grayson said. 'OK, let's get our fill and find our seats. The marathon hasn't even started yet, and I already feel knackered!'

'Aden,' Joanie called. 'Which drink do you want?'

Aden wandered over towards Joanie, leaving Lorelai and Grayson alone. Grayson reached out and tugged a strand of her wet hair.

'You need fresh clothes,' he said softly. 'And probably a shower.'

'Tell me about it,' Lorelai said as lightly as she could manage. *Breathe, Lorelai. Breathe.* Before she knew what she was doing, she had placed her hand on Grayson's arm. He looked down at it for a second, before placing his hand over hers, strong and heavy. His skin was warm, surrounding her hand, and it made her breath catch for a second before she said, 'I'm really glad you're staying.'

◆

It took Lorelai a few years to figure out exactly what it was she was seeing when she kissed someone. Before that, endless questions would run through her mind. Was it an Ebenezer Scrooge in *A Christmas Carol* kind of deal? Was she being shown a version of the future that could be changed if these people did something differently or mended their ways? Or could she do something to prevent their deaths? At thirteen and eighteen she'd been too young to think seriously about 'preventing their deaths'. It sounded crazy. She started to believe that maybe she *was* crazy. Was it even the future she was seeing? Perhaps there was something wrong with her, mentally?

It was when she was at university that Lorelai got her answer. News of Thomas and Arthur's deaths reached her. They had both tragically died within six months of each other: Arthur while drink-driving and Thomas had been stabbed outside a club – exactly the ways in which Lorelai had seen them go years before. So she wasn't crazy. She *had* seen their future deaths.

Now another question burned through her: was Lorelai simply a witness to their future deaths through her kiss, and did she have the power to intervene? Or had her kiss been the thing that sealed their fates, once and for all?

◆

Eight

Event nights were often long and slow. Lorelai had changed into her spare set of work clothes and had done the best she could with her hair in the ladies' toilets, but after the initial excitement of the evening, she didn't have much to do when the movies were on. This marathon in particular was dragging on longer than usual, and in her heart she knew it was because Grayson was close by. So close, yet she wasn't able to talk to him. She sat at the back of the screen for some of the first movie but spent the majority of it staring at the back of his head, desperately wishing for him to turn around and look at her. She thought he might come and find her between the movies but, frustratingly, Grayson and Aden were cornered by Wesley during every break, who continued to ply them with freebies.

Lorelai gripped the edge of the sink and looked at her reflection in the mirror of the staff toilet. The dim lighting made the dark circles under her eyes look even darker.

'Come on, Lorelai' – she pointed to her reflection – 'you're acting like a schoolgirl. Just stop it, OK? You've made your decision – love, romance, all of it is off the table. You've been doing it for this long, you can carry on doing it. Nothing has changed.'

Yes, it has. Lorelai squeezed her eyes shut, and Grayson's face appeared. His kind eyes. The way he looked at her. The curve of his smile. 'Nothing has changed,' she repeated. 'Nothing's changed. Nothing's changed. Nothing makes Grayson any different.' *That's not true.* 'Yes it is! He isn't different. He can't be. This is what I need to do. I can't put myself through it again. Especially for someone who may not stick around. And he wouldn't. Not if he knew...' She took a deep, long, steady breath. This was working. 'So that's that. It's a no and will always be a no.' Lorelai stepped back from the sink and gave herself a final, firm nod. She felt better now. No more nonsense. She would focus on herself. Nothing was missing and she didn't need anyone to complete her. Lorelai *was* complete.

She strode back out to the foyer, head held high, confident she was making the right choice. And then she saw Grayson and her resolve weakened. He was leaning against the counter, looking out of the doors, watching Soho slowly begin to spring to life. Soho didn't sleep for very long each night, but it was quite something to watch it go to sleep, only to awaken a few hours later.

'Has it got to a boring bit?' she asked, making him jump.

'Aden fell asleep, and when he woke up he was furious I didn't wake him up sooner and I got fed up with his sulking. Plus the last movie is *loooong*.' He rubbed his bleary eyes.

'At least you're still up. That's an improvement from last time, right?'

'To be honest, I may have had a snooze during the second movie but only for about ten minutes before the girl behind me screamed at an orc. Flung her popcorn everywhere.' Grayson shook his head for effect, but a little piece of popcorn did in fact fall to the ground.

'Well, at least you don't have to clean it up!' Lorelai ducked underneath the counter for a dustpan and brush. She took a deep breath to steady herself, before standing up. *If I'm fine by myself then why does being with him feel more exciting than being on my own?*

'True but I get my fair share of that where I work too.'

'Which theatre was it again?'

'The Palace. Just around the corner actually.'

'One of the ones on Shaftesbury. Cool.' Lorelai never really visited the theatre. It was only round the corner but when the tickets sometimes cost ten times more than the tickets at the cinema, she could hardly justify the price when she only just about made rent each month as it was.

'Less popcorn but lots more plastic wine cups and empty sweet packets.'

'Just as glamorous as here then. So that's why you come here on a Saturday? It's so close?'

'Well, I have a few reasons for coming here.' Grayson's voice dropped to what she could only describe as a bedroom whisper and she promptly got to her feet, almost dropping what she'd collected in her dustpan.

'The excellent events, obviously.' She quick marched around to the other side of the counter where he couldn't follow her but he leaned on his elbows and leaned in closer.

'That's one of the reasons but admittedly not the main reason. Don't tell Wesley… Guess again.'

'I'm out of ideas.' She shrugged and tried to look anywhere but at him, but he was leaning in close and it was hard to avoid him. Her eyes fluttered to his lips. The thought of kissing them was almost too much to bear and just as she found herself leaning in with reckless abandon, the door behind them opened with a squeak. Lorelai jumped back as if she'd been electrocuted but Grayson stayed exactly where he was, smiling.

'Not interrupting, am I?' Riggs said. He had his jacket on and his bag was slung over his shoulder.

'We thought you'd left ages ago. Have you been back there this whole time?' Lorelai couldn't quite meet anyone's eye.

'Dad didn't want me out front anymore tonight. For obvious reasons.' Riggs glanced at Grayson. 'He had me doing inventory out the back but...' Riggs took a deep breath and Lorelai could hear it shake in his throat, 'when I couldn't even do that right, he fired me.'

Lorelai gasped. 'He *fired* you?'

'Yup. So... that's that, I guess.' Riggs shrugged.

'Where the *fuck* have you been?' Joanie yelled at Riggs, storming through the doors that led to the screen. 'You get one bollocking and then disappear all night?'

'Joanie...' Lorelai began but Joanie held up a finger.

'No, Lollie,' Joanie interrupted.

Lorelai's eyes darted to Grayson to check if he'd picked up on that nickname and his raised eyebrows suggested he had. She groaned inwardly.

'No, I'm done,' Joanie ranted, in full flow now. 'I have no more fucks to give. My fuck field is barren. My river of fucks has runneth dry. I am fresh. Out. Of fucks!'

Riggs, who had already been defeated, looked so completely beaten back by her words.

'*Joanie!*' Lorelai hissed.

'*What?!*' Joanie spun round to face Lorelai.

'Riggs just got fired,' Lorelai explained.

Riggs let his gaze slide to the floor, his head hanging in embarrassment.

'Oh,' was all Joanie could say, the wind knocked out of her sails.

'You can keep staying with us until you find another job,' Lorelai told Riggs gently.

'He's staying with you?' Grayson finally spoke up.

'Just for a bit,' Lorelai said quickly. 'He had nowhere else to go.'

'You can stay for a few more days,' Joanie said. 'But I want you gone by next week.'

'Joanie—'

'No, Lorelai.' Joanie was firm. 'Look, Riggs, I'm sorry you got fired, but this can't have been a shock to you. It's time for you to figure things out, and stand on your own two feet.'

In her heart, Lorelai knew Joanie was right. Riggs would never find out what his dream was if they kept coddling him. And poor Wesley. For all the time she'd worked at The Duchess, Wesley had talked at great length about how his son would take over and run the cinema one day. It was his dream that the business would be passed on from father to child, generation after generation. His legacy continuing until cinemas became obsolete. Firing Riggs was not only a father firing his son, it was also the final nail in the coffin to his life's dream.

'Listen,' Grayson said to Riggs, 'I hope you don't think I asked for you to be fired. I promise it wasn't like that.'

'Whatever.' Riggs made his way around the counter. 'I'm going for a walk. I don't know when I'll be home.' And then he was gone.

✦

Lorelai awoke abruptly in a bed that wasn't her own and found herself staring at her jeans, which were flung over the back of an unfamiliar desk chair. She was clammy and her head was pounding harder than it had in a very long time. She wanted so badly to blame alcohol, but she knew by the visions swimming around her mind that it was another nightmare. The blood-red numbers of the alarm clock glared 4 A.M. Lorelai rolled over to see the face of the man she'd spent the night with and couldn't stop herself from smiling. Michael.

Lorelai had admired Michael during her fresher's year but had never found the courage to speak to him. He had an understated kind of confidence she envied with her whole being. He was never afraid to show off his knowledge but was also the first to admit when he was wrong. He would throw up his hands and laugh like it didn't pain him to admit defeat. Lorelai was attracted to him in a way she'd never felt before.

Finally, in her final year, she'd bumped into him at a coffee shop and she had somehow found the right words to say. She had been happily surprised when Michael had known her name, known who she was. He offered her a seat at his table and they'd talked for over an hour before either of them had realised how much time had passed.

It was the beginning of something, even if Lorelai wasn't prepared to admit it. Being near Michael made her feel like someone else. Someone who wasn't constantly worried about what people would think of her. Someone who didn't have a secret to hide. It was easy to forget about all of that with Michael close by because he made her laugh and made her feel clever. He made Lorelai feel normal. He made her feel comfortable and as someone who had never felt hugely comfortable with anyone before, Lorelai basked in that feeling.

But then her nightmares would come, each one worse than the one before it. Night after night she would jolt awake, the images replaying vividly, and her head feeling as though it would split in two. She didn't know why her nightmares were becoming so vivid, and lingering for so long when she was awake, but she knew it couldn't be anything good.

Her smile dissolved into a hard, thin line. Now that she was in Michael's bed, lying beside him, the painful realisation that she could never be normal, could never have whatever was between her and Michael came crashing down around her.

Lorelai felt the sudden urge to leave, to flee, to put as much distance between her and Michael as she could. Being close to him felt so comfortable and so right and yet so terrifying. Being close to someone in the way she felt she wanted to be with Michael would mean being honest. It would mean not having secrets. Secrets so big they could destroy a relationship. She panicked. She couldn't find enough strength to stay calm. All she could think about was getting as far away from Michael as possible. She kicked off the covers, grabbed her clothes and ran out of his room. Lorelai could hear him calling out after her, but she kept running.

Whatever they were couldn't happen. She'd let herself get too close. She'd let things go too far. She'd let herself develop feelings for someone. And how could she be close to someone when she might be the reason they died?

No. It could never happen. Not now. Not ever.

✦

Nine

It was half nine in the morning, and Lorelai was making her way to the tube station with Joanie, Grayson and Aden. Lorelai loved Soho best in the morning. The way that Soho began to rumble into life as the morning trundled on, and the vibrant colour of the party the night before drained away and turned into the slate grey of business suits, as they hurriedly weaved in and out of tourists. At 6 a.m., you could still spot the last vestiges of the previous evening. A couple of hobbits walking through Soho at that time would barely turn one head. But at half past nine, things were different.

'You are both far braver than I am.' Lorelai laughed, wafting Grayson's green cape behind him.

'It takes a very secure person to dress like that and walk with as much purpose as you do,' Joanie called over.

Grayson held his chin high and began to strut down the street. Aden gave his brother a shove.

'Oh, come on, you're not still angry at me, are you? You looked so cute when you were asleep, I couldn't possibly have woken you up!' Grayson went to pinch his cheeks but Aden shoved him away again.

'I missed half of the second movie! I slept through so much good stuff.'

'Pfft, you've seen them all before and you woke up again long before they got to Mordor. There's always next time!' Grayson laughed but Aden pointedly pulled his earbuds out of his pocket, stuffed them in his ears and walked on ahead.

'So, Graaaaayson.' Joanie sing-songed the words and Lorelai shot her a sideways glance, knowing this meant she was up to mischief. 'Are you free sometime soon? Saaayyyy tomorrow?' She looped her arm under Lorelai's.

'Maaaayybbee,' Grayson sang back. 'Why?'

'Lorelai has Mondays off, so I was wondering if you fancied taking her for dinner?'

'Joanie!' Lorelai groaned, trying to pull her arm out of Joanie's iron grip.

'Shh, the grown-ups are talking,' she said, patting Lorelai's hand.

Grayson darted a look at Lorelai, who rolled her eyes in her friend's direction. Clearly these plans were out of her control and so he took her shrug as the go-ahead to continue using Joanie as the middle woman.

'I can't do dinner as I work in the evenings on Monday.' Grayson smiled. 'I could do brunch, though?'

'Brunch?!' Joanie shrieked, startling a few nearby pigeons. Even Aden pulled out one earbud and glanced back in their direction.

Grayson laughed. 'What's wrong with brunch?'

'Brunch. As in the meal between breakfast and lunch?' Joanie asked. 'Brunch... as in the meal that consists of a measly amount of avocado smashed to a pulp, shoved on wafer-thin gluten-free bread served with a coffee that comes in a cup the size of my little toe? All for the extortionate price of our monthly rent?'

'I don't think I've ever met anyone who's felt so strongly about a meal before.' Grayson rubbed his eyes, his brain groggy from a night of very little sleep and not quite up to the task of tackling Joanie's ferocity.

'Don't even get her started on elevenses...' Lorelai muttered, and she enjoyed the sleepy smile he threw her way.

'You'll need to do better than brunch.' Joanie wagged a finger at Grayson.

'I like brunch!' Lorelai protested.

Joanie disentangled her arm and playfully shoved Lorelai away. 'You're made for each other! Alright, then. Grayson, just call up the cinema and ask for me because this one has no follow-through and we can organise a time and a place. I'm gonna go and bother Aden and give you guys some... *alone time.*' With that she skipped off, and pulled a bud out of Aden's ear and placed it in one of her own.

'Wow. Is she—'

'Always like that? Yeah.'

They both slowed their pace to create more distance between them and Joanie and Aden.

'So... no follow-through?' Grayson pushed his hands deep inside the pockets of his linen trousers.

'You caught that.' Lorelai dipped her mouth down below the lip of her scarf.

'Listen, Joanie's sweet and I really appreciate her putting in a good word for me but if you don't want to go out next week,

I get it.' Grayson bumped her shoulder with his. The warmth of his voice was so inviting but she couldn't let herself become distracted by that. This was too confusing.

'Look… it's not you.'

Even though Grayson had said he got it, his shoulders fell, as if he'd been holding onto a bit of hope, waiting for her to answer.

'I know the "it's not you, it's me" line is overused but it's true. I've not dated anyone in a while now because I've got… stuff.'

'Like emotional baggage?'

She looked up at him and, for the briefest of moments, wondered if she could tell this man her secret. She quickly dismissed it. Of course she couldn't. The burden was hers to bear alone. It was time to shut this down, before it got out of hand.

'Sure. Let's go with that. Emotional baggage. I don't date. I have my reasons and I don't ever expect anyone to understand them,' and then, as Grayson took a breath to ask a question, she added, 'which is also why I never tell anyone what those reasons are. I'm happy as I am.'

'OK, fair enough. That's pretty refreshing, though – you know who you are. I like that.' Grayson ran a hand through his hair. 'Well, how about just as friends then?'

'What? What do you mean *friends*?' she said it as though the word was alien to her.

'I *mean* that it doesn't have to be a date. You have friends, right?' He gestured to Joanie who was now dancing outside of Leicester Square station to whatever music Aden was playing. 'And going for coffee or a meal with a friend is a normal thing to do, right?'

'It is but... I am serious about not wanting to date you,' Lorelai clarified.

'Yes, I did hear you the first time,' Grayson said, laughing.

'And I'm not going to change my mind.'

'You seem like a woman of your word. I wouldn't expect you to.'

'Sex is off the table too.' She stopped and turned to him.

'Woah, who said anything about sex?!' Grayson stopped, his eyes darting around them to see if anyone had heard her.

'I'm just making myself completely clear. And if that's a deal-breaker for you and you're just going to disappear and never—'

Grayson held up his hand. 'Are you telling me that of all the men who've asked you out that you've turned down, not a single one of them... Well, no one stuck around to get to know you just... because? The end game was sex and if that was off the table they walked away?'

'You sound surprised,' Lorelai said.

'I suppose I am. I'm sorry, first and foremost. That sucks. Secondly, I just think you're pretty cool. I like spending time with you.'

Lorelai couldn't think of anything to say so she smiled and picked up the pace again.

'No, seriously! You love movies as much as I do. You love to read. You were kind to your friend even after he behaved like an idiot. Do I need any more reasons? You're cool. Why wouldn't I want to be friends with someone cool?'

'Indeed,' was all Lorelai could manage.

Grayson had an innocence to him. He was upbeat where most people were pessimistic. Lorelai knew she was a little pessimistic.

Had she ever been as positive as Grayson? He seemed unburdened by the world, not because he was naive but because he chose not to be weighed down by responsibility. Choosing to make friends with Lorelai seemed foreign and strange to her. *You make friends with people because you work with them or you went to school together,* she thought. *You don't find someone who you like and then proposition them for their friendship. Who does that?*

Grayson did that and she liked it.

Before Lorelai could think of an excuse to turn down Grayson's offer of friendship as well, she said, 'Alright. Brunch. But not tomorrow. Wesley always makes us do the late Sunday shift after a Saturday night marathon so I don't think I'll be up in time for brunch tomorrow. But the Monday after? Call up the cinema and ask for me or… well, that weirdo.' She gestured to Joanie who was now attempting to floss next to a very concerned-looking Aden.

◆

'I still can't believe you said yes. You said YES!' Joanie yelled, turning the key in the lock. Lorelai shushed her before she disturbed their neighbours.

'I can't believe it either,' she admitted. 'But it's just as friends. It's not going to become messy or horrendous and the start of my worst nightmare.'

'Save some of that positivity for your date, Lollie. I'm sure Grayson won't be able to resist your optimistic zest for life.'

'It's not a date!' Lorelai insisted. 'I've been very clear. We're going to be friends and that's it.'

The sound of glass clinking against glass made them both freeze. Lorelai raised her eyebrows at Joanie. Riggs was home.

'Riggs,' Lorelai called out, but she was met with silence.

Joanie marched into the living room, with Lorelai hot on her heels. Riggs was sat in darkness illuminated only by the light of the kitchen, which spilled onto his slouched form on the floor. There were several empty beer bottles scattered around him. Four more were lined up on the coffee table in front of him, their caps removed, ready to be consumed.

'Everything alright?' Lorelai's redundant question startled Riggs. He looked up at them with red, puffy, sad eyes. His face crumpled and he let the tears flow hot and freely down his face. 'Oh, Riggs.'

Joanie looked at Lorelai in alarm. Joanie was all fire and heat when she thought Riggs was shirking his responsibilities, but this was something else. She didn't know what to say or how to comfort this broken man in front of her.

Lorelai knew this was all on her. 'Why don't you let me speak to Riggs alone for a bit?' she whispered to Joanie. Joanie eagerly nodded in agreement.

'I'll make us some coffee,' Joanie declared before disappearing.

Lorelai took off her coat and scarf, placed it over the arm of the couch and sat on the floor beside Riggs.

'Not my best night,' he said, reaching out to peel a green metallic label off a bottle.

'Was it your worst night?' Lorelai let her shoulder bump against his and left it there.

'It's up there but... no.' Riggs laughed sadly at himself. 'Not my worst.'

'Damn. I had a whole inspirational speech ready for when you said yes. Then I would've said something enlightening, like, "It's only up from here!" Or, "You've survived your worst day, so now you can get through anything".'

'Sorry. Didn't mean to spoil the pre-planned encouragement.' Riggs picked up a full beer bottle and began to drain it at worrying speed.

'How much beer have you had?' Lorelai asked, looking at the debris.

Riggs ignored the question. 'I have no plans for the future. No real interests to pursue. No money. No home. No job.' He paused. 'No girlfriend,' he said more quietly.

'You can have all of that. It'll take time but this is a huge turning point in your life. You're still young. There's plenty of time to figure out what you want to do.'

'Who's going to love me?'

So he's really hung up on the girlfriend thing.

'You've had girlfriends before… right?' Had he? Lorelai had no idea. She'd never seen him with any girls but then she didn't often see him outside of work. No friends and no girlfriends seemed unlikely and, yet, here he was, sat on her living room floor.

'As soon as they realised I lived with my parents they disappeared pretty quickly.' He folded the label over and over, creasing the edges with his fingernails.

'You don't live with your parents anymore. And if a girl cares about where you live then she's not the girl for you.'

'Would *you* care?' he asked after a moment.

'If someone I was dating lived with their parents, you mean?'

He nodded. Would she care? Perhaps a little, but not enough to put her off dating them. She had other reasons for that... 'No... no I wouldn't.'

'Really? You wouldn't care if someone had no job, no money and still lived with their parents...?'

'If I really liked them, no. That's not a deal breaker. But if they weren't happy with the life they had I think I'd probably encourage them to—'

Lorelai couldn't quite fathom what happened next. Her vision went quickly black, the breath knocked out of her as she fell backwards into a dark abyss. Images started to flash through her mind. Several bottles of whisky surrounded by small white dots. Everything was a blur – she couldn't focus on anything for long enough. The images danced around, hazy and unclear. She heard groaning and something rattling. The small white dots. They were pills being poured from a plastic pill bottle into a pair of dirty hands. But everything was so confused. This wasn't like the other times.

Lorelai struggled to open her eyes, and saw Riggs above her.

'Riggs...' she mumbled.

'Oh, Lorelai.' Riggs pulled back for a second, before kissing her again.

This time she was keenly aware of Riggs's rough, chapped lips finding hers. But the images were different than before. Now she saw an old man, alone, asleep in bed. He awoke, a hand clutching his chest, before collapsing back down again, gone forever. The vision slammed into her brain several times and she felt a tightening in her own chest. It took her far too long to realise why she had seen two potential futures.

As the pain in the back of her head subsided she tuned back into the weight that was on top of her, the breath on her neck and the smell of beer.

'GET THE FUCK OFF ME NOW!' she yelled against his mouth, pushing him back, trying to sit up.

'WHAT THE FUCK IS GOING ON!' Joanie flew into the room so fast she skidded into the coffee table, knocking the full bottles of beer onto Lorelai and Riggs who were tangled together on the floor. Joanie grabbed Lorelai by her underarms and slid her out from under Riggs. His expression cleared as he realised what he'd done.

'I'M SORRY! I'm sorry! I thought… I just—' Riggs was on his knees, soaked in beer, his head in his hands.

'Don't you dare try to justify this!' Joanie hauled Lorelai up from the floor and stood in front of her, arms outstretched.

'I misread the situation! I thought you were coming on to me!'

'Coming on to you?!' Lorelai shrieked, a tear catching in the corner of her mouth.

'You said you didn't care if I didn't have a job or money or lived with my parents!'

'I wasn't talking about *you,* you arrogant idiot! I was saying it hypothetically about someone I might be dating, Riggs! But I'm not dating you, am I? Nor do I want to!'

'I'm sorry, I'm sorry.' Riggs kept repeating his apology as he pushed himself up onto the couch, still wobbly from the amount of alcohol in his system.

'Jesus Christ. Did he kiss you?' Joanie span around to face Lorelai. She held her by the shoulders, checking her over for signs of damage. But the damage was already done.

'God forbid anyone kisses me,' Riggs muttered, rubbing his temples.

'This isn't about you!' Joanie shouted.

'That wasn't OK, Riggs,' Lorelai said through her tears. 'I didn't want that.' She wiped her mouth, but she could still feel his lips on hers.

'Why didn't you say?' Riggs mumbled, his hands covering his face in shame.

'When exactly was I meant to mention it? When your tongue was already in my mouth?'

'He slipped you the tongue?' Joanie exclaimed.

'Not now, Joanie,' Lorelai said, and Joanie nodded, understanding.

'Why, Riggs? I was just trying to be nice to you. I wasn't coming on to you.'

'You were nice. The nicest anyone's been to me in a long time.' He looked up at Lorelai, mournfully. 'I'm... I'm really drunk.'

'Is that meant to be an excuse?' Joanie snapped. 'Actually, you know what? I don't care. Out. Get out. Now.'

'Joanie...' Lorelai put a hand on her friend's shoulder, thinking about what she had seen when Riggs had kissed her. Riggs kissing her hadn't been OK, and she'd make sure he knew that, but the visions kept coming back to her. She was disorientated and needed to be alone for a while.

'No. No, no, NO! You cannot seriously still be defending him?!'

'I'm not! I'm not but... when we wake up later this afternoon, we'll discuss this. Right now, we're sleep-deprived from working all night and we all need some rest. We need to sleep on it. In separate rooms. Away from each other.'

Joanie's face softened when she looked into Lorelai's tired, red eyes. Joanie sighed and nodded, and then turned to Riggs.

'You heard the lady. Clean up this mess and then you're sleeping on the sofa or the floor or anywhere that's in the vicinity of this room. You are to go nowhere near Lorelai. Or me for that matter. You hear me?'

Joanie grabbed Lorelai by the hand and led her towards her bedroom. Lorelai held onto her friend's cool hand, soothing against her sweaty palm. She knew Joanie was ready to kick Riggs out but Lorelai was relieved that he would be in the flat, at least for another day. She could keep an eye on him here.

Because for the first time in seven years she had been kissed, which meant for the first time in seven years she had seen the way someone was going to die – and that person was Riggs.

PART TWO

The Messy Middle

Ten

Telling Joanie her secret had been entirely unplanned. Lorelai would have taken it to her grave had it not been for Joanie being unbelievably nosy on a morning when Lorelai felt too tired to make excuses. There were only so many nights out you could have with someone before they started to notice your complete disinterest in anyone, ever, and began to ask questions.

'OK, OK. Don't be cross with me but… I *need* to know,' Joanie said one morning about six months after they had met. Lorelai adored Joanie more than any friend she'd ever had but her heart momentarily stopped, praying what she thought was coming next, wasn't. 'You can tell me to sod off because it's really none of my business but know that if you don't answer I will become insufferable,' Joanie said, adjusting her position so she was sitting back on her knees.

'Noted.' Lorelai swallowed a mouthful of her hot tea.

'How is it that you're single?' Joanie said quickly, and then covered most of her face with the hood of her dressing gown, only her wide eyes visible.

Lorelai felt a wave of heat rush up her body but she pulled

as much fabric of her own dressing gown around her, hoping it would protect her from this conversation.

When Lorelai didn't say anything, Joanie spoke again. 'Seriously, you could make a killing!'

Lorelai flinched. Joanie's choice of words would have been insensitive had she known Lorelai's secret.

'I've seen a fair few people try their luck with you over the last few months and most of the time there's been nothing on your end. You've sent them all packing. Or do you do everything secretly? Have you been having all your cheeky kisses in the toilets where I can't see?'

'Don't be daft.' Lorelai was blushing and she knew it.

'Babe, whoever you are, own it. Take it from someone who was closeted until the age of twenty. It was *agony* pretending the *Pretty Woman* poster in my bedroom was there because I loved Richard Gere and not Julia Roberts.'

'I'm just not interested in seeing anyone right now,' Lorelai said eventually.

This wasn't the first time she'd had this conversation. Every time her well-meaning mother called, it usually ended in a short and awkward argument that Lorelai would shut down by saying she wanted to live a bit more before she thought about settling down. She'd often heard Lila say she'd wished she'd seen more of the world and ticked off a few more things on her bucket list before she'd got married. Playing on that lost dream of her mother's felt a bit manipulative but if it meant feeling less guilty about never giving her parents grandchildren then it was a necessary evil. She'd thought about telling her parents the truth. They'd attempted to pry once or twice but every time she thought about broaching the subject she felt instantly exhausted. She knew just how much it would take to explain and it was an ordeal she'd never been able to gear herself up to go through. The one person who might have understood was her grandma, but she'd left it far too late and had missed her chance. The thought of having that conversation with her parents stirred up all kinds of troubling feelings, so it was best to just avoid the entire idea altogether to save a lot of unnecessary pain. Especially when a positive outcome wasn't guaranteed. After bringing someone into the world, raising them and watching them grow, they must've thought they knew all there was to know about their daughter. They had no idea she was a harbinger of death.

'No, it's more than that,' Joanie continued. 'I've seen the way you flirt with people a couple of times.' She narrowed her eyes, her cogs visibly turning. 'There's interest there. You just never act on it.'

'Please can we not talk about this right now? My head is splitting,' said Lorelai, changing tack. What would it take to make Joanie back off?

Joanie's voice became gentle. 'Lorelai, you can trust me. Whatever it is I swear I won't tell another soul. I just think… secrets can make you lonely.'

Ouch. Joanie's words made the weight of Lorelai's secret bear down on her harder.

'And the last thing I'd want is to think you were struggling with something on your own. Because you're not. On your own, I mean. At least, you don't have to be.' Joanie's eyes shone with concern.

Lorelai had never told a soul yet somehow she could feel the confession creeping its way to the tip of her tongue. Why did she feel she could trust Joanie? What was it that made her want so much to tell her? Why had she attached herself to Joanie in the first place? Then she remembered. Wesley had never found out that Riggs was to blame for the cinema being burgled the day he'd forgotten to lock up. He never found out because the CCTV tapes from before the robbery had *mysteriously* been erased. One person had been sent to check the CCTV cameras and only one person could have tampered with them: Joanie. She could easily have got Riggs fired. She had every right and every reason to throw Riggs under the bus, but she'd known that if Wesley saw that footage it could have resulted in more than a firing. Wesley's visible disappointment in his son would've been soul-destroying for Riggs, and Joanie just didn't have the heart to be the person to do that to him. She'd given Riggs a second chance, and that was why he'd been on thin ice with Joanie ever since. Joanie's kindness towards even those she didn't like very much reminded Lorelai of her grandma and she wondered if that's why she felt so inclined to trust her. Joanie was almost a second chance at confiding in the person she'd thought would best understand.

Lorelai let her head fall back onto the sofa, knowing full well that this was it. This was the moment when she was finally going to tell someone her secret. If Joanie heard her out and accepted her as she was, Lorelai might not have to live such a lonely life after all. If Joanie ran screaming from the flat, Lorelai would know once and for all that she couldn't trust anyone with her truth. Either way, it was time.

'It's going to sound insane,' Lorelai said, rubbing her stinging eyes.

'Insane is so much more fun than whatever's on the telly or

the news. So would you just tell me?! I'm about to explode from the suspense.' Joanie bounced on the sofa, causing Nora to slide out from underneath it, hiss and run off towards their bedrooms.

Lorelai breathed in and out slowly, wondering how to begin.

'I haven't kissed anyone since I was eighteen,' she said quietly.

Joanie's shoulders sank. 'Is that it? That's not a big deal at all! I half expected there to be a dead body under your bed and you needed help getting rid of it. At least *try* to shock me.'

Lorelai knew Joanie was playing a game and she hated that it was working. Now there was a part of her that wanted to see how far she could push it before Joanie went quiet with shock. 'The reason I haven't kissed anyone in that long is because when I do… I see how that person is going to die.'

There it was. That moment of silence. Lorelai held her breath.

Joanie didn't say anything. She stared at Lorelai, her expression unreadable. Lorelai began to panic because the silence didn't end. She'd never known Joanie to be so quiet for so long. What had she been thinking? She shouldn't have said anything to Joanie.

Finally, Joanie shifted position and opened her mouth to speak.

'No but… no? Shut up. OK, you're not saying anything but still SHUT UP.' She yelled those final words, and Lorelai felt something inside her shift. Joanie didn't look like she thought Lorelai was mad. Did she… *believe* her?

'I told you it sounded insane,' Lorelai said.

'It does.' Joanie nodded, staring off into the distance, her brow creased with concentration. 'So, hang on… I need more info. How does it work?'

'The details are a little fuzzy. I've only kissed two people in my life, and I've vowed never to kiss anyone again so it's uncharted territory.'

'Never?' Joanie gasped. Lorelai nodded. 'Why?'

'If you knew what it was like, you wouldn't be asking me that.'

'So, you have absolutely no idea how it works and yet you're willing to change the rest of your life based on the very little you know?'

'Again—' Lorelai inhaled deeply, trying to vanquish the morbid images from her mind '—if you'd seen what I have seen, I guarantee you'd be unwilling to engage with whatever this is, too.'

'Tell me, then,' Joanie said.

'What do you mean?'

'Tell me,' Joanie said again, simply. 'Tell me what it's like. It's one thing telling me what your secret is but it's still lonely having to bear the burden on your own. You're the one who has to live with it so it's never going to be the same for me. But you can still tell me about it. You don't have to go through it alone anymore.'

Whatever reaction Lorelai had been expecting, it hadn't been this. Joanie had accepted her secret as truth, without question. How could that be?

'You're taking this all very well,' Lorelai said, fighting the urge to cry from the tremendous waves of relief crashing down on her.

Joanie laughed and shrugged. 'Do I think you're the sort of person to make something like that up? No. Am I going to be a little bit sceptical until I get cold, hard proof of your witchy powers? Maybe. Do I absolutely love the idea that my friend is a superhero? Yes. Yes, I do.'

Lorelai glanced at her bookshelves. She'd never likened herself to a character in a movie or a book. She felt too troubled by her secret to compare it to the powers of the heroes in movies who always saved the day. How could Lorelai think of herself as a hero if all her 'superpower' did was bring about death? If anything, she was the villain of the piece.

'Also,' Joanie said, interrupting Lorelai's train of thought, 'I'm still waiting for my letter to Hogwarts, I still check the back of my wardrobe just in case Narnia has appeared and if ever I happen to see a white rabbit, I will follow it just in case it leads me to Wonderland. This is like… the next best thing.'

Lorelai smiled and for that she was grateful to Joanie. Whenever things felt foggy, Joanie was good at shining a light and making everything brighter.

'All I know is that whatever I see comes true. The guys I kissed when I was younger are both dead now.'

'I'm so sorry. That's really awful.' Joanie put a hand on her shoulder.

'But… what scares me the most is… it might be me,' Lorelai said.

'What do you mean?'

She took a short sharp breath and began to explain before she could talk herself out of getting into it too deeply. 'I've always wondered… well, what if they might not have died if I hadn't kissed them? What if my kiss was the thing that sealed their fate?' It took Joanie a few moments for that to sink in.

'Oh…' Joanie said quietly.

'Yeah. Oh.'

'And that's why you've not kissed anyone? Because you think

you're causing their deaths instead of just… witnessing them prematurely?'

Lorelai could feel herself squirming against the questions, but she knew it was because it felt so alien to her to be sharing anything in this way. The actual act of sharing, though, was blissful. It was as if she'd been hibernating and was feeling the sun on her face for the first time.

'It's twofold, I guess. It's partly for my sake because if I'm kissing someone, I like them enough to not want to watch them die.'

'I wouldn't want to see anyone die, whether I know them or not,' Joanie said. 'That's not something I think I'd ever get over.'

Lorelai nodded, knowing exactly what she meant. 'But also, if it *is* my fault that those boys died, then how could I knowingly inflict that on anyone else?' She hadn't realised she'd been hoping Joanie might have an alternative theory until she'd nodded in reluctant agreement, and the disappointment washed over Lorelai.

'That's a sensible thing to do but surely you can't sacrifice your happiness for something that may or may not be true. You need to find out exactly how it works and *then* decide what to do from there.'

'Potentially killing someone is a bit of a big risk to take.' Lorelai couldn't believe she was having an actual conversation about this with another person. It felt… good.

'Of course but surely… I mean… surely there's a way around it? Like… I don't know, kissing an animal?'

'That's still pretty cruel, Joanie. I'll have the RSPCA coming after me.'

'But less cruel than killing a person? A person who might be destined to cure world hunger? A hamster's not going to do that.'

'Are you suggesting I kiss a hamster?' Lorelai laughed but when Joanie shrugged she realised she was serious.

'Not specifically a hamster. You can pick a different animal if you're that fussy.'

'I'm going to regret telling you about this, aren't I? I should have found someone who would have had a little more to say than, "Why not kiss a hamster?"' Despite Lorelai genuinely wondering if telling Joanie was a bad idea or not, she smiled affectionately at her friend, who was now the only other person in the world who knew.

'Would you settle for a guinea pig?' Joanie asked.

Lorelai began to laugh hysterically, and she couldn't be sure if it was because of Joanie's idea, or because of the sheer relief of finally talking about her secret so openly.

'Ooh! Ooh! DO ME! DO ME!' Joanie threw herself at Lorelai, her lips puckered.

'What?!' Lorelai shrieked as Joanie barrelled into her, knocking her backwards onto the sofa.

'I want to know how I'm going to die!' Joanie made kissing noises as Lorelai pushed her away by the shoulders.

'Are you crazy?' Lorelai laughed. 'First of all, this is very aggressive. Is this how you ask all women to kiss you, because this is a lot.' Lorelai shoved her back onto the sofa where Joanie flopped and pouted. 'Secondly, I'd rather not be the one to seal your fate and cause your death. And finally... why? Why on earth would you ever want to know how you were going to die?'

'Because then I'd know I was invincible through everything

else! Please, please, please, please.' Joanie clasped her hands together in prayer.

'I don't think that's how it works.' Lorelai's stomach flipped and her voice cracked.

'How *does* it work, then? I want to know everything. *You* need to know everything.' Joanie must have sensed the change in atmosphere because she shook off the pout and reached for Lorelai's hands. She interlaced her fingers with Lorelai's and squeezed.

The relief Lorelai had felt a moment before disappeared. Joanie was right – she did need to know more. She knew very little about what she could do, but the truth was she wasn't sure if she wanted to know any more than that. And where would she even start looking for those answers?

Eleven

Riggs settled down on the sofa under a thick blanket and was soon snoring. Joanie dragged Lorelai into her bedroom and as soon as the door was closed behind them, the barrage of questions began.

'Are you alright? What was he *thinking*?! Did he get you? Did he *kiss* you? Was it horrible? Not the kiss. Actually, was the kiss horrible? Was what you saw worse?'

Joanie flung herself at Lorelai and wrapped her arms tightly around her friend, stroking her hair with such tenderness that Lorelai started to cry again. The affection was more than Lorelai was accustomed to, but it was moments like this that made her grateful that she had trusted Joanie with her secret.

'Joanie! Joanie. I'm OK,' she said between her sobs. 'I mean, I'm not OK but I'm… fine. It wasn't that bad.' Joanie went still and quiet for a noticeable moment. 'You can ask about it if you want.'

'Oh, good,' Joanie said, relieved. She pulled back and looked Lorelai in the eye. 'How does he go? I need to know everything. Is it horrible? Is it peaceful? Is it soon?'

'Joanie! Would you relax?! You're meant to be calming me down, not the other way around!'

'Sorry.' With her fingers outstretched, Joanie swept her hands down in front of her face, closed her eyes and took a deep breath. 'First question. How?'

'I don't know. It kept changing.' Lorelai tried to understand what she had seen but it had been so unusual.

'What do you mean? Is that normal?'

'At first it was bad. Really bad. I think… I think he was taking his own life.'

Joanie gasped and threw her hands over her mouth. Joanie and Riggs weren't close, but she would never wish him any harm.

'I can't be certain but that's definitely what it looked like. He looked young, too. Exactly how he looks now and there were lots of whisky bottles and pills but then…' Lorelai's voice trailed off as she struggled to make sense of it all.

'What?'

'But then it… flickered. Like strobe lighting. Between the images of… that…' Lorelai said, not wanting to say those words again, 'and images of an old man in bed having a heart attack. He died in the middle of the night. It must have been Riggs when he's older. His skin was leathery and tanned, as though he'd spent too much time in the sun.' Lorelai paused again. 'He looked like he'd lived a really good life up until that point.'

'Has that happened before? With the other people you've kissed. Did what you see, the images, did they change in the middle of things?'

'No.'

'Why did it all change, do you think?' Joanie looked thoughtful, and then her eyebrows shot up as something hit her. 'Oh my god, do you think it was you? Do you think your kiss *changed* his future?'

'No way,' Lorelai said instinctively, but something in her brain faltered.

'But your visions of the future began to change mid-kiss.'

'Oh my god.'

'I'm right, aren't I? Aren't I right?!'

'Maybe. But I don't see how I could've done this.' Lorelai's brain was racing a million miles an hour but she couldn't grasp onto anything solid. Nothing was sticking. She massaged her temples and took some deep breaths, hoping that everything would slow down so she could think straight.

'You said it yourself. You have no idea how this, whatever it is, works.' Joanie stood and began to pace. 'You thought that kissing someone sealed their fate and they had no way out, but what if whatever you see is their fate regardless of your kiss, and you just see it. You don't influence it; you're just an innocent spectator?'

'OK…' Lorelai nodded, trying to follow.

'What if, when it comes to someone you know, someone who loves you, a kiss is more than just a kiss. Riggs said he thought you were coming on to him, right? So, a kiss from you was more than just a kiss. It was hope. You gave him hope for a better future, Lorelai. That's why the images changed! He was on a path of self-destruction but then you showed him some kindness and kissed him—'

'He kissed me,' Lorelai corrected.

'I know, I know, but you heard him! He thought you were coming on to him. He thought it was mutual and that made him think maybe life was worth living, after all. Maybe you and your kiss *saved* him.'

Joanie's words hung in the air, and Lorelai's mind, finally, stopped spinning. She'd spent so long believing that she may have killed those boys, Thomas and Arthur. Believing that whoever she kissed would die because of her. But the truth was that she didn't know enough about what she could do, that everything she thought she knew was based on theory and speculation. It was time to stop running away; she couldn't ignore it any longer. If she had been the one to change Riggs's future, then she needed to know that for certain. She needed to be more prepared, so it was time to understand whether her kisses influenced someone's future or not. Did she have the kiss of death?

Joanie's theory made so much sense. Lorelai couldn't see how it could be any other way. Riggs was in a bad way when they had come home and found him. Being jobless and homeless would send anyone into a downward spiral but being jobless and homeless because your own father kicked you out of the house and fired you from your job… it was a lot to cope with.

'Riggs must have been feeling so desperate. He couldn't see any other way out, could he?' Lorelai's voice cracked.

'No, I don't think he could. Until he kissed you. I'm not saying he should have kissed you. That was presumptuous and the actions of a stupid man, and it shouldn't be excused. But knowing the little that we do about your kisses, the sweetness to the bitter pill is that you may have just saved Riggs's life by showing him some kindness when he needed it the most.'

Lorelai let Joanie's words sink in. Could she be right? It *did* make sense, but if that was the case then Joanie had been right about something else too. She had been right when she had suggested that Lorelai needed a deeper understanding of what she could do if she was to live her life to the full. Whether it was a gift or a curse, understanding it was a step she needed to take.

'Fuck,' Lorelai said with a sigh. The thought of what came next was daunting.

'Yeah, I know. Amazing, right?' Joanie grinned.

Lorelai allowed herself a wry smile. 'As much as I *hate* to admit it, you're right. I do need to figure out what's wrong with me.'

Joanie rolled her eyes. 'What's *wrong* with you?! There's nothing wrong with you! Lorelai, this could be the best thing that ever happened to you! We don't know!'

'Exactly. We don't know. It could also be a lot worse than we think, so—'

'So… what? The default is pessimistic defeatism?' Joanie folded her arms across her chest.

'That's my default, yeah. You can be as annoyingly positive as you like but there's something else on my mind.' Lorelai adjusted herself on the bed and Joanie sat by her. 'We went pretty off the handle after what happened. What if we undid everything? What if we made everything worse and his fate went back to what it was before?'

Joanie's eyes went wide. 'Oh god. Can that happen?'

'I don't know! But surely if a fate can change mid-kiss to something more positive it's going to be the same the other way around, right?' They both looked at each other, unblinking.

'I'm going to go check on him.' Joanie scrambled off the bed.

'Be nice.'

'I know, I know.' She sighed, and then plastered a giant

comical grin on her face for Lorelai's benefit, before leaving the room.

Lorelai took a deep breath and leaned her head against the wall. Had the last twenty-four hours really happened? She thought of Grayson and the time they'd spent together, and immediately felt a warmth rush through her. But it wasn't just Grayson – she'd also kissed someone for the first time in seven years and discovered that her kisses might not be what she'd always thought them to be. She closed her eyes and tried to put her thoughts in order. With her mind still, and the room quiet, she had a moment of peace to make sense of all of this. Maybe she could—

'LORELAI!' Joanie yelled, crashing down the hallway. 'Lorelai!' She burst through the door, her cheeks red and her coat half on. 'Riggs is gone!'

✦

Lorelai's heart felt heavy as she and Joanie raced out of the flat and onto the street. As soon as they were outside, they both started screaming Riggs's name.

'Have you tried calling him?' Lorelai asked, pulling her coat tightly around her. She rubbed her hands together and blew into them, trying to generate a little warmth. The memory of the first vision of Riggs's death flashed through her mind, and a wave of nausea hit her. They needed to find Riggs. Now.

'It's ringing but it's just going to voicemail.' Joanie hung up and immediately hit redial. A few seconds later, she sighed in frustration, and repeated the process. 'When we find him, I'm going to kill him.'

'If we don't find him quickly you may not have to,' Lorelai said.

Joanie's anger dissipated and then her face cleared. Riggs had answered her call. 'Riggs? RIGGS! Where are you? Where did you go?'

'Leave me alone,' Lorelai heard him say, his voice muffled against Joanie's ear.

'Give it to me,' Lorelai said and Joanie handed over her phone without hesitation, knowing that Lorelai was the one who had the best chance of talking him down.

'Riggs, it's Lorelai. Please come back. We're worried about you.'

'I don't want anyone to worry about me anymore. I'm done.' His voice sounded small and sad.

'You're done?' Lorelai tried to keep her voice steady, but she could feel the panic begin to rise.

'Yes. I'm done.' Riggs was slurring more than before. How much more had he had to drink?

'With what?' Lorelai knew she had to keep him talking.

'Everyone. Everything. It's all bullshit.'

Lorelai heard the slosh of liquid in the background. 'Call Wesley!' she whispered to Joanie, shoving her phone into Joanie's hand.

As Joanie made the call to Wesley, her voice urgent, Lorelai took a deep breath and tried to remain calm.

'Riggs, tell me where you are and I'll come and get you.'

'No.'

'Riggs, please. We care about you. *I* care about you. Your dad would be devastated if anything happened to you. So would I, we all would. Please just tell me where you are, so we can talk about everything properly.'

She did care about Riggs – just not romantically. She wondered if he would misunderstand her words again but the only thing that mattered was finding out where he was before he hurt himself. She'd deal with any fallout later. She just needed to make sure Riggs would still be around for that fallout. Lorelai felt Riggs hesitate and began to feel hopeful that he would agree to let her help him.

'No,' he said finally with conviction. 'And no one is going to find me because I'm where no one would ever expect me to be.'

Riggs hung up without another word. Lorelai stared at the phone for a second, and then grabbed Joanie's arm, who was still on the phone to Wesley.

'Tell Wesley he's back at the cinema.'

Twelve

Wesley found his son in the darkness of the storage room, curled up in a foetal position, clutching an empty bottle of whisky. Riggs had passed out before he could hurt himself, and for that everyone was grateful. He'd have a raging hangover for a while but he was alive.

Wesley was devastated. He'd had no idea his child had been feeling this way, that things had become so dark for Riggs, that he'd considered taking his own life. Lorelai could feel the guilt coming off Wesley. Both Lorelai and Joanie felt guilty that they hadn't spotted the warning signs either, but to be Riggs's father and not have known how much your own child had been struggling; Lorelai knew it was something that would haunt Wesley for the rest of his life.

'I… I had no idea.' Wesley's shoulders fell under the weight of it all, but there was a determined look in his red-rimmed eyes. 'But now that I do, we can get him home and get him the proper help he needs. My boy is never going to feel alone again. Take the Sunday evening shift off, girls. I'll do some switching around. Consider it a thank you.'

✦

Later that night, too tired to cook, Lorelai and Joanie picked up fish and chips from the chippy across the road for their dinner.

'Do you think Riggs will be OK?' Joanie said, unwrapping the steaming packages. Joanie's eyes were red and puffy, so Lorelai knew she'd had a weep when she hadn't been looking. Lorelai was close to crumbling herself. They both needed to take their minds off the day's events.

'He's with his dad now. Wesley will take care of him, and we can check in on him too. We need to be there for him, without overwhelming him. Let him know we're here if he wants to talk, without making him feel pressured into it.' Lorelai rubbed her forehead. The memory of Riggs's first death would be forever etched in her mind, a constant reminder that you never truly knew what was going on inside someone's head. 'Shall we talk about something else? Distract ourselves, just for a little bit? It's been an intense day.' Lorelai made this request for Joanie as much for herself.

Joanie thought for a moment and then turned to Lorelai with a tired smile. 'How about we talk about the fact that *someone has a date*? I need to know *everything*. What are you going to wear? How are you feeling about Grayson? How are you feeling about the idea that you may be able to change someone's death, that your kisses aren't the end of the world, after all?'

Lorelai groaned. 'It's not a date! And I meant let's talk about something light-hearted. Or at the very least sit in silence and watch a film or something?'

'I want to talk about you and Grayson. We *never* talk about you, Lollie!'

'I don't have anything to say!' Lorelai stuffed a handful of chips into her mouth.

'Of course you do! You've got an actual *superpower*, Lollie.'

'Please don't call it that.'

'Do you know how many kids dream of having what you have?'

'No, they do not. Kids dream of being super strong, flying or becoming invisible. They don't dream of seeing blood and broken bones and people in pain every time they have a kiss. Whatever I have, it is not a superpower.'

'But it *is!* You could start a business. Charge people money to tell them how they're going to die,' Joanie said.

'I don't think so.'

'It would be like being a doctor. You might be saving people's lives!' Joanie said, pointing a chip at Lorelai.

'You're ridiculous.'

'I think it's a great idea.'

'I'm not doing anything until I know more.'

'So does that mean you are going to do some research?' Joanie asked.

'I think I might have to,' Lorelai said slowly. 'I'm just not sure what that would look like.'

Joanie brushed the crumbs off her lap. 'Talk me through it,' she said. 'What do you already know?'

Lorelai thought for a moment, before speaking. It felt so strange to be talking about this. 'Well... I saw Riggs die in two separate ways in the space of what, thirty seconds? One self-inflicted, one natural. But it looks like we stopped the first vision from coming true. So if fate can be changed even after I've kissed someone, that might mean I'm not the one *sealing* their fate, I'm merely a witness to it before it's even happened. Outside forces can still intervene even after I've kissed them.'

'That's what I said. You gave Riggs some hope so that caused his fate to change.' Joanie nodded in agreement. 'So, you're more like a psychic?'

'That doesn't feel accurate, but I guess that's the best word to describe me, at least for now. It's just very specifically tuned into death and I can only see those things when I kiss someone.'

'You don't seem excited about this.'

'I'm not.' Lorelai shook her head.

Joanie rolled her eyes. 'Are you kidding me? Not even a little bit?'

'No!'

'You're not even a smidge excited that there's something about you that sets you apart from every other human?'

Lorelai tried to think about the best way to articulate what she was feeling. 'Am I excited about the idea of watching lots of unsuspecting people die? No. It doesn't sound like a very fun thing to do. But—' Lorelai hesitated '—I can't ignore this anymore. My kisses with Riggs showed me that I might be able to change fate, and that's a huge responsibility. I need to know if it was a one-off.'

'And if it isn't a one-off?' Joanie asked, reaching over to squeeze Lorelai's hand.

'That I don't know.' Lorelai stared down at her food, her appetite suddenly gone.

'OK, OK, I get it,' Joanie said. 'But for the record, I think this *is* exciting, and that you're amazing. And I'm here to help you figure this whole thing out. But Lorelai, if you can do what I think you can, then you won't have to be just friends with Grayson. You could make that "just friends" brunch an actual date.'

This had been at the back of Lorelai's mind too, but now that Joanie had said the words aloud, Lorelai allowed the twinge of excitement in her chest to grow. She had never dared explore what she could do or what it meant because she'd never had reason to. She'd avoided meaningful romantic attachments but as she recalled her conversations with Grayson, the way he looked at her sometimes, and how he made her feel, she knew that, for the first time in her life, she did have a reason and that reason was Grayson.

✦

The Duchess felt eerily quiet when they came back to work on Tuesday morning, the absence of Riggs making itself known. Both Lorelai and Joanie were subdued, and things with Wesley were awkward and strained.

'Well, you two,' he said, his hands clasped behind his back. He walked towards them slowly, his head bowed. 'Erm, thank you for what you did yesterday. Riggs is, well, we've got some things to work through as a family. He's having a rough time right now so a little bit of privacy is probably for the best.' He couldn't meet their eyes, too ashamed to have failed his son in this way.

'Wouldn't having his friends around be more helpful?' Lorelai said. 'To show him that he's cared about?' The words came out more firmly than she had meant them to.

'It's all just a bit much for him right now. When he's feeling stronger, we'll arrange something. Perhaps you both can come over?'

Lorelai took in Wesley's tired eyes, and heard the quiver in his voice. This was hard on him too. She glanced at Joanie who gave her an imperceptible nod. She was thinking the same – they needed to go easy on Wesley too.

'That sounds like a good idea,' Joanie said.

Lorelai nodded. 'OK, but would you please let Riggs know that we were asking after him?'

'Of course I will.' Wesley gave them a nod and slowly trudged off back to his office.

'I know I gave him a hard time but it is weird that Riggs isn't here. It's not like it's left us with any more work to do as we always picked up his slack anyway, but it's just odd, you know?' Joanie fiddled with the straw dispenser.

'I know what you mean. Part of it could be the way he left too.' Lorelai gave Joanie a playful shove. 'I think you just miss having someone to pick on. You had better not turn that attention onto me now,' she warned.

'Maybe I will, maybe I won't. Now that I know your kisses aren't going to kill me, you have no protection!'

Lorelai hurriedly shushed her. 'Would you keep your voice down?!'

Joanie raised an amused eyebrow and then leaned in to whisper, 'It's time to find the bright side in all of this, Lollie. You deserve to be happy.'

The phone rang, interrupting their conversation. Joanie looked at her pointedly as Lorelai answered the call, feeling flustered.

'Hello, The Duchess,' she said distractedly.

'Lorelai? Is that you? It's Grayson.'

On hearing his happy voice, Lorelai's cheeks flushed. One glance at Joanie's grinning face confirmed that she had caught who was on the other end of the line.

'Hello? Lorelai, are you there?' Grayson laughed nervously, and the sound brought Lorelai to her senses.

'Yes, hello. Sorry, I'm here. Hey.'

Why did she feel guilty? Lorelai hadn't made Grayson any promises, and she had been clear they were just going to be friends. But the kiss with Riggs kept replaying in her head, and knowing that there was a chance her ability may not be what she'd always feared it was, she wished that her first kiss in years had been with Grayson. There. She admitted it. Joanie would've been beside herself if she could read Lorelai's mind.

'Hi. So, shall we say Monday? Eleven?'

'Monday at eleven?' Lorelai said blankly.

'For brunch?' Grayson's voice faltered. He coughed.

'No! Yes, I know! Sorry, so much has happened since I saw you last, and it's only been a couple of days. Plus, my brain hasn't fully woken up yet.'

'Is everything OK?'

If only Grayson knew how loaded a question that was. Things were *not* OK, but they might be eventually, and Lorelai needed time to get her head straight before she saw Grayson again.

'Grayson, to be honest, things have become a bit… complicated all of a sudden. I might need to take a rain check on our brunch.'

Lorelai's heart squeezed but this was the right thing to do for now. She was being pulled in so many different directions with Riggs, and Grayson, and finding out more about her abilities.

She need to focus on one thing at a time, and that was figuring out more about herself and what she was able to do, before she could start moving forwards.

'Really?'

'Yeah. I need to sort through some things and I need a bit of headspace,' she explained. She knew her words were hollow and weak, but couldn't see what else she could say beyond these platitudes.

Grayson was quiet for a moment and then said, 'OK, no worries.'

Lorelai had expected some pushback, for him to try to change her mind but he'd accepted her excuse without question. Suddenly, she wondered if maybe she'd got the wrong idea. But *he'd* called *her,* hadn't he? Or was he just being polite? *Stop overthinking and say something!*

'Thanks for understanding,' she said, as neutrally as she could manage.

'Sorry, that sounded like I'm not disappointed. I am. I really wanted to see you but I get it. You're a busy woman. As you should be.'

Lorelai could hear the smile in his voice and was instantly relieved. He was teasing her.

'It's not that! Please don't think I'm the sort of person who can't make any time for anyone. It's just a lot has been going on here. Ask Joanie, she'll vouch for me.' Lorelai held the phone in Joanie's direction.

'She's telling the truth, lover boy!' Joanie yelled.

'See?' Lorelai said.

Grayson chuckled. 'I believe you. You don't have to prove anything to me.'

138

'I know. I just wanted to see you too.'

She *had* wanted to see him. She wanted to be close to him again, to hear his voice, and watch his eyes crinkle when he laughed. There was no getting away from how he made her feel. Grayson was different. He stirred something inside her, something she'd kept pushed down since Michael. But even this felt different to what she'd felt for Michael. She was entirely unable to control how Grayson made her feel.

'Another time.' His voice dropped a little, and Lorelai could tell he wasn't angry with her. 'Let me leave my number and you can call me.'

Lorelai jotted his number down and said, 'Thanks, Grayson. Bye now.'

'Bye now?' Joanie yelped once Lorelai had hung up. 'Bye now?!'

Lorelai shook her head and waited a beat before she spoke. Once she had said these words aloud, Joanie wouldn't let her go back on them. 'I really like Grayson. This brunch thing we're meant to be going on... we said we'd go as friends but I'm not sure I want that with him.'

'What *do* you want with him?' Joanie asked carefully, knowing not to push too hard.

'I don't know, but friends doesn't feel like enough.' Joanie squeaked with excitement at Lorelai's admission. 'I know. I don't know what I'm doing and this might be a huge mistake but things have changed, and I can't move forward with Grayson until I know what's going on with me. And I refuse to let Grayson be my guinea pig.'

'I get that. So, who will be your guinea pig?' Joanie grabbed a handful of popcorn from the machine and began to munch.

'Well, if we think we've established that I'm not going to actually kill anyone by kissing them, then let's go out this weekend. I think I'll need to kiss more than one person to test out our theory, so the drunker everyone is, the less likely someone will notice how strangely I'm behaving.'

'Oh man.' Joanie grinned from ear to ear. 'This is going to be so good. Going out with you is always fun but this will be the first time you've properly let loose.'

'You know what, Joanie?' Lorelai smiled back at her friend. 'I'm looking forward to it.'

For the most part, Lorelai had found it relatively easy to shut off her feelings when it came to relationships but that didn't mean there hadn't been moments when she'd found it difficult. Joanie and Lorelai enjoyed their nights out together, but this sometimes led to Lorelai finding herself entangled in unwanted situations with men who were pushy or who didn't like hearing, 'No.' Some took every sway of the hips, every polite smile and every glance in their direction as an invitation. Other times, Lorelai found herself being reckless. Dancing close to the line, without crossing it, before backing off when something inside her jolted her sober. It was a constant tug-of-war, and all she wanted was to be normal.

One particular Valentine's night, the urge to be 'normal' was overwhelming. She drank too many cocktails, sang loudly to songs she didn't know the words to and danced with anyone who would let her. She quickly picked up the attention of a handsome man who had the kind of bone structure you only see on red carpets. His face swam in and out of her blurry vision as they moved together to a bass-heavy beat. She felt his hands curl round her waist and she let herself sink further towards him.

Be normal. Be normal. I just want to feel normal.

He began to move more slowly and she followed suit, intertwined in between all the other writhing bodies. Lorelai's heart beat loudly in her ears, drowning out the music. Her head was spinning, and as he dropped his head, his eyes on her lips, everything around Lorelai fell away.

What are you doing? You're not ready for this! You can't handle what you're about to see! Get out of here! Don't let him kiss you! DON'T LET HIM KISS YOU!

Lorelai pushed away from him, gently at first and then more forcefully as his grip around her waist tightened. He let go abruptly and she knocked into someone dancing behind her.

'What the—' the woman said, annoyed, and then stopped when she saw the panicked look on Lorelai's face. 'Are you alright?' She reached out to steady Lorelai.

'What the fuck is your problem? Stupid little cocktease.' The man Lorelai had just been so close to had hardened, his face contorted in anger. The woman swept Lorelai behind her with one move of her arm.

'She owes you nothing. Now fuck off and leave her alone.'

The woman's friends crowded round, holding Lorelai up and ready to defend her if they needed to. Clearly outnumbered, the man slunk off but not before spitting on the ground at their feet.

Once the coast was clear, the woman and her friends shepherded Lorelai out of the club, the night air hitting them all like a two-tonne truck. They didn't say much to each other, but they held hands and didn't let go of one another until they all felt more stable.

'Thanks,' was all Lorelai could manage to say.

The woman smiled back and it was a smile that said so much.

We've all been there. We'll take care of you. We've got your back.
But, as grateful as she was, Lorelai knew the woman who'd helped her would never understand the extent of what she was feeling. Sitting alone in the cab on the way home, Lorelai watched London's glitzy night lights twinkle through her tearful vision, knowing that no matter how much she wanted it or how hard she tried, she would never be 'normal'.

◆

Thirteen

Liberty was heaving. After waiting ten minutes outside in the cold night air in their thin dresses and heels, which had already numbed Lorelai's toes, Lorelai and Joanie stepped through the doors and Lorelai began to survey the crowd. She didn't intend to drink. It might cloud her judgement and her understanding of what she might see but, for once, she was going to make an effort to talk to people. Lorelai was used to sitting on the sidelines during nights out. She would usually sit at the bar and watch Joanie flirt and make everyone fall madly in love with her. Tonight was going to be different. That night's crowd seemed the same as it always did. Lots of twenty-somethings grouped together, champing at the bit to win a flirtatious glance from at least one person. Lorelai wasn't planning on ending up in anyone's bed tonight, but she did want some good, old-fashioned making out.

'Anyone catch your eye?' Joanie gave Lorelai's waist a tickle.

'Not at the moment, no.'

Joanie dropped her hands by her sides. 'Come on, Lollie. You don't need to be picky. Surely anyone with a pair of lips will do?'

Joanie had a point, and it wasn't as if Lorelai was here to

make a connection with someone. She was here because of her connection with Grayson, after all, but she was nervous about the evening ahead and what she might see. 'There are too many people here.' Lorelai wiped her sweaty palms on her dress.

'Shall I get you a drink?'

'Don't worry, I'll get these ones.' Lorelai stood, her legs shaking. 'See if I can find anyone drunk enough to kiss me right off the bat.'

'Go forth into the night, fair maiden, and return with a porn star martini and less lipstick than you originally applied!' Joanie grinned and gave her a thumbs up, and Lorelai felt the butterflies in her stomach flutter again.

She stood at the bar as seductively as she could. She gently rested an elbow on the counter, popped her hip and bevelled her leg but the only vague whiff of interest she received in the ten minutes it took to get served was from a tall blond man who sneered at her over the top of his Corona. She realised she probably looked more like she needed the toilet than a seductress. She readjusted and stood normally, feeling silly.

'What can I get you?' the bartender asked.

'A pair of flats and a fluffy dressing gown?' she said, clutching the bar unsteadily. He laughed hard at her lame joke, and her interest was suddenly piqued. If he was interested enough to laugh far too hard at a joke that wasn't funny, then he might be a potential candidate.

'A porn star martini and a Diet Coke, please.'

'Let me guess, you've been dragged here by a friend on the pull?' He pushed his hair back from his face and pulled two glasses from underneath the counter.

'Who says I'm not on the pull?' She flashed him what she hoped was a sexy smile, but feared she looked a bit mad instead. *Who even are you?* Lorelai scoffed at herself. She needed to get all of her bad flirting out of her system tonight. Just in case.

'Are you?' The bartender was unflustered by her forwardness, obviously used to women flirting with him. Lorelai gave him the once-over. He had sparkling grey eyes, and long hair that was smoothed back neatly. He had some stubble, which Lorelai imagined she wouldn't like after Riggs's stubble had left her lips and chin sore. Riggs had come at her quite forcefully, though, so maybe it would be different with…

'What's your name?' she asked.

'James.' He smiled, a dimple appearing in his left cheek.

'Just James?' Lorelai raised her eyebrow suggestively. At least she hoped it was suggestive.

'Is there meant to be anything else to the name James?' He laughed but it had a nervous edge to it, which she very much enjoyed.

'Just James it is then,' she said.

James placed the drinks on the black rubber mat in front of her. He didn't say anything.

'How much?' she said eventually. He gave a subtle shake of his head and discreetly waved her card away. 'Oh, OK. Thank you.' Lorelai tried to sound as if getting free drinks happened to her all the time. As if men always fell at her feet because she oozed confidence. She gave James another smile, and then walked back to Joanie, free drinks in hand.

'Anyone?' Joanie asked, reaching out with both hands for her martini and shot glass.

'Him.' Lorelai nodded towards the bar.

'James? Nice. Do you think you've got a chance?'

'Of *course* you know the bar staff here. And yes, I reckon I've got a chance. The drinks were free.' Lorelai blushed as she took a sip of her Coke.

'Excellent work! Go back and talk to him. Find out when his next break is.'

Lorelai glanced over at James. He was serving someone else but he kept looking over to where she and Joanie were standing.

'Is it really that simple?' Lorelai's confidence wavered. 'I might have got the wrong end of the stick.'

'Lollie, don't make this complicated. He likes the look of you, you like the look of him. That's it. It *is* that simple and it doesn't have to be any more than one cheeky kiss.'

'It'll always be more than one cheeky kiss.' Lorelai sighed.

'He doesn't know that and he doesn't have to know that.' Joanie knocked back her shot of champagne and then downed almost half of her martini in one gulp.

'Slow down! I'm not carrying you home tonight!'

'I'm single now,' Joanie said without an ounce of sadness. 'I may not be coming home at all.' She handed Lorelai her glass and danced away, disappearing into the crowd.

Lorelai took Joanie's advice and asked James when he would be getting a break.

Twenty minutes later, she found him in the alley round the side of the club. It really was that simple. James clearly wasn't there for conversation because he said two words to her before pulling her close and those words were, 'Come here.' All signs of nervousness had left him and Lorelai wondered if that was because his confidence didn't lie in his chat, but in what he was capable of physically.

Lorelai knew then that had she been interested in James, it would never work out between them. She longed for conversation in a relationship more than she longed for anything else, and that only made her think of Grayson. He was curious about her, was always asking her questions about herself, wanting to learn about who she was as a person. She remembered how surprised he had been when she had told him that most men disappeared when she took anything physical off the table. Lorelai felt a sudden wave of guilt, as though kissing James would be a betrayal towards Grayson. She quickly pushed the thought away. She was doing this *because* of Grayson. He was the reason she wanted to find out more about her ability. She needed that knowledge if there was to be any future for them.

James's lips were warm and soft, his kiss impatient and hungry. It took a few moments for a vision to appear and then Lorelai saw James riding on a bicycle, barely any older than he was now. A second later, a car sped through a stop sign and ploughed straight into him. As she watched him fly off his bike, Lorelai felt all the breath leave her body. She heard the thud as James's broken and lifeless body hit the ground, and the screech of the tyres as the car sped off. Lorelai's mouth was suddenly dry and she groaned.

'I know, I know,' James whispered, mistaking her groan for one of pleasure. He wrapped his arms around her waist and pulled her closer into him but she didn't want him near her. She didn't want to be touched or caressed. She wanted to be alone and to regain control. Seeing death felt so intrusive, like her mind was no longer her own. James was leaning in for a second kiss but she pulled back, grimacing.

'Is everything OK?' James said, confused.

Lorelai didn't know how she managed to keep it together, but she did. She took a step back, tipped her head to the side and looked up at James. 'More than OK. But you know what they say. You can never have too much of a good thing.'

She turned and walked away before James could respond. She concentrated on walking slowly, when all she wanted to do was run home. She could still hear the sound James had made when the car had hit him. She'd remember that noise always, and she already knew it would become the soundtrack to her next nightmare. She stifled a sob, knowing she needed to keep going. For her, and for Grayson.

◆

Lorelai made her way back inside. She spotted Joanie dancing on a podium and began walking towards her. As she made her way across the dancefloor, she was intercepted by a skinny man dressed all in black, wearing skull earrings. He took her hands and began to dance with her. She hesitated for a moment, the images of James's death still lingering, and then she relaxed into moving with him, ready to take a plunge into darkness again.

The more she allowed him to spin her around, the closer he got to her, and eventually he kissed her. The image that Lorelai saw was simply of an elderly man, asleep in a bed, who never woke up. The stranger pulled back from their kiss, and he was suddenly swept away from her by a group of people she assumed to be his friends. Lorelai stood for what felt like a lifetime, the crowd around her gently jostling her. Her breath caught as the two different deaths flashed in front of her. She squeezed her eyes shut, but she could still see every detail, and she felt hot and queasy.

Eventually Lorelai opened her eyes, and saw Joanie looking at her in concern from one of the podiums. Joanie clambered down onto the main dancefloor and beckoned her over. Lorelai made her way towards her friend.

'Are you OK?' Joanie had to shout to make herself heard over the music. 'How's it going?'

Lorelai took a breath to steady herself. 'Two kisses down. I think I could manage a couple more before I'm done for the night. It's... I'm... I'm starting to feel it, you know...'

Joanie looked at her with sympathy. 'You sure you don't just want to go home now?'

'No,' Lorelai said quickly before she changed her mind. 'I need to do this for a bit longer.'

These two kisses had wounded Lorelai, just as she knew they would. But she'd discovered she had a steely resolve and was strong enough to endure such awful visions, if the reason to do so was important enough. *Grayson.* But not just for Grayson; for herself too. She felt stronger, more determined, and dare she say, more hopeful for her future. It was also a relief to learn that not everyone would die a horrific death, only she would never know who would and wouldn't. It wasn't a lot more new information, but it was a start.

'Joanie!' A tall man with a closely shaved head, wearing a silver silk shirt grabbed Joanie around the waist and pulled her into a hug.

'Of *course* you're here! Lorelai, this is my friend Darren. Darren, Lorelai.'

Lorelai waved a hello, and Darren leaned in to kiss her cheek.

'Just a heads-up, ladies,' Darren said in a thick Liverpudlian accent. 'I've watched that bloke over there harass a few women tonight.' He nodded towards a man wearing a tweed jacket. He was sweating profusely under the lights. 'Do you want to come and sit with me for a bit? All my mates are outside smoking and I'm lonely upstairs in my booth.'

Lorelai and Joanie agreed, and followed Darren upstairs.

'Oof,' Lorelai said, sitting down heavily. 'My feet needed the break!'

'I'll be back in a bit.' Joanie disappeared and Lorelai knew that she was going to sneak a cigarette from someone outside.

'Don't worry, Lorelai,' Darren said, smiling. 'You're safe with me, I promise.'

As they settled down together, Lorelai felt a wave of tiredness wash over her and was grateful for the reprieve. *This is hard work,* she thought.

'I reckon that bloke downstairs is doing the *play*,' Darren said, stroking the top of his head. His fingers were adorned with several rings that sparkled in the light.

'The… play?' Lorelai drew a blank.

'You haven't heard of it? I'm sorry to be the one to tell you but I feel it's my duty as your new best friend.' He paused for dramatic effect. '*The Play* is this book, all about how to play girls to get them to sleep with you. There are a bunch of guys that hang around Piccadilly Circus and Soho late at night, trying to pick up young tourists or unsuspecting locals, using the rules of *The Play*. It's pretty gross.' Darren grimaced.

'That's grim.'

'Yeah. The book also encourages negging.'

'Is that when someone gives you a backhanded compliment?'

'Or a shit sandwich, yeah.'

'A what?' Lorelai laughed.

'A shit sandwich! They say something nice, which is the first slice of bread. Then something horrendous – the shit. And then something nice again. It's meant to lower self-esteem, which is all part of the play.'

'Let me try.' Lorelai flicked her hair behind her ear. 'Your American accent is so sweet. Oh wait, you're English? Argh, I usually hate English men but you're actually not too bad.'

Darren threw his head back and laughed. 'Yes! Exactly! Or how about this?' He cocked his head to the side, and looked up at Lorelai with a glint in his eye. 'I love how you're hot but like... really dorky. It's cool; it means you're more relatable.'

'That one was subtle. I might have missed that one.'

Darren shook his head gently, shaking away his new persona. 'I'm ashamed of myself for being such a natural arsehole.'

'Don't be – you seem alright, Darren,' Lorelai said, wondering if Darren could be her third and final kiss of the night. She wasn't sure she could handle any more after that.

'Speak of the devil...' Darren nodded towards the man in the tweed jacket who was swiftly approaching. He stopped at their booth, and stared at Lorelai.

'Can I help you?' she said as politely as she could.

'I'm going to give you my phone and you're going to put your number in.'

'I don't think I am.'

'You're feisty, aren't you? That's hot. Usually I don't like overly aggressive women but you make it work.'

Lorelai and Darren looked at each other and then burst into laughter.

'Oh, mate. That was terrible! Do you really think you had a shot?' Darren howled.

'What, and you do?' the man sneered. He looked Darren up and down.

'I've got way more of a chance with Lorelai than you do.'

The man rolled his eyes and scoffed. Lorelai didn't like the way he was dismissing Darren. Who did he think he was?

'Actually, he does. He's got more going for him than you do,' Lorelai said, shuffling closer to Darren.

'What? The man in the woman's shirt and drinking the girly cocktail? Oh please,' he said incredulously.

Darren looked at Lorelai then and raised his eyebrows as if to ask, *May I?* Lorelai's response was to lean in without hesitation. As their lips touched, Lorelai felt a warmth emanate not just from his body but from his soul. She let herself sink into him, momentarily forgetting that kissing for her wasn't as simple as it was for everyone else.

An image of Darren in a hospital bed started to come into focus. Lorelai barely recognised him as the same person she was kissing. His form had diminished, his skin was grey and sallow, his face gaunt. He was unconscious and hooked up to numerous machines. There were cards and flowers on every surface in the room. Lorelai heard a sudden beeping, and she saw Darren's heart rate flatline. A woman old enough to be his mother was holding his hand but by the time she had realised what was happening and called for help, it was too late. Darren had already slipped away.

Lorelai didn't know what had killed him, but it looked like something unforgiving and devastating. Instead of making her want to pull away from their kiss, Lorelai deepened her touch. Darren had limited kisses left, limited time in which to give and receive love and affection, so Lorelai wanted to give him something to remember, another happy memory he could cling to in his final moments. Lorelai was so lost in what she was doing, that she didn't know the man in tweed had walked away until Darren eased away from their kiss.

'That showed him!' Darren laughed, unperturbed by her sudden intensity.

'Sorry. I got a little carried away.' Lorelai wiped a tear from the corner of her eye, hoping it looked like a laughter tear, rather than one of sadness.

'Don't apologise. Those lips are quite the weapon! Use them wisely.' Darren sat back and grinned at her.

Her heart squeezed; he had no idea what was coming.

'Sound advice!' Joanie appeared above them, leaning on the back of their booth. 'Looks like I've been replaced as your best friend though, Lorelai!' she huffed in mock outrage.

'I think I've got a long way to go before I could ever replace someone as glorious as you!' Darren said, smiling.

'Oh, alright. You're forgiven.' Joanie grinned.

Lorelai leaned her head back and looked up Joanie. Joanie frowned a little, noticing the expression on Lorelai's face and so she kissed her on the forehead.

'Time?' Joanie said quietly into Lorelai's hair.

'Time.' Lorelai began to stand, and Darren gently took her hand in his. Lorelai gave it a squeeze back.

'You're not leaving, are you? Let me buy you a drink? The party's only just getting started.'

'Next time,' Joanie promised Darren. 'We got the party started but now I've got to get this one home.' She ruffled Lorelai's hair, and gave Darren a peck on the cheek.

'I'd ask for a kiss goodbye, Lorelai, but I think we've already covered that!' Darren chuckled to himself, and a lump rose in Lorelai's throat. She said goodbye, gave his hand another squeeze, and then followed Joanie out onto the street. Lorelai sincerely hoped she'd see Darren again one day.

'How are you?' Joanie asked.

'Exhausted,' Lorelai said.

'Do you want to talk about it, tell me what you saw?'

Lorelai shook her head. 'I will but not yet. I'm still processing.' Lorelai looked across the street, and spotted James in the alleyway again. His cigarette glowed in the darkness. 'Before we go home, there's one more thing I need to do. Joanie, I need a favour. A big one.'

'Name it.' Joanie straightened up, ready for action.

'See that bike there? The blue one?' Lorelai gestured across the road to a bike rack. 'That one on the far left is James's bike.'

'How do you know that?'

'I recognise it from when I kissed him.'

'I'm not sure I like where this is going.'

'I need you to, I don't know, slash his tyres or something.'

Joanie's eyebrows shot up. 'You've lost it. I can't do that!'

'I'm serious. He gets hit by a car when he's riding his bike

– that's how he dies, and he looked the same age he is now. I need you to do something to his bike that might delay his death. Then I'm going to kiss him again and see if anything has changed. It's a sure-fire way to know if I'm sealing fates or not. I'm almost certain that is the case after what happened with Riggs, but this would confirm it once and for all.' Lorelai could see Joanie's resolve wavering. 'Plus, plus, plus… you might save his life and let him live another fifty years! *You* would be a hero.'

Joanie's eyes flashed for a moment and then her shoulders dropped in resignation. 'Fine, you hooligan. But I'm doing this for the greater good.'

'And for me?' Lorelai gave Joanie a nudge.

'Don't push it.' Joanie rolled up the sleeves of her jacket and casually walked towards the bike rack. Lorelai waited until she was kneeling by the bike before crossing the road and heading towards James.

'James?' she called.

'Hey. Hi. Hey.' He quickly stubbed his cigarette out on the wall and pushed his hair back. 'You disappeared so quickly earlier. Is everything OK?'

'Yes, yeah. It's just… can I ask you something?'

He walked towards her. 'Sure.'

Lorelai closed the distance between them, her lips inches from his. 'Kiss goodbye?'

Lorelai felt sick at the idea of seeing the car hit James again. What if she did see the same thing? That would mean her kiss had sealed his fate, made his cause of death inevitable. *But what if you're wrong?* That little voice in her head was getting louder. She had to know, for her sake. Grayson's face suddenly flashed in her mind. She wanted to be close to him. She wanted to know what it was like to kiss him, but she'd never be able to if she didn't learn the truth. Lorelai was shaking as James's lips touched hers. This was it.

'OH MY GOD!' Lorelai yelled into James's mouth as the vision became clearer.

He stumbled backwards, clutching his chest. 'Jesus Christ! You scared the shit out of me! What is it?! What's wrong?'

'Nothing! Sorry! No, nothing's wrong. Nothing's wrong at all! I have to go. Sorry. Thank you! Yes! Thank you!' Lorelai stumbled over her feet as she ran from James, waving at him wildly. She found Joanie loitering in a doorway further down the road.

'Joanie!' she shrieked.

'What? What is it? How'd it go?'

'He didn't die on his bike! He's going to die in a hospital somewhere *decades* from now. He looked a lot older. We changed things! *You* changed things!'

'Hooray! I mean, not hooray, but... oh, you know what I mean!'

'So what did you do? Did you let down his tyres?'

'How was I going to let down his tyres? All I've got in my handbag are a few hair pins and a lipstick!'

'Then what did you do?'

Joanie took Lorelai's hand and led her around the corner. James's bike was propped up against the wall. Joanie rang its bell.

'The fool hadn't even chained it up, so you'll be getting a cab on your own tonight because... I've already got my ride home.'

Fourteen

What had Lorelai learned? She had learned that even the deaths
of complete strangers would always have an impact. She would
never not feel the weight of it press against her chest. She would
never forget a single one. Lorelai had replayed Darren's death
in her head over and over. What illness would eventually take
him? Would he suffer for long before death came? Why was the
ending so bleak for someone so clearly loved? Lorelai had been
up half the night wondering and worrying, and when she had
fallen asleep, her sleep had been filled with nightmares.

'Here you go, sunshine.' Joanie set two mugs of tea down
on the bedside table and hopped up onto Lorelai's bed. 'So tell
me one thing you know now that you didn't know yesterday.'

Lorelai groaned and sat up. She'd barely been awake when
Joanie had barged into her bedroom and slipped under the covers
with her. Lorelai had demanded tea before she could even think
about the night before.

'Well? Come on.' Joanie prodded Lorelai.

'I guess… I guess I know I'm capable of pushing the bounda-
ries far more than I thought.'

'Good. What else?' Joanie pushed.

'I'm not sealing anyone's fate when I kiss them. You stealing James's bike changed his death, which means I'm not creating a fixed end point when I kiss someone. It can change depending on what they do with their lives, the choices they make. I'm just able to see it, and what I see is determined by the path they're currently on and that point in their life.' Lorelai said it in one breath, quickly, as though it might not be true if she didn't get the words out fast enough.

'Which is a huge win, right?' Joanie gave her the thumbs up.

Lorelai nodded, feeling her shoulders relax. It *was* huge. Her biggest fear had been that she was some kind of modern-day Grim Reaper, but that wasn't the case. She rubbed her temples. If only she could get these nightmares to stop. It was hard to see the positive side when images of death continued to haunt her in her sleep.

'Anything else?' Joanie sipped her tea, and snuggled in closer to Lorelai.

'I'm still having nightmares,' Lorelai said and Joanie squeezed her arm in sympathy. She thought carefully about what she wanted to say next. 'I'm desperately sad about what I saw when I kissed Darren, but I don't feel the same way about the other two deaths I saw. I'm glad we changed James's fate, but Darren's death has hit me harder. Maybe it's because I got to know him a little bit and there was a connection there *before* I kissed him.'

'Right…' Joanie knew where this was going.

Lorelai's voice was shaking. 'Which means I don't think I'd ever be able to have a meaningful relationship,' she said in a rush.

'Lorelai…' Joanie said in a warning tone.

'I'm serious. If just a brief conversation with Darren has left me feeling this way, how am I going to feel if I fell in love with someone? How could I put myself through seeing what end is currently mapped out for them and feel that kind of heartbreak every time I kissed them?'

'Are you thinking of Grayson when you say that?' Joanie's eyes lit up.

'Are you even listening to me?' Lorelai sat up and reached for her tea.

'Answer my very intrusive question and then I'll listen.'

In truth, Lorelai had been thinking only of Grayson throughout this whole ordeal. She had conducted her experiment last night *because* of Grayson.

'Yes, Joanie.' Lorelai rubbed a hand over her tired face. 'I am thinking of Grayson.'

'Knew it. I knew it, I knew it, *I knew it*.' Joanie punctuated each word with a prod.

'But you're not listening. I *can't* think about him anymore. My life works best the way I was living it before. Alone.' Lorelai felt a tightening in her chest. This was the right decision. This was how she could protect herself, and everyone else. So why did she feel as though her heart was breaking?

Because it is.

'No, Lollie, you can't honestly think that's for the best,' Joanie pleaded.

'It is. Say I fall hard for Grayson and kiss him and see how he dies. Then what? I just live with that pain, carry it with me every day? What if he's only got a couple of years, or months, left? What if he dies a horrible, tragic death that completely changes everyone's lives? How could I stay with him *knowing* where

it was headed? How am I supposed to live with that? I can't.'
Lorelai didn't realise she was crying until her voice cracked.

Joanie turned to face Lorelai, and began to wipe away her
tears with her sleeve. 'Look at you, you snotty mess. Come here.'

They sat in silence for a while, Joanie holding Lorelai, letting
her cry it all out. Joanie didn't speak again until the tears stopped,
and Lorelai's breathing returned to normal.

'Sweetie,' she began, 'if Grayson is going to do die of old age in
sixty years or so, then there's not going to be anything you can do
to change that and it's still going to be sad for everyone who knew
him. Death is a part of life and we all have to deal with people we
love dying. It's inevitable. If there's one thing we can all be certain
of, it's that we're all going to die one day and you can't stop that
from happening. Yes, you can do something no one else can. But
if you see that he's going to die young in some kind of preventable
accident or tragedy, then you might be able to stop it. You have the
gift of foresight, so you could make sure he gets the old-age death.'

Joanie's words hung in the air. Joanie only ever spoke of what
Lorelai could do as a positive. Lorelai had thought Joanie said
these things to balance out Lorelai's negative views on it all, on
how she saw her ability as something that made her less than
everyone else. But ever since Grayson had entered the picture
and they spoke of it more and more, she realised Joanie genuinely
thought of it as a good thing. Something to be embraced.

'This doesn't feel like a *gift*. It feels like a dirty secret, and this
huge responsibility all at once. I just want to be normal.'

'There's no such thing as normal!' Joanie threw up her hands,
exasperated. 'Everyone thinks they're not normal. Newsflash –
normal is in the eye of the beholder.'

Lorelai shook her head. 'But you don't know how this *thing* feels! It's too much.'

'My dear sweet friend,' Joanie continued, 'how do you not realise just how many people would be desperate to know when their loved ones were going to be taken from them? I think you'd be surprised at how many people would want to know so they could relish their final days, and say all the things they never got to say. To be able to plan a proper goodbye. People spend their entire lives wondering, *What if I'd said that? What if I'd done this? Maybe if they'd known I felt this way things would be different.* You will never have to deal with that if you choose not to. One kiss and you and your loved ones can prepare for the day everyone always feels unprepared for.'

Lorelai took a few sips of her tea and thought about what Joanie was saying. She was making valid points, and was offering a point of view Lorelai hadn't considered before, but Lorelai knew it couldn't be as simple or as straightforward as that. People were different. There was no blanket rule for everyone. One person might want to be prepared for the day they died, while the next person could find that knowledge a burden and end up spending their life waiting for the axe to fall.

'So, you'd want to know, would you? If I kissed you right now, you'd want to know how you were going to die?' Before Lorelai had even finished her sentence Joanie was nodding fervently.

'Yes! I've said it before and I'll say it again, if I knew how I was going to die, I'd know I was invincible through everything else.'

'It doesn't work like that!' Lorelai exclaimed.

'Why not?'

'We now know that your fate can be changed.' Lorelai began to explain, realising this was as much for herself to try to understand as it was for Joanie. 'Say I kissed you now and saw you die peacefully in your sleep at the age of a hundred. What if you then decided, based on that knowledge, to take up extreme sports or become an adrenaline junkie and go bungee jumping and sky diving and swimming with sharks and alligator wrestling because you thought you could survive it. Surely your death would change because your whole lifestyle has changed? You would have died in your sleep as long as you stayed on the path you were on. But telling you how you were going to die created a fork in the road and you chose a different way, which therefore gives you a changed death.'

'Huh.' Joanie sat back, processing Lorelai's theory. 'So you're saying someone's life decisions have an impact on their death.'

'You stole James's bike and now he no longer dies on a bike.'

'Then surely that means you never have anything to worry about?'

'What do you mean?'

'If death is ever-changing because life is ever-changing, surely the deaths you see won't always come true? Because people are constantly making choices that change the course of their life. One tiny moment or insignificant decision could change everything and suddenly it means someone who was meant to die in a... a... boat explosion at twenty-two, dies in their sleep at *eighty*-two because they forgot to set their alarm and didn't make it to the airport in time. Small things that we don't think twice about have the power to impact the outcome of our entire lives. Which means... you have the chance to change what you see. Exactly like you did last night.'

Lorelai couldn't deny that this all made sense but there was still so much to explore and she had no idea how to begin to understand better. There wasn't a handbook or a manual that she could read. She had to figure this out for herself and it was daunting. How was she meant to figure out her next step?

'This is all so confusing.'

'Because life and death are confusing.' Joanie tapped her nose and pointed at Lorelai, confident she had it all figured out.

'Both people I kissed in my teens died in the ways I saw them die.'

'They probably stuck to the book.'

'What book?'

'The book of… death? Death's book. Of names. Of people who are going to die. And… how?' Joanie held up her hands in a half shrug.

'I'm starting to think you may not the best person to talk to about this stuff.' Lorelai smiled mischievously. 'The book of death?!'

'I don't know! We're both just making this up as we go along. Besides, I'm the *only* person you can talk to about this.'

Joanie was right, and Lorelai was usually fine with that, but something had changed, and now Lorelai wanted to tell Grayson. Confess everything. Lay it bare. She wanted him to see her as she really was, and that terrified her. But how could she explain it to him when she didn't fully understand it herself? And what if she lost him? Lorelai's heart wasn't ready to make that kind of sacrifice. She had to keep her secret, no matter the cost.

◆

After she heard the news that Arthur and Thomas had died in the ways she had seen, Lorelai sank into a pit of despair. She shut herself away and barely spoke to anyone. She had been thrust into a dark and confusing world, and it haunted her. Why had she seen those things? What did it mean? She had no answers and no one to talk to. The loneliness seeped into her bones, and became so much a part of her that even when she was in a room full of people or wrapped in her mother's embrace, she still felt alone. Seeing those visions had terrified Lorelai, but Arthur and Thomas dying in exactly the way she'd seen, knowing she'd witnessed the future, set Lorelai on a path of self-destruction. She was adrift, on her own, and falling apart.

One night, while Lorelai was at university, she had a particularly brutal nightmare. She jolted awake, mid-sob, tears running down her face in hot rivulets.

Cries of pain.

Dripping blood.

Crunching metal.

Bones breaking.

Lorelai gulped, trying to steady her breathing, and waited for the images to fade. Laying there, the eerie silence of night pressing down on her, Lorelai had never felt more helpless. She didn't have anyone to talk to. Just when she felt she might be making friends, her nightmares would pull her back into the death spiral she now lived in. It kept her separated from the world she so desperately longed to be a part of. A world where she could go out with her friends, fall in love, kiss someone and have it not matter. Lorelai's sobs deepened and she wept for herself, for Arthur and Thomas, and for everything she would never have.

Enough was enough. She needed to tell someone. She needed to know what was happening to her. She needed help. Lorelai picked up her phone and dialled her mother's number with trembling fingers.

'Lorelai?' Her mother's voice croaked down the line, thick with sleep.

Lorelai tried to say, 'Mum,' but it came out as a cry. Lorelai rubbed at her face and tried to calm down.

'Darling? Is everything OK? What's wrong?' When Lorelai didn't respond, Lila's voice rose in panic. 'Are you hurt? Has someone hurt you? David! David, wake up! It's Lorelai. Something's wrong. Come on, we've got to go and get her.'

That jolted Lorelai into action. What was she thinking? She couldn't tell her mother; she couldn't tell *anyone*. Her mother had panicked just hearing Lorelai cry, and had jumped to conclusions. She'd send Lorelai away to some awful soul-destroying facility if Lorelai said anything about her secret. She'd be labelled as 'crazy'.

'No,' Lorelai said suddenly, her sobs lessening. 'I'm OK. I just got a bit overwhelmed. I'm working too hard and was just having a moment. I just... ' Lorelai breathed deeply to staunch the flow of tears, 'I just wanted to hear your voice and say hello to take my mind off things for a little bit.'

'It's almost three o'clock in the morning, sweetheart. Have you been working through the night?' Lila's voice was stern, yet filled with concern.

Lorelai looked at her tear-drenched pillow. Hearing herself say that she'd had a nightmare so she had called her mother made her feel pathetic and weak.

'Yeah. Sorry, I lost track of the time. Didn't realise it was so late. I'll call properly tomorrow.'

'Please do. We've not heard from you in so long and I hate hearing you like this.'

'I'm fine. Honestly,' she lied unconvincingly, still sniffling.

'You know we're always here.' Lila's voice was kind. 'On the end of the phone, or we can always come and bring you home at the drop of a hat.'

Lorelai felt like a child again, unable to look after herself. 'I know. Thank you. Look, I'm sorry I called.'

'Don't say that. I'm glad that you called.' Her mother sounded hurt.

'I mean, sorry that I called so late,' Lorelai corrected. 'I promise that I'll ring you tomorrow. Please don't worry about me though. I really am OK.'

They talked for a few more minutes, about nothing very important, and then Lila said goodbye, making her promise once more that she'd phone her again soon.

She placed her phone on the bedside table and stared at it.

The nightmare had made her feel vulnerable. She really had planned to tell her mother what was going on because in the immediate seconds after she awoke, with the nightmare images still fresh, she didn't feel strong enough to cope with this alone. But the longer she was awake, the more those images faded, and she found the strength to stay quiet about her ability. She was able to convince herself that she could maintain the charade of being normal. Once she revealed her secret, she'd be giving in to it, and it would take over her life entirely. She didn't want that. No, it needed to remain her secret, so she had the freedom to find some form of normality.

Lorelai didn't know then that staying silent was the thing making her miserable. In staying hidden and not sharing her true self with the world, Lorelai would lose herself a little more each day.

◆

Fifteen

Lorelai wrestled with whether she should see Grayson again, but in the end decided that brunch couldn't possibly make matters worse, so she had called him to rearrange. And the truth was she *wanted* to see him, to be near him, spend more time with him. She couldn't shake it. Despite the confirmation that having a relationship was never going to be a good idea, Lorelai couldn't make peace with the idea of Grayson not being part of her life at all. She would need to keep a huge part of herself private, but she was used to that. Meeting him had felt like fate, and she couldn't ignore that. Keeping good people close was important, and helped her feel less alone.

Lorelai often thought of the night she'd almost told her mother her secret. Would she have understood? She liked to think that both of her parents would have, but in reality she couldn't see them believing her. It scared her to think about what might have happened if she had come clean. Would Grayson understand if she told him? Would he stick around long enough for her to explain?

'Where are you meeting your lover boy?' Joanie draped herself seductively against the door frame of Lorelai's bedroom.

It was a couple of days later. Lorelai had several outfits laid out on her bed and yet she was still in her pyjamas, twenty minutes before she was due to leave.

'The Duchess,' Lorelai replied

Joanie's mouth fell open. 'Why on *earth* are you meeting your beau at work, of all places?'

'Because we both know where it is, and he said it's not far from where we're going for brunch. Why, is that weird?' Butterflies fluttered in Lorelai's stomach. She was already nervous, and Joanie wasn't helping.

'I guess not.' Joanie shrugged, and perched on the edge of the bed. 'Just not the most romantic of places. But, actually, if you happen to see Wesley, can you ask him how Riggs is?'

'I texted Wesley last night. He said that Riggs is still a bit shaky but doing better. We should try to visit him soon.' Joanie nodded in agreement. 'And anyway,' Lorelai continued, 'Grayson is not my *beau* or my *lover boy*. He's a friend. That's all.'

'Alright, alright. But I don't see you blushing when you talk about your other *friends*. It's OK to admit you have feelings for him.'

'It doesn't matter how I feel about him, he can't be anything more than a friend right now.' Lorelai swallowed hard. She reasoned that she didn't have to suppress her romantic or physical feelings towards Grayson. No, she just needed to work on turning them into platonic ones. She took a yellow dress from the pile and put it back in her wardrobe. It was too bright for a casual brunch with a friend.

'Right now? Did you just say "right now"? Does this mean there's hope for the future?' Joanie asked, excitedly.

Lorelai groaned. 'Can you just help me decide what to wear please?'

Joanie rolled her eyes. 'OK, fine. If we were going out for a casual bite to eat, what would you wear?'

'Jeans and a T-shirt,' Lorelai said immediately, 'because the places you take me are dives.'

Joanie looked at the clock on the wall. 'Go ahead and make jokes. I'm not the one who has to leave in less than fifteen minutes. Just pick something!'

'Fine.' Lorelai let out a huff. 'I'd wear black skinny jeans and a slightly nicer top.'

'And that's what you'll wear now.'

And that is what Lorelai wore. Which is why when Grayson arrived, dressed casually in jeans and a sweatshirt, she felt foolish.

'You look nice,' Grayson said, smiling down at her.

'Thanks. You too,' Lorelai said, her cheeks growing hot.

'The place I wanted to take you to is just up Shaftesbury Avenue. Shall we?'

Lorelai nodded, and tried to calm her nerves. *This is not a date. This is not a date. This is not a date.*

They started walking, and made polite conversation until Grayson led her down a road that was all too familiar.

'Ta da!' he said, spreading his arms wide with a flourish.

'Angel's Diner?'

'Yeah! I love this place! And they do brunch until twelve-thirty. Is that… is this not OK?' Grayson rubbed the back of his head and peered in through the window, rethinking his choice.

'It's great!' Lorelai said too brightly. 'It's just amusing.'

'Amusing? Do explain before the embarrassment really has time to set in.'

'This is where Joanie works. When she's not working at The Duchess.'

'Oh, right. So you don't want to eat here?'

'No, it's fine,' Lorelai reassured him. 'I've never actually eaten here. Joanie banned me because she has to wear a pink wig, a silver miniskirt and serve food on roller skates. For some strange reason she thinks that's embarrassing!'

Grayson laughed and opened the door for her. Lorelai stepped inside and immediately fell in love with the place. It had every-thing a classic American diner should have. The jukebox in the corner was blasting out 'Jailhouse Rock', the spinning dessert cases were filled with huge wedges of lemon meringue pie, and Lorelai watched the pink-wigged wait staff rolling by on their skates. Joanie was going to get an earful about keeping this place from her.

'This looks just like the Frosty Palace from *Grease*,' Lorelai said, as they slid into a booth by the window.

'*Grease* is a great movie. Such a classic.'

'Yeah, it is. I love it and always will, but I have an issue with the final message. Isn't it saying that you'll only find love if you change everything about yourself and become a completely different person?' Lorelai pulled a menu from the stand. 'I don't think I'll be squeezing myself into a catsuit or taking up smoking anytime soon, just to please a man.'

'And there was me singing "You're The One That I Want" at the top of my lungs at the last singalong without a care in the world!'

'*You* came to the *Grease* singalong?' Lorelai eyed him over the top of her menu.

His lips twisted into a cheeky smile. 'You know,' he said, 'you always seem surprised by me. Is there a preconceived version of me in your head that's feeding you false information?'

The truth was that Lorelai fought so hard to push thoughts of Grayson away that she didn't let herself think too deeply about the kind of person he was. That was a daydreaming rabbit hole she wouldn't allow herself to fall into. So it was a surprise each time he revealed a bit more about himself. A very pleasant one.

'No…' She lifted her menu a little higher between them.

'There is! You've already decided what movies I like, what I watch on the telly, whether I prefer beer over wine, what I like to do on the weekends.'

'I haven't! It's safer for me not to think about you at all!'

Grayson went very still. 'Safer?'

Lorelai's heart was hammering. What did she say that for? 'I, um, that's not I meant. It's just that…' Her voice trailed off. She couldn't think of anything that would explain away her comment.

'Lorelai.' Hearing her name on Grayson's lips was an arrow straight to her heart. He reached over and pushed the menu down so he could see her face. 'Why is thinking about me unsafe for you?'

'It was a bad choice of words.' Lorelai's voice was too high. 'Sorry! Shall we order? What are you going to have? Hmmm? Everything looks so good!'

Smooth.

Grayson looked at her seriously for a beat, weighing up

whether to push her on it, and then he smiled and picked up a menu. They sat in silence for a few minutes before he said, 'So how is that guy? The one who got fired? He seemed pretty upset when he left.'

'Riggs?' Lorelai, grateful for the subject change, pondered how much to say. 'It got a bit hairy there for a while. He had a *really* bad day and then he tried to kiss me and it quickly spiralled from there.'

'Oh. Were you two…?' Grayson asked casually, not quite meeting her eye.

'Me and Riggs? Oh my god, no. Absolutely not. No. No way. No.'

'Oh, that's good.'

Lorelai couldn't help but feel happy at the look of relief on his face.

'Riggs is sweet but we're just friends. He took something I said the wrong way, and misread the situation.' Lorelai wanted to get off the subject of kissing Riggs. 'Anyway, he's dealing with some personal things now, so he's taking some time out to figure out what's next for him.'

'I see,' Grayson said. 'But the two of you are definitely just friends?'

'Definitely.'

'Good.' Before Lorelai could think about *why* Grayson was so happy that she and Riggs were just friends, he pointed his menu at her and raised an eyebrow. 'So, tell me. What do you think about the gherkin theory?'

'Excuse me?' She laughed.

'The gherkin theory! Don't tell me you've never heard of it?

It's a cutting-edge scientific theory that neurobiologists have been working on for years.' He nodded seriously.

'Oh yeah?' She mimicked his serious nodding.

'Yes. The theory is that two people are only completely compatible if one of them likes gherkins, and the other doesn't.'

'This sounds legit.' Lorelai put her chin in her hand but then quickly sat up straight again. She didn't want to look like a doe-eyed teenager. *We're friends.*

'Hear me out! It's so when you both order burgers with gherkins, one gets the satisfaction of handing over their gherkins and making the other happy and the other takes away the thing that makes the other unhappy.'

'Are gherkins really that much of an issue in relationships?'

'It's symbolic.' Grayson batted her hand with his laminated menu.

'Symbolic of what?'

'I have no idea. I didn't read that far down the BuzzFeed article.'

Lorelai whacked Grayson with her menu. 'Idiot,' she said affectionately.

The waitress skated up at that moment and they placed their order – a blue cheese burger for Lorelai, and a bacon cheese burger for Grayson.

'So much for brunch!' he said.

'I'm too hungry for brunch.'

'Me too. So. Tell me about yourself.'

They were four simple words but they had the power to make Lorelai sweat.

'Why can't you tell me about *your*self?' she asked.

'Well… I will.' Grayson laughed, sitting back in his seat. 'But right now this feels very one-sided. You know about my love of nerdy movies. You know I have a brother. And, most embarrassingly, you've seen me dressed as a hobbit. I think it's only fair that now I get to know you a little better.'

His tone was jovial but the look in his eyes was determined. Lorelai's stomach flipped. He was interested in her. Grayson wanted to know about *her*. She needed to give him something.

'I guess the first thing you should know about me is I don't much like talking about myself.'

That was so lame.

Grayson wasn't letting her off the hook. 'Just give me anything. Tell me something about, I don't know, your childhood?'

He crossed his arms, the muscles in his biceps shifting underneath his sleeve. Lorelai wondered what it would feel like to hug him, to have those arms wrapped around her.

'I'm an only child,' she offered up.

'OK…' He nodded encouragingly.

'Both parents are still around and still together,' she continued, uneasily.

'Do you see them a lot?'

'Not as much as I should. We talk. On the phone. Every now and then.' Lorelai felt a pang of guilt.

'That must be hard. I don't know what I'd do if I couldn't see my mum and Aden every day.' Grayson shook his head.

'What about your dad?' Lorelai asked, thankful the conversation had moved back to him.

'Dad has always travelled for work. He's a pilot and he's in his last year of flying before he retires. Even though he categorically does *not* want to. We hear from him every night he's away though. At six o'clock on the dot, he calls no matter where he is in the world, no matter the time difference. When he's home it's like Christmas every day!' Grayson laughed, reliving these happy memories of his family. 'My auntie has always lived with us. She moved in when we were kids to help out when Dad was travelling, and she never moved out. My mum and aunt are hysterical. My favourite people. Family is pretty important to us.' Grayson's face lit up as he spoke of his relatives, and Lorelai thought it looked good on him.

'I can see that. I don't have that kind of relationship with Mum and Dad.' Lorelai surprised herself. Why had she admitted that?

Because you like Grayson. You trust him. He makes you feel safe.

'How come?' Grayson asked softly.

'My parents are great parents, don't get me wrong. But I was quite a reclusive teenager and I think they didn't know how to handle that. They didn't want to pry or push too hard so they let me get on with things by myself and they never stopped. I've always been pretty self-sufficient. I can feel my mum trying sometimes though, you know? Trying to get me to open up. I'm just not sure how to let her in now. It's been too long.'

'It's never too late,' Grayson said gently.

'So I'm told.'

The waitress arrived with their food, for which Lorelai was grateful. If she hadn't interrupted them, who knows what Lorelai would've admitted next. She might have felt compelled to tell Grayson her secret, and that could never happen. She needed to steer things onto less complicated territory.

She looked pointedly at her burger, and Grayson grinned.

They each lifted their burger buns, revealing several gherkins. They both placed them onto a napkin.

'It's make or break time,' Grayson said. 'You ready?'

'Ready.'

Grayson took an exaggerated deep breath, closed his eyes and gently slid the napkin towards himself. When he opened his eyes, Lorelai smiled and said, 'The demon cucumbers are all yours.'

Sixteen

The rest of their non-date was less fraught and Lorelai managed to avoid sharing anything too personal. Grayson was perfect company – he was funny, had a laugh that was a little too loud, he loved good conversation and had strong opinions. There was no denying that Lorelai was drawn to him, and she tried to ignore the voice in her head telling her she wasn't good enough for him. *But it doesn't matter*, she told herself. *We're just friends. This is purely platonic.* And yet she felt a thrill when he offered to walk her to the station; he wasn't ready to leave her yet. His hand brushed against hers and it was electric. Lorelai glanced at Grayson to see if he'd felt it too, but he just smiled at her.

'So, this wasn't so bad, was it?' Grayson bumped her shoulder with his.

'No, it wasn't. It was very nice.'

'Nice? Woah, big compliment,' Grayson said, laughing. He stopped laughing when he saw the look on Lorelai's face. 'Sorry, sorry. Yes, it was nice. It's just… you don't give much away, do you? About how you're feeling, I mean.'

Lorelai tensed. 'It just takes a while for me to trust people. But

I really did have a lovely time. As friends,' she added, sneaking a glance to see his reaction.

He tilted his head to one side, in agreement. 'As friends. Of course.'

'The gherkins will be ever so sad.'

'I think that kind of compatibility – or com-pickle-bility if you will – isn't necessarily restricted to romantic relationships. The gherkins don't lie,' he declared to Trafalgar Square. 'We're bonded for life now whether that's as friends or... whatever.'

'Or whatever,' she repeated, not daring to look at him but feeling the weight of his gaze on her. *Lorelai*, she warned herself. *Don't play with fire.*

As they approached the National Gallery, the sound of a guitar filled the air. The sun was high above them now but the air was still chilly. Lorelai pulled her coat around her and shoved her hands into her pockets to avoid any further accidental hand grazes. Any more of that and she knew she'd cave right then and there.

'He's not bad, is he?' Grayson paused next to the small crowd gathered around the guitarist.

Lorelai listened for a moment. The young boy's fingers darted up and down the fretboard, plucking a delicate and melancholic melody. The boy's eyes were closed; he was completely lost in the emotion of whatever this song meant to him.

'Very,' Lorelai agreed. 'But that's coming from someone whose only musical experience is two singing lessons in primary school.'

'Just two? Why did you stop?'

'I gave it up after my teacher told me I couldn't carry a tune even if it had handles.'

Grayson barked his laughter, startling an old lady in front of them who tutted and shook her head at him, as she walked away.

He's got the biggest, happiest laugh. I could just— Lorelai shook herself. Enough of that.

'I trust your instinct though.' Lorelai gestured back to the boy. 'You work in the theatre and spend all that time around musical types; you must have a much better grasp on what's good and what's not.' She was leaning in towards him, closing the distance between their walking bodies. Their shoulders pressed together and she liked the way it felt. Solid. Strong. *Normal.*

'Sometimes I just look at young kids like this and think what if he's the next Ed Sheeran and none of us know it yet? What if we're watching TV in a few years' time and he's on it and all these people just wandered past without so much as a glance?' Grayson was nodding along to the rhythm.

'Or what if he has the capability to be the next Ed Sheeran but the right people don't discover him?' she said, becoming more entranced by the song too.

'Exactly. Not many people get their big break. That's why I pay attention to these street performers. They're doing what they feel they were born to do, and so I think they deserve a bit of our attention.'

The song ended and they clapped their appreciation. They pulled away from the crowd before he began his next song and wandered towards the fountain. Their pace had slowed, both aware their time together was coming to an end, their hesitant steps a silent pact to draw out these last few moments for as long as they could. Lorelai spotted a couple sat on the edge of one of the fountains, playfully splashing each other until the moment swept them into a kiss. Lorelai looked away, a lump in her throat. What must it be like to kiss someone so easily, for a kiss to just be a kiss?

'So what were you born to do, Grayson Brady?' Lorelai asked in an effort not to dwell on her thoughts for too long.

'Good question.' Grayson looked thoughtful. 'I was born to look after people, I think.'

'So a doctor or a nurse? Or a carer?'

'Nah, I'm too squeamish for anything like that. I even fainted during my flu jab last year.' Lorelai liked how he was comfortable being vulnerable, and laughing at himself. 'But there are other ways to look after people. Making them feel loved and valued. Making sure they're warm and listened to. Even if it's just the few people around you. Nothing makes me happier than making sure Mum, Dad, my aunt and Aden are well cared for.'

That warmth again. A pang of guilt squeezed Lorelai's heart. What sort of daughter had she become, to have pushed her loving parents so far away?

'What about you?' he asked 'What were you born to do?'

That wasn't the same question as what do you *want* to do. She wanted to adapt books and write scripts and spend her life on film sets. But what was she *born* to do? Was her ability something she was born with because she was meant to use it somehow? What was its purpose? To prophesise about death? To what end? Was there someone somewhere who was meant to know their death date to try to stop it? Lorelai realised she'd not spoken for a few moments. Grayson must be seconds away from waving a hand in front of her blank face.

'I don't know,' she said quickly. 'I'm one of those people who will inevitably spend my life aimlessly wandering around, without really figuring it out.' She laughed but the sound was sharp and strangled.

'You'll figure it out, Lorelai.' Grayson paused by one of the fountains and hopped up to sit on its damp edge. 'You're too cool not to.'

She leaned next to him. She'd misjudged the distance between them and was leaning at an angle that meant they were now very close. Moving away would look awkward and rude. The devil in her, the wild and carefree side of her, loved being this close to him but the cautious side of her, the angel on her other shoulder, was telling her to walk away as quickly as possible. To head back to the flat, back to where life was safe and made sense.

The angel won. 'This has been lovely,' Lorelai said. 'It's nice to make new friends.'

'Hmmm,' he said, non-committally. The way his eyes shone at her made the devil on her shoulder very excited.

'Did you know the artist who made the lion statues got something slightly wrong?' she said quickly, giving herself something else to focus on, other than his beautiful, full lips.

'What?' Grayson shook his head, confused. Her complete one-eighty even had her head spinning. One minute she's saying they're friends and the next she was thinking about his lips.

Get your act together, Lorelai, said her angel.

But he's so wonderful and maybe, just maybe… said her devil.

'Yeah, the artist was commissioned to make lions and was using a dead lion from London Zoo as a model. By the time he got to the paws, the lion had decomposed so badly he couldn't really make them look realistic. So the paws look more like house cat paws than lion paws. That was all he had to work with,' she rambled. She stared straight ahead, at one of the great, bronze lions, but she could *feel* Grayson looking at her.

Lorelai knew it was a bad idea but she glanced at Grayson who was looking down at her, his face arranged into an expression of slightly amused adoration. A look she'd never seen focused on her before. Lorelai could feel that pull in her chest and for the briefest of moments, she leaned in. Grayson raised his eyebrows, asking the silent question. Lorelai couldn't stop. The kiss was inevitable, they were at the point of no return. His eyes were closing and he'd stopped just centimetres from her face, allowing her to come to him in her own time. He was so beautiful, and kind, and he made her laugh. She could just—

Cries of pain.

Dripping blood.

Crunching metal.

Bones breaking.

The images were like bullets to her brain. What was she doing?! As much as her body yearned for that physical touch, the feeling of being kissed by Grayson, it couldn't happen. She couldn't watch him die. She couldn't open herself up to that kind of pain and grief. It didn't matter about the angels and devils whispering in her ear. She had feelings for Grayson; she was falling for him. Watching the life leave this man's eyes would be the end of her.

Lorelai pulled back, and then she ran.

She ran back up the steps towards the National Gallery, past the Garrick Theatre and kept going until she got to Leicester Square station. She flew down the steps and she didn't pause for breath until she was on the first train, any train, that would take her far away from Grayson Brady.

Seventeen

When she returned home, Joanie wanted to hear everything about her day.

'Where did you go? What was he wearing? What did you talk about? Are you seeing him again?' She was holding a can of gin and tonic. Lorelai grabbed it and drained half of it in one mouthful.

'I've had enough with the questions for one day, Joanie. Let's not do this now, OK?'

'What does that mean? Did he ask a lot of questions? Did you ask him a lot of questions? Is he amazing? Is he too good to be true? Is he a serial killer?'

Lorelai massaged the bridge of her nose, a headache brewing behind her eyes. She pushed her way past Joanie into the living room, drained the last of the tin and sat down heavily on the sofa.

'Joanie. Calm down. It's over.'

There was a long silence. Lorelai hoped Joanie would take the hint and leave her alone but no such luck.

'What do you mean "it's over"? What did you do?' Joanie stood over her, hands on her hips.

'What did *I* do? What did *he* do?' Lorelai pressed her face into a cushion.

'What *did* he do?!'

'Hmm trmmm tom kimmm mmm,' Lorelai mumbled into the pillow.

'Lollie!' Joanie sat down next to Lorelai and whacked her on the arm.

'OW! Joanie!' Lorelai stood up. Feeling her headache press against the back of her prickling eyes, Lorelai turned away and faced her bookshelves. 'He tried to kiss me.'

'What happened to the "just friends" thing?' Joanie asked.

'We *were* only friends!' A hot tear trickled down Lorelai's face. She felt numb.

'Was it the same way Riggs tried to kiss you? Did he force himself on you?' Joanie came up behind Lorelai and wrapped her arms around Lorelai's waist, resting her cheek in between her shoulder blades.

'No. It wasn't like that. He didn't actually kiss me. I didn't let him.'

'Why not?'

'You know why.'

'But he was going to kiss you, and you said no?'

Lorelai nodded.

'What happened then?' Joanie asked.

'Nothing.'

'No, I mean what happened when you said no?'

'Yeah, nothing.'

'OK, I need more detail.' Joanie gently turned Lorelai to face her and guided her back over to the sofa.

'Nothing happened. I didn't say no. If anything, I said yes.' Lorelai paused and Joanie waited patiently for more but when

Lorelai didn't continue, Joanie prodded her hard. 'OK! We were saying goodbye at Trafalgar Square and there was a *moment*, and I leaned in. So he closed his eyes and leaned in to kiss me… and I panicked and just walked away. Well, I ran away, actually.' Another silence but this time Lorelai wished Joanie would say something. Joanie not saying anything was never a good sign.

'Wait a second. I need to process this. You were saying goodbye…'

'Yeah.'

'You gave him the green light, he closed his eyes and leaned in for a kiss…'

Lorelai nodded miserably.

'And by the time he opened his eyes you'd evaporated into thin air.'

'It sounds horrible when you put it like that,' Lorelai mumbled.

'Wow.' Joanie was at a loss for words and Lorelai's stomach dropped. Joanie *always* had something to say.

'I really am the worst,' Lorelai said sadly.

'You're not the worst you're just… in unchartered territory. But you're going to have to call him.'

'I can't!' Lorelai wailed.

'Lorelai, even if you don't want to see him again, the decent thing to do is to call him and explain that the reason you ran away is because you're new to this and you panicked. He's a nice guy! He'll understand! If it had got to the point of a goodbye kiss, then I'm guessing you had a nice time up until that point. And if you leaned in first—' Joanie held up a hand to stop Lorelai from speaking '—which is totally fine, by the way, you giving into your feelings is OK, you know? Anyway, if you leaned in first then he may have thought that a kiss is what you would have liked, too.'

'It is what I would have liked,' Lorelai admitted. 'More than anything. I spent the whole time trying to push my feelings away, but I couldn't carry on doing it. I felt like a regular girl spending time with a regular boy, and I didn't want that feeling to end. The more time I spend with him, the more I like him, and the more terrifying this all becomes. I don't think I'm ready to handle this kind of thing.'

Lorelai remembered how she'd felt sitting next to Grayson by the fountains, the easy way they'd talked for hours, the feel of his hand touching hers. She had got carried away and she'd been a fool to lead him on. He had responded to her invitation and then as soon as the moment had arrived, she'd run. Literally and figuratively. Lorelai knew deep down that her abstinence from romantic interaction wasn't strength. It wasn't a choice she had made because she thought it was for the best. It was a choice she had made because she thought it would be easier. Less traumatic, messy and complicated. The truth of the matter was simple. Lorelai was scared. She always had been and now she knew she always would be. At a moment when a whole new chapter of her life could have begun, just when she thought maybe she was ready, she proved to herself she was a coward. Lorelai covered her face with her hands and began to sob. She felt like the tears may never stop.

'Oh, Lollie.' Joanie wrapped her arms around her, and Lorelai sank into her, her heart breaking. 'I know it's a lot to handle,' she said quietly. 'I can't pretend to understand what this is like for you, or know how it feels to meet someone who makes you rethink your life choices. But Grayson is a good guy and it's not fair to play games with him.'

'I'm not playing games.' Lorelai tried to pull away from Joanie but she held her tight.

'I know you don't mean to mess him around. That's not who you are. You know what's right for you and how you to deal with this situation in a way that protects you and your heart. But from his perspective, he's just a guy... standing in front of a girl... asking him to love her...' Lorelai smiled at the *Notting Hill* reference. 'Seriously, though, he likes you and he must be so confused right now. You need to have a think and make some decisions. If you think you can't handle a relationship because it would be too painful then you need to figure out whether you can just be friends. And if you don't think you can be just friends because of how you feel about him, then you need to let him go.'

Lorelai's face crumpled. 'Is there another option?' she asked quietly.

'There is, but I don't think you're going to like it.'

'What is it?'

'The other option is to go for it — start a relationship with Grayson. All relationships are complicated and messy, period. Sometimes the best thing to do is just surrender to it and enjoy the ride.'

They sat there together, arms around each other, for a few minutes and Lorelai found comfort in the silence.

'You know,' Joanie said tentatively, 'you could always tell him. About your secret. That would make things simpler. If he knew what you were going through, he might be able to help. Offer a different perspective.'

Could she tell Grayson, trust him with her biggest and most protected secret? She did trust him, and a part of her wanted to come clean and tell him everything. But she knew that she never would. Despite all the hurt and confusion, running from Grayson was much less painful than Grayson running from her. She didn't want him thinking she was some kind of monster. Someone who needed to be locked away. She imagined how he might react, his playful expression changing to one of distrust and fear. It was another cowardly move on her part but she needed time to decide what to do next.

'I'll think about it but…' Lorelai had no idea which of her worn-out excuses to use. In the end she simply opted for, 'I'll think about it.'

Eighteen

'Hi Grayson, er... I know I'm the last person you want to hear from right now. But I wanted to explain what happened the other day. Just... give me a chance? The bottom line is I'm sorry. You didn't deserve that and I promise I have good reason it's just... a little strange. Call me back? Bye. This is Lorelai, by the way. Umm, yeah. Bye.'

Lorelai pulled the phone away from her ear. The screen was damp from perspiration. She wasn't used to reaching out to someone she had complicated feelings for.

'You're really bad at that.' The voice startled Lorelai, almost making her drop her phone.

'Riggs?' She walked out to the front counter.

'Yeah, hey.'

He looked different. He'd had a shave and he was wearing a suit. He'd lost some weight too, but it suited him, and he held himself differently too. He was standing a bit straighter, and there was a determined gleam in his eyes.

'You look... well. You look really well.' She meant it, and smiled warmly. It was good to see him looking so *alive*.

'Thanks. I've got an interview round the corner. Just to be

a runner at a voice-over studio. They do audiobooks and video games mostly but it's the TV and filmmaking stuff they do that I find interesting. Turns out I like movies a lot more than I thought I did.' He smiled and it changed his whole face. He looked happy.

'You can't be missing it here, surely?'

'No, I'm not.' He laughed a genuine laugh. One that didn't sound forced or fake as they so often used to be. 'But I miss the films and the audience they attract so I thought that would be a good place to start.'

'Well, good luck. I really am happy you seem to be doing so well.' Lorelai slipped her phone into her apron pocket. 'I was worried about you after, er, well after everything.'

Riggs blushed in embarrassment. 'Can we talk?' he asked after a breath. 'Outside? I have something I want to say to you.'

Lorelai nodded and followed him as he walked towards the street outside.

'I just wanted to formally apologise.' Riggs reached up to one of the 'Now Showing' signs either side of the door, where a bouquet of lilies lay. He handed them to her, bashfully looking down at his feet.

'Oh, wow. Thanks. Lilies are my favourite.' He was trying. Really trying.

'Yeah, Joanie said.'

Lorelai almost choked on her next breath. 'You talked to Joanie?'

'Only briefly but it was OK. I apologised to her as well.' He paused. 'So, I'm sorry. I wasn't in a great place. Which isn't an excuse but it's an explanation and the truth. I had liked you for a really long time, I'd just lost my job and had nowhere to live and it all just got… too much. I've got a therapist I'm working with now, and things with Dad are better, so I'm trying hard to become someone I'm proud of. But I can see now that you were just trying to be a good friend to me that night, and I should never have kissed you like that. It wasn't something you wanted, and I'm sorry I did that to you. I never want to do anything to upset you, and I promise I won't do it again – to you or to anyone else. I'm sorry.'

The words were rehearsed, and Lorelai knew he would have spent some time preparing this. A lump rose to her throat. Seeing Riggs take responsibility for his actions was humbling. And it inspired her to do the same. She reached out and took his hand.

'You're forgiven,' she said, squeezing his fingers. They stayed like that in silence for a few moments, London passing them by and letting whatever was broken between them mend.

'So that Grayson made an impression on you, huh?' Riggs avoided her gaze, staring straight ahead. Lorelai took a few seconds before responding.

'Yeah. He has. But that's over, I think.'

'Why?'

Lorelai just shrugged.

'OK, you don't have to tell me. But you deserve to be happy, and I think this Grayson makes you happy, so maybe you can find a way to make it work. He must be special if you're leaving him bumbling voicemails. I only want the best for you, Lorelai.'

'Oh, Riggs.' She hugged him, and tried to stop the tears that had begun to escape.

'Lorelai…'

'Yes?'

'Lorelai, stop. Stop, stop!' Riggs whispered fiercely. He wriggled out of her grasp,

She let go immediately. He was looking past her to something further up the street. A feeling of dread crept over her. She turned slowly and locked eyes with Grayson before he turned on his heel and disappeared around the corner. She stared at the empty street, not knowing what to do. Eventually she walked back inside, her feet heavy.

'Why aren't you going after him?'

Lorelai hadn't expected Riggs to follow her inside.

'Because there's no point,' she said helplessly. 'He hasn't answered any of my calls so he probably wasn't even coming here to speak to me. But if he didn't want to speak to me before he definitely doesn't want to speak to me now.' She slipped behind the counter and looked to the computer, praying someone had emailed. A request, a question, a complaint, anything to focus on before she burst into tears.

'Fucking hell, Lorelai.' Riggs rubbed his face, exasperated.

'What!' Lorelai snapped. 'What exactly am I meant to do here? Chase him down the street like a lunatic? Yell after him, arms waving?' Lorelai turned away from Riggs's hard stare to arrange and rearrange the popcorn buckets in order of size.

'Yes! Have all these movies and books taught you sod all? You must have watched and written countless number of scenes where someone chases their love interest down the road, or towards the gate at the airport, or in the rain, and the outcome is always a good one. Do you know why?'

Lorelai was in no mood to appreciate Riggs's new-found optimism and positivity, not when she felt this helpless.

She sighed. 'Because it's fictional and everything has to work out for the best or box office sales plummet?'

'Because those who chase their dreams get rewarded. You need to believe in the romance of it all!'

Riggs was talking to her about romance? Everything was upside down.

'There's nothing romantic between me and Grayson.' They were her words, but they still made Lorelai's heart ache.

'It's not about him. It's about you. You're looking for a connection with someone deeper than just casual dating or sex, right?'

Lorelai's mouth dropped open. Now Riggs had insight? And he had articulated the specific longing Lorelai felt so perfectly.

'How exactly do you know that?' she croaked.

'Because no one can be *that* obsessed with movies and books and not be a hopeless romantic, and I know very few hopeless romantics that don't want that kind of movie romance for themselves. But that's not the point. It's something deeper for you. Whatever has been stopping you from finding your own love story all these years is starting to fade. That fog has cleared enough for you to consider the idea of you and Grayson. That's enough, Lorelai. *Go after him.* Even if it doesn't work out, it's better to regret trying than to not try at all. Take it from someone who, before you talked some sense into them, had never bothered trying, himself.'

How was Riggs the one standing in front of her, telling her this? Lorelai hadn't realised her romantic avoidance had been so obvious that even Riggs had picked up on it. He was right; all the walls she'd put up to protect herself from pain were starting to crumble. Grayson had got under her skin, and she'd thought more about the possibility of being with him than she had with any other man. Was Riggs right – was it better to try, than not try at all?

'Thank you—' Lorelai squeezed his hands over the counter '—but I think I'm done with being a hopeless romantic. It's exhausting.'

'I get it. It *is* exhausting,' he said pointedly.

'I didn't know you'd been harbouring feelings for me for so long.'

'I know you didn't. I'm just saying… I get it. I really do understand. Being in love with someone takes a lot of time and energy but it also takes a lot of courage.'

Something caught in the back of Lorelai's throat. 'Love?' she whispered.

She thought it had been a simple crush. But love? It had certainly taken her by surprise, but who was she to deny him how he felt? After all, what did Lorelai know about love?

'Yes, love.' Riggs's eyes were sad. 'I know nothing will happen between us, and I'll settle for your friendship, which is still pretty special. But Grayson, Lorelai, that could be the real thing. I saw the look on his face when he saw us hugging, and I saw your face when he walked away. There's something between you, and you both feel it. Do you know how rare that is? So just think about it, Lorelai. Please?'

What *did* Lorelai know about love? She had watched enough movies and read enough books to know about the fairy tale; that you fell in love at first sight with your one true love, had true love's kiss, and lived happily ever after. That was how it was supposed to go, right? That's what everyone was searching for, and it had to be possible, didn't it? That's what Lorelai believed in when she was growing up, until, when Lorelai was twelve, her grandmother explained what love was truly like.

Lorelai was sitting at the kitchen table nearing the end of yet another novel.

'Another romance, is it?' Her grandmother laughed as she put a tray of cupcakes in the oven.

'It's not soppy!' Lorelai insisted.

'Let me guess? Girl meets boy. They fall in love. La-di-dah-di-dah, they live happily ever after?' Sylvia put her hands on her hips and shook her head with a wry smile.

'Something like that,' Lorelai mumbled, hiding the book under the table so her grandmother couldn't see that that was exactly what she was reading.

'Those stories are wonderful to escape into,' Sylvia said gently, 'and you should enjoy as many of them as you wish. But that's not how love works in the real world, sweetheart. Love is messy and complicated. Listen, let me tell you a real love story.' She sat down at the table. 'Have I ever told you how I met your grandfather?' she whispered, mischievously. Lorelai shook her head and stifled a laugh behind her hands. 'Well, your grandfather was engaged to be married when I met him.'

'No!' Lorelai gasped.

'He was. Poor girl. I did feel bad for her. She was sweet but your grandfather's heart wasn't in it. He was working at a big newspaper company and I was their new receptionist. Before I knew it, I couldn't shake him off. He was always turning up for something or other.' Sylvia puffed out her chest and lowered her voice to do her best impression of her husband. '"Have I got any mail? How about now? Can I borrow a pencil?"' She laughed. 'He'd walked three floors down just to ask to borrow a pencil! Of course, I knew he was engaged and so I always dismissed him, although he never came out and said he was interested in me. To be honest, I was too distracted to pay him much mind. I'd not been sleeping well around that time, but even so, I knew what he was up to. The problem was so did his fiancée. One night she turned up to meet him after work. Straight away she was eyeing me up and as soon as I told her my name, she slapped me clean across the face! In front of everyone! Goodness knows what your grandfather or anyone else had said to her about me but clearly it was enough for her to slap me. Well, she broke off the engagement and I lost my job because of it. So I left and I thought I'd never see him again.'

Twelve-year-old Lorelai leaned in, eyes wide, knowing there was more to come.

'So anyway,' Sylvia continued, 'I manage to get myself a job as a receptionist for a dentist on Harley Street and, one day, Doctor Gill says he has a spare ticket for a show in London that he now can't go to. I snapped it up. I love a bit of theatre, me. What he didn't say was that I'd be sitting next to the person he was meant to be going with.'

'And it was Grandpa?!' Lorelai squealed.

'It was your grandpa.' Sylvia nodded, smiling at the memory. 'He apologised all night about me losing my job, but I wasn't having any of it! That poor woman he was engaged to! My heart went out to her. She must have been so humiliated. I stayed for the show, which was marvellous, but I got out of there pretty sharpish and lost him in the crowds on Shaftesbury Avenue. I didn't see him for a few months and then, one day, I'm walking along Oxford Street and someone steals my purse! Pinches it right out of my hand and runs off with it down the street. Someone starts chasing after them and manages to wrestle the bag back off them. The mugger got away, but without my purse. And who was it who rescued my purse and brought it back to me?'

'Grandpa!' Lorelai exclaimed.

'Grandpa, would you believe it?! So I begin to think the universe is playing a little game here. I believe that things like this always happen in threes so I thought, how about I see if one more coincidence happens before I give in and ask him out for dinner.'

'And it did? Of course it did because I know how the story ends!' Lorelai clapped her hands together.

'Yes, darling. It did. As you know, I love my photographs. I had a beautiful camera that I used sparingly. Only took photos I really wanted to take and I'd get the roll of film developed when I had the money. Well, I'd been waiting for a roll of film to come back for a while and when I finally got it, I was excited to see a specific picture I'd taken in Trafalgar Square of one of the lions covered in pigeons. On the day I'd taken the photo, I'd been so focused on getting the lion's head in the shot that I hadn't realised someone had been sitting between the paws of the lion eating his lunch.'

'No! You're joking?!' Lorelai's mouth dropped open.

'I'd taken a photo of your grandpa without realising. After that, I couldn't deny it any longer. The universe was pushing us together and I tell you something, my darling girl, the night that we finally went out to dinner was like… magic.' Sylvia had a faraway look in her eyes.

'I thought you were trying to convince me that love at first sight doesn't exist?' Lorelai asked.

'All I'm saying is that your books make it sound so simple. Your grandpa and I had lots of highs, but we had lots of lows, too. Books end at happily ever after but the rest of the story, what happens next, is long, hard and can be incredibly bumpy. But if you really love each other, it's all worth it.' Sylvia gave Lorelai's hand a little squeeze.

'And was it? Worth it?' Lorelai looked at her grandmother, her eyes full of hope.

'Darling, there's not a second of my life with your grandpa I'd change. Not for all the riches in the world.'

'Grandma, you've done a *terrible* job at convincing me real life isn't like my stories. That sounds like a fairy-tale romance to me.'

The following year, Lorelai kissed Arthur Trent and she realised that a fairy-tale romance was something she would never have.

◆

Nineteen

'So what did Grayson say?' Joanie asked. She and Lorelai were in The Duchess storage room.

'When?'

'When you went after him, obviously!' Joanie gave Lorelai a playful shove.

'Well, I didn't actually...' Lorelai's words fell away as she opened the door and began to retreat from the room.

Joanie caught the door before Lorelai could escape. She threw her weight against it, pulling it out of Lorelai's grip, and slammed it closed. 'Lorelai Sanderson. Are you telling me that you didn't go after him, that you didn't try to explain the misunderstanding? That, after all the messages you left him, and a pep talk from not only me but Riggs as well, that when he finally turned up... *you gave up?*'

Joanie looked furious. She rarely lost her temper and it was even rarer for Lorelai to be on the receiving end.

'I haven't given up! I've just... I've...' Lorelai floundered.

'Lorelai Sanderson,' Joanie growled.

'Will you stop full-naming me?'

'Not until you give me a reason. Why didn't you go after Grayson?'

'I'm tired! OK! I'm tired.' Lorelai sank to the floor until she was sitting, her back against the door.

'You're tired? You're *tired*?!' Joanie was yelling now. Lorelai tried to shush her but nothing would stop Joanie now. 'Tired isn't an excuse! If you're tired, have a nap! Being tired does not justify throwing away your future happiness.'

'And I'm scared,' Lorelai mumbled.

'Oh boo-fucking-hoo, Lorelai.' Joanie's words were a slap in the face. She had never spoken to Lorelai like this before, but she'd had enough of watching Lorelai be her own biggest barrier. 'Poor Lorelai who has fallen for someone who actually likes her back! It's what most people dream of finding, but here you are, running away. Again. I've watched you back away, time after time, not just from romance but from your own parents! Your mum is desperate to speak to you. She calls the flat every week because you never answer your phone and I end up talking to her for an hour, filling her in on *your* life.'

Joanie's face was pink and, despite the fact that Lorelai was crying, she wasn't going to stop until she had said everything she had to say.

'People have been trying to reach out to you for years and you keep pushing everyone away. You're making yourself miserable. Can't you see that? You're not happy and you know you're not happy but you're letting the fear take over. Life is scary, Lorelai. For everyone. Not just you. Everyone deals with fear on a daily basis, but do you know which fear is the scariest of all? The fear of the unknown. Of not knowing what's coming next. But you do know what's coming next, and you have the power to do something with that knowledge, but you keep pushing that away too. So you know what, Lorelai? It's time for you to deal with it.'

Lorelai expected Joanie to push her out of the way. To storm off and not speak to her until she had calmed down. She did not expect Joanie to plant her hands either side of Lorelai's face and pull her in for a kiss. The shock of it momentarily forced her mind into a dark abyss where she could see nothing at all. When she tried to open her eyes, the darkness deepened. Lorelai couldn't find the light. And then she heard a voice. A voice she instantly recognised as her own. It was frail and quiet, full of trepidation, but undoubtedly her voice.

'Do you know me?' Lorelai heard her voice say. 'Joanie. Do you recognise me?'

The black abyss began to lift and the images came into focus. Joanie was lying in a bed, with three or four pillows behind her head so she was almost completely upright. Her skin was grey and sallow, and she was an old woman now. It was then that Lorelai realised she was seeing Joanie through her own, aged eyes. She wasn't an observer of this scene; she was *in* the scene. She and Joanie were still together. Still by each other's side. Joanie looked at Lorelai with glassy eyes.

'I'm sorry, Lorelai. Joanie may not recognise you but I'm sure she loves that you're here.'

Lorelai's older eyes turned to take in the room. Six other people were there, their focus on Joanie. She looked at the two young children on the lap of a woman, who looked to be in her thirties. She was smiling as she wept. No one seemed to carry the desperate sadness Lorelai associated with death. Instead,

Lorelai could *feel* their love for Joanie and it filled the room. Young Lorelai didn't recognise anyone in the room but she could feel the warmth her older self held for them. She would come to know them, she realised, and they would become important to her. She felt a hand touch hers. She looked down as Joanie interlaced her fingers with her own. Lorelai began to cry but she didn't know if those tears belonged to old or young Lorelai; she couldn't tell in that moment. All she cared about was Joanie. She looked up from their hands to find Joanie staring at her, as though she was *seeing* Lorelai for the first time.

'Lollie,' she whispered, her voice croaking.

'I'm here,' Lorelai sobbed.

'You never needed to worry.' Joanie paused to cough. 'Don't be scared, Lollie. It's all going to be just fine.' She closed her eyes.

Lorelai felt the life slipping out of her friend but Joanie wasn't done yet.

'Go to Grayson. I know you're listening, you silly git. Go to Grayson.' Joanie smiled her last smile and then she was gone.

'What did she say?' one of the men in the room asked.

'I think she said go with God?' said the woman with the children.

'No.' Lorelai's laugh caught in her throat as she stroked her friend's lifeless hand with her thumb. 'It was a message for me because she knows I'm listening. Well, she knows that I was listening a very long time ago.'

Lorelai felt Joanie's lips release hers, but she needed a few seconds before she opened her eyes.

'Hopefully, that'll teach you that you're strong enough to—'

'Joanie, shut up.' Lorelai still couldn't open her eyes so she opened her arms instead and reached out, hoping that Joanie would come to her. She did.

'Everything OK?' Joanie's voice softened when she felt how hard Lorelai was clinging to her.

'Yes, everything's OK. At least… I think it will be.'

Twenty

Lorelai was running. It had been several hours since she'd seen Grayson but she hoped he would be at work by now. The problem was that she didn't recall which theatre he worked in. Did he ever say? She was sure he had but she couldn't remember.

She pushed past tourists posing for photos. It was unlikely that Grayson would be in the crowds but that didn't stop her scouring every face. Up ahead she saw one of the theatres on Shaftesbury Avenue towering above her. She'd never be lucky enough to find him working in the first one she came to. How would she even go about figuring out which one he might be in? A queue was forming outside the theatre. Was it nearing showtime already? She'd whiled away so much of the day fretting and feeling sorry for herself.

Joanie was right: Lorelai's comfort zone was self-pity. She felt comfortable wallowing in her own misery because the alternative – to face her situation head on and try to change it – terrified her. The fear of the unknown was paralysing and so she had done nothing about it. It was only recently that she had tried to learn more about herself and what she could do. She had spent so long ignoring it, trying to be 'normal', whatever that meant, and wondering why it had never truly worked. Lorelai was a hopeless romantic, always had been, and she was finally admitting to herself what had been missing all these years. She wanted to be loved and she had so much love to give to someone else. She needed to be touched and held and… kissed.

She had become a master at suppressing all her urges but Grayson was changing everything. Suppressing them was becoming impossible and all these feelings she had tried to push away were fighting their way to the surface. It was overwhelming, unbearable, and exhilarating. Enough was enough. Lorelai was ready to let herself feel it all – thanks to some not-so-gentle pushing from Joanie. Lorelai didn't know how she was going to deal with the physical and emotional fallout of giving in to her deepening affection for Grayson, but she was ready to try, whatever that ended up meaning. Especially if it meant Grayson would be with her through it all. Lorelai was formulating a plan as she quick-marched across the road.

I'm going to kiss Grayson, she told herself. *Well, first I'll explain what happened with Riggs and then, if he's OK with it, I'll kiss him. And if all goes well, I'm going to tell him. I'm going to tell him about me and what I see. If he runs a mile, it wasn't meant to be but that's OK. This is good. This is the start of a new chapter. A new me. I need this. This is good. This is good. This is good.*

The theatre was beginning to let people in and was heaving with excitement. Four front-of-house staff stood either side of the main entrance, checking everyone's tickets.

'Excuse me!' A huge burst of adrenaline overcame Lorelai and pushed her forward. She leaned over the rope where ticket holders were queuing, the front most woman giving her a very pronounced tut. A staff member politely stepped forward to speak to her. 'A Grayson Brady doesn't happen to work here, does he?'

'No, sorry, love.' The woman shook her head, her ponytail swinging from side to side. Hope crumbled away.

'OK. No worries.' Lorelai knew it had been a long shot but she really had hoped that he'd be at the first theatre she tried. It would've meant that fate or destiny or stars were aligning for a perfect movie moment.

'Do you know Grayson?' the woman asked. The glimmer of hope restored itself back into Lorelai's heart.

'Do *you* know Grayson?!' Lorelai asked eagerly, and the woman laughed.

'Yes, I do. Not well, but some of these guys—' she gestured around at her colleagues '—they know him so we've all ended up at drinks together before. He works at The Palace.'

'Buckingham…?' Lorelai said it without thinking.

The woman cackled. 'No, The Palace Theatre. End of Shaftesbury Avenue.' Lorelai remembered now that Grayson *had* told her where he worked. 'Keep walking that way and you won't be able to miss it. But I'd hurry up because as soon as the show starts at seven-thirty he'll be harder to find if you don't have a ticket.'

'Thank you!' Lorelai called out, as she broke into a run.

Maintaining the run was virtually impossible, with eager theatregoers filling every inch of Shaftesbury Avenue. Lorelai had to keep stopping and starting and huffing and apologising and dodging and swerving. She moved as fast as the crowds allowed and was doing all she could to get a bit more momentum behind her. After what felt like an eternity, The Palace Theatre came into view and it was bigger and grander than she had ever realised.

Have I ever walked past this place before? I'm sure I would have noticed, Lorelai thought, but in reality she probably wouldn't have. She never took much interest in London's architecture because she very rarely looked up. She would make a point of doing so now. The building was beautiful. Theatres, Lorelai realised, were beginning to look like London's elderly relatives, wise and with hundreds of stories to tell.

The crowds deepened and Lorelai had to squeeze herself through to get close to the building. Finally, she was close enough to try to grab someone's attention.

'Excuse me!' Lorelai waved madly at the man on the door taking tickets. 'Hello! Yes! You! Hello!' He had caught her eye, but she saw him bend his head to his shoulder and lift his hand to press a button on a walkie-talkie. There was no doubt that he was warning someone inside that she might be an issue. 'I just want to ask a question! I won't be a moment!'

The man held up a finger to the person who was holding out their ticket and just as he stepped off his position at the door, Grayson appeared behind him. Lorelai couldn't hear what they were saying but if Lorelai's lip reading was correct, it looked like Grayson said, 'I'll deal with this.' Lorelai immediately felt on edge. Grayson was treating her like a nuisance, not someone he held any affection towards. Not that long ago he had wanted to kiss her and today she was a problem to solve? Lorelai knew she was in his bad books but even so, this stung.

'What's up?' Grayson said without much feeling.

'What's up?' Lorelai repeated, her face burning.

'Yeah. I need to get back to work.'

'So do I,' she snapped.

'Right.' Grayson looked behind him, distractedly. Lorelai sighed.

This wasn't why she'd come here. She needed to pick her battles, so she tried to ignore how annoyed she felt.

'I came to explain,' she said.

'Explain why you disappeared or explain about you and Riggs?'

'All of it but firstly, there is no "me and Riggs". What you saw was him coming to apologise to me for behaving so badly and me accepting his apology.'

'Right,' he said again. He still looked unconvinced, but the hard edge to his voice had softened.

'He's been through a hard time, but he seems to be back on his feet and… it was just a hug, Grayson. It wasn't anything more than one friend accepting an apology from another friend. It didn't *mean* anything. Not like that.'

Grayson simply nodded, but Lorelai saw his shoulders drop, as though he'd finally let go of a breath he'd been holding in.

'As for the thing the other day. Me leaving you in Trafalgar Square.'

'Yeah, that was…' Grayson raised his eyebrow, trying to find the right word.

'It was weird. I know. And I have an explanation. But it's going to take longer than a couple of minutes outside of your work to explain properly. Could we maybe meet for a drink after you've finished here?' It was Lorelai's turn to hold her breath. Grayson didn't say anything. He looked over his shoulder at the hundreds of people filtering in through the theatre's doors.

'OK.' He nodded. He gave her a small smile, but it was enough.

'OK.' Lorelai smiled back.

All she had wanted was a chance to explain, and now she had it. She just hoped that Grayson would understand.

Twenty-One

It was almost half past ten that evening, and Lorelai was waiting for Grayson to finish work. She was standing at the back of the theatre, near its stage door. She watched the crowd leaving the theatre and envied them all, clutching their glossy souvenir brochures and reeling from the live experience they had all witnessed individually, but also together. Whatever happened in that building had happened to them as a group and it had brought them together. Occasionally, a cheer would go up as one of the cast left via the stage door, and they were met with hugs or a wave of programmes and pens. They smiled and chatted and scrawled an illegible signature that no one would be able to decipher on the way home. Life was happening all around her, and Lorelai was ready to grab some of it for herself.

Fifteen minutes went by, and still no Grayson. The crowd was thinning out, as people headed home or on to post-show drinks, and Lorelai began to worry. Each time the stage door opened, her heart leapt into her throat, but it was never the face she was waiting for. Lorelai was about to cut her losses and walk to the station, already preparing what she'd say to herself on the way. That Grayson wasn't worth the heartache if he wasn't willing to hear her out. That just because Grayson didn't give her a chance didn't mean she shouldn't give someone else one in the future. That she shouldn't give up on the idea of a relationship because she was now ready to open up to someone. That this wasn't the be-all and end-all. *Grayson* wasn't the be-all and end-all.

And then all of a sudden he was there, standing in front of her, and all of those thoughts disappeared into the wind. A thrill ran through her when she saw his eyes light up at the sight of her.

'Hi,' she whispered, smiling up at him.

'Don't make me smile at you. You're still in the doghouse.' He was grinning but there was an edge to his voice. He was still unsure.

'I'm not doing anything!'

'Yes, you are. You're being you.'

'Oof. That was a good line.' The warmth of the compliment settled over Lorelai. Maybe it would be OK. 'Where shall we go?'

'There's a place just down one of these side streets. It looks dodgy from the outside but that's what keeps it so well hidden from tourists.'

'That sounds perfect.'

For a moment Lorelai thought Grayson was going to take her hand. They both hesitated, and then he stuffed his hands in his pocket.

'It's this way,' he said, embarrassed.

They wove their way deeper into Soho, making small talk. *How was your day? How was work? What was the show like? Any good movies on at the moment?* It was excruciating. Eventually they came to a stop outside a black building. It was a slim London townhouse, squeezed in amongst the other bars and shops. While other businesses were busy and bustling, with outdoor tables full of people, this building appeared silent and empty. Black blinds were pulled down over every window and only one singular light shone out over the front door. At first glance it looked like someone's home.

'Are you sure this is the right place?' Lorelai hung back as Grayson started walking down the brick steps.

'This is the place! The people who work on the show get free membership. I reckon a few of the cast have probably beat us here.'

Lorelai's stomach flipped. She hadn't realised they wouldn't be alone tonight. The idea of meeting new people always unsettled her, but she was more concerned that she might not get to say all the things she needed to say.

'Don't worry, we don't have to sit with them,' Grayson reassured her quickly on seeing her face fall.

'Am I dressed right for somewhere like this?' Lorelai was wearing her cinema attire and a pair of bright-white trainers that glared obnoxiously against the inconspicuous building. Grayson walked back up a couple of steps, offering her a hand.

'They get people coming straight from the theatres all the time, so they don't really care as long as you spend money at the bar.'

'That I can do.'

Lorelai curled her fingers around his and revelled in the electricity his touch sent up her arm. She hoped it wasn't just her who could feel the spark between them and by the way he lingered before gently pulling her down the steps towards him, she suspected that he had felt it too. Although his hand didn't feel as clammy as hers. Nor was he breathing as heavily, and she couldn't hear his heartbeat as loudly as she was certain he could hear hers. Lorelai couldn't remember ever feeling like this, and she knew it wasn't just her nerves. It was Grayson, being this close to him, holding his hand. It did something to her insides. She had always hoped she'd be cool and suave, like Margo Channing in *All About Eve* who said things like, 'Fasten your seatbelts, it's going to be a bumpy night.' But she was behaving more like the Cowardly Lion.

Grayson knocked on the door, and Lorelai noticed the gold plaque on the wall.

'The club is called Charlatans?' *How apt.* 'And you have to knock to get in?' Lorelai laughed but it came out in a strangled breath.

'You have to knock because it used to be a house and you always knock at people's houses.'

'A club that demands manners. Can you sneak me in here more often?'

'Depends on how good your explanation is.'

Lorelai tensed before Grayson shot her a teasing look. The door opened a crack and a man with piercing blue eyes looked out at them, before opening the door fully. Lorelai looked past him, into the long, dark hallway behind him. Ornate, antique sconces shaped like hands held lanterns that shone a subtle light down the corridor. The rest of the decor was a mix of black and a red that was so dark it was only a couple shades away from being black itself. The inside of the building was as inconspicuous as the outside. All except for the man at the door who was dressed head to toe in white. His poker-straight hair was dyed an intense platinum blond.

'Come in, Master Brady. Lovely to see you again.'

'You too, Enoch. This is my guest this evening. Lorelai.'

'Hi,' Lorelai said, but when she was met with a slight raise of the eyebrow she added, 'How do you do?' She'd seen enough period dramas to guess what the appropriate thing to say might be. Enoch nodded at her, seemingly satisfied now, and as he turned away to write their names in an oversized ledger, Lorelai mouthed, 'Enoch?' to Grayson. He smiled and gently waved her away as if to say he'd explain later.

'This way, sir. Ma'am.'

Enoch led them down the corridor to a coat check where a woman took their coats and bags. She was also dressed head to toe in white, with white roses in her hair and a dusting of silver glitter around her eyes that sparkled with every turn of her head. Lorelai looked around. The place seemed quiet, so perhaps Grayson's colleagues hadn't arrived yet. The only thing Lorelai could hear was the faint tinkling of classical music coming through on the speaker system.

'You come here a lot?' Lorelai inspected each painting they passed, unable to shake the feeling that each pair of painted eyes were following them they carried on up the corridor.

'Not a lot. It can be a bit much if I come too often, but… well…' He gestured around him. 'But when I have… special guests… I like to show them this place. Bit of a hidden gem really.'

'Would you like to sit in the garden?'

Lorelai jumped. Enoch had been so silent she had forgotten he'd been walking behind them. *Get a grip*, Lorelai scolded herself. *Stop being so tense.* Enoch gestured at another gold plaque. It said, *Fairy Garden*.

'Actually, the library would be great if there's a table free,' Grayson said.

'Of course, sir.' Enoch turned down a corner and led them to another black door, its plaque reading, *The Enchanted Library*. 'There's no one in this room this evening so don't be afraid to wander at your leisure.' Enoch opened the door to a breathtaking number of books. Each wall had floor-to-ceiling bookshelves with little wooden ladders that wheeled from side to side. In the corner was a small bar that also doubled as a bookshelf. The room smelled like old, weathered pages and Lorelai loved it.

'Oh, wow,' she said, which was met with a wry smile from Enoch. He gave her a little bow and left the room, closing the door behind them. Lorelai spun around to face Grayson. 'OK, where are we? Because I feel like we just left London and have ended up in some Narnia-type world that no one else knows about.'

'I felt like your explanation needed the proper setting.'

'Somewhere deathly quiet and exposing?' Lorelai felt her mouth go dry.

'Exactly. But first drinks. What do you fancy? This place is renowned for its Old Fashioned but they're pretty lethal.'

'Sounds yummy.' *Did you just say yummy?* Lorelai wanted to smack herself on the head. Her nerves were starting to get the better of her. She cleared her throat. 'How do you order here?'

'If it's not busy they don't usually have someone at each bar but there's a dumbwaiter in the corner. You write your order on the pad and paper, put the order in there and send it to the downstairs bar.'

'This place is *wild*.' Lorelai laughed, taking a seat at the bar.

'In a good way?' Grayson paused, pen poised above the pad.

'In a… new and different way.'

'I can make my peace with that.' Grayson sent their order down in the dumbwaiter, which clattered as it descended. Not long after, they heard it rumble into life once more and their drinks appeared in the little hatch.

'Voila!' Grayson said with a flourish. He slid her drink across the bar into her open and waiting hand.

Lorelai took a sip and tried to collect her thoughts. It was time. 'So.'

'So…?' Grayson prompted. He wasn't going to give her any more than that.

Lorelai stared into her drink. 'Where do I even begin?'

'Just talk,' Grayson said.

'OK. Look, I like you a lot. And I told you right from the start I only wanted to be friends because friends is all I do. But then I've never met anyone I like as much as you which… changed things. It made me act differently around you and it made me want more from you and from us. Every time I've been around you, I've been at war with myself. Wanting you but knowing I can't have you.' She was babbling but it felt good to start letting some of this out.

'Why can't you have me? Isn't that—' Grayson began but Lorelai held up a hand.

'Please let me finish. There's more to this than you realise. It's complicated, and I don't really know how to say this all without sounding crazy.' Lorelai took another sip, the alcohol burning her throat on the way down. 'I shouldn't have run away from you. I'm sorry about that. Really, I am. I'm just so used to pushing people away because that feels safer. I've become accustomed to keeping people at arm's length, so being just friends has always been instinct. It's my go-to, and it's never been a problem. Until now. I guess you can't ignore how you feel, no matter how much you try to. But I shouldn't have led you on, and I definitely shouldn't have run away when... well, you know. I should have kept it purely platonic, just like I said – friends. Or...'

'Or?' Grayson had been slowly deflating in his seat with each word Lorelai said. Now, he was sitting upright again.

'Or I should have listened when my instincts told me I could trust you. That maybe you'd understand me when no one else really has. Other than Joanie, of course.'

'Well, of course.' Grayson absentmindedly traced circles in the condensation on his glass. 'So you're going to stop running away from me? Because I really can't deal with any more of that. I'm not one for playing games. I don't do all of that. Treat 'em mean, keep 'em keen, playing hard to get. It's all such a waste of time, and I don't see the point in any of it. I just want good, upfront honesty. So, no more running, no hiding and no games.'

'I get that and I don't like that stuff either, but there's still a lot about me you don't know.' Lorelai fiddled with the napkin underneath her glass.

'I'd like to get to know you, though.' His voice was so earnest it made tears spring to her eyes.

'And I want to get to know you too, I really do, but you have to understand that my secrets aren't like normal-people secrets.'

'You haven't murdered anyone, have you? Because I do draw the line at hiding dead bodies.'

Lorelai tried to keep her voice light. 'No, no murders.' *But plenty of dead bodies.* 'I want to tell you the truth, Grayson, but it's hard. These are things I've never told anyone.'

'Other than Joanie, of course.' Grayson rolled his eyes gently and smiled softly.

'She knows now, but I didn't even want to tell her initially. I kept it from her as well at first.'

Grayson raised his eyebrows, the smile fading. 'OK, so this *is* serious, then?'

'It's very serious and not the kind of thing I would tell someone without knowing I can really trust them first. I know I ran away from you, and that this is a big ask, but I need to trust that you won't run away from me.'

Grayson placed a calming hand over hers to stop her from ripping her napkin to shreds.

'You can trust me. On both counts. I promise you can. Cross my heart and hope to die.'

Lorelai turned to face Grayson properly. Her knees brushed against his and instead of jolting away, as though she'd been burned, she leaned into the heat between them instead. She looked into Grayson's eyes, and took in his hopeful-looking face. Could she trust him?

'There is something I want to try first, and then I'll explain everything to you.' Lorelai slid her arm along the bar and gently touched his thumb with her finger. He responded by taking his hand away from his glass and letting his fingers intertwine with hers. Her whole body was aflame.

'Is it… is it something you might…' she began, breathless, leaning in closer.

'I might…' Grayson responded, closing the distance and

meeting her halfway. He paused just before the tips of their noses touched. She could feel his hot breath on her face. Or was it her breath? They were so close now, she couldn't tell. Her heart was thumping in her chest, and her head felt light. Her body was heavy with longing and if Grayson didn't press his lips to hers soon she felt like she would explode. 'Are you sure?' he whispered against her mouth, and she answered by closing the gap until their lips were touching.

Finally.

Grayson's lips were soft and full, and Lorelai squeezed her eyes tight, falling hard into their kiss. The other kisses she'd had didn't compare to what she was feeling now. Every movement, every touch, felt like a lightning bolt through her heart. They were standing now, arms wrapped around each other, pressed together so tightly no air could pass between them. They were one.

'We have breaking news just in from Heathrow Airport.'

The sound of the news reporter's voice was faint in Lorelai's ears, and it took her a moment to realise what was happening and focus in on the words. *No, not now. Please. Just let me have this.*

'A plane containing over three hundred passengers has crashed on the runway after two of its engines failed and one quickly caught fire. We don't yet have confirmation on how many passengers were injured or if there are any fatalities...'

The voice faded away but Lorelai knew there was more to come. Her arms were still locked around Grayson's neck but the joy and desire she'd felt just seconds before had disappeared. Now, in her mind, she was on the plane.

It was chaos. Shouting, screaming, people moving and pushing, the sound of fire crackling and blazing, smoke already choking her lungs. Among it all was Grayson, barely any older than he was now. He was in the middle of a crowd of people who were by the doors in the middle of the plane, in front of the wing, desperately clawing at the giant red handle to get the door open. A steward pushed through to help but before Lorelai or anyone else on the plane could call out to tell them to stop, the door was open and the flames from outside were upon them. The steward was claimed first. The passengers tried to outrun the fire, but it moved faster than the bodies scrambling up the aisles and climbing over seats. They were ablaze. Lorelai didn't want to watch but she had no choice. Grayson was clambering over seats, pushing people towards the back of the plane, his voice carrying over the hellish sounds of people screaming. But he just wasn't fast enough. In his attempt to undo an elderly woman's seat belt, the last thing he could do was shield her from the fire as it claimed them both. Grayson was gone.

'Lorelai?' Grayson's voice brought her back to now.

Her eyes flew open and she saw him, alive and well. Unharmed. But it brought her no solace. He wouldn't be this way for long. Lorelai's throat had closed, and she couldn't sob or speak. All she could do was shake her head and avert her gaze as she stumbled back, tripping over the bar stool. Of all the deaths she had seen, this was by far the worst. It wasn't just *how* Grayson had died, but how she had felt watching it play out. In that moment, Lorelai's heart and soul had shattered into a million pieces and there was no way to put it back together. She was destroyed, devastated, inconsolable.

'Lorelai, you're freaking me out… what's going on?'

'I have to go,' she mumbled.

'No, not again.' Grayson gently took her hand. 'You need to explain to me what this is or—'

'I can't do this. I'm sorry. I really thought I could, but I can't. I'm not strong enough. I'm so sorry.'

'Lorelai, no! Wait! Talk to me. What happened?'

Lorelai met his desperate stare with her own, and became locked in his gaze for a painful moment. He was so kind, so ready to love and be loved. She thought of his family, of Aden, when they heard the news of his death. Would they ever recover from losing someone like Grayson? She'd known him for the smallest fraction of time and she already knew this was something she'd never get over. Something that would haunt her for the rest of her life.

'I'm so sorry,' she whispered and he let her go.

She turned and fled. Her eyes were blurry from the tears, her heart was crashing in her ears, her mouth was dry, everything was numb. London was a blur around her as she ran. People instinctively moved out of her way as she ran and ran and ran. The plane, the flames, the screaming... it was too much. Why did the man she had fallen in love with have to die in such a way? Was this the price she had to pay for having this power? She'd dearly hoped to see Grayson quietly and peacefully slip away, after living a full life. She'd prepared herself to handle the best-case scenario because what were the chances she'd be dealt the worst? Why did Grayson have to be taken so painfully and so very soon? With every thundering footstep on London's wet pavement, she could feel the little time Grayson had left slipping away and it was so much more than her heart could handle.

◆

Lorelai didn't bother folding her clothes. She simply grabbed armfuls out of her wardrobe, hangers and all, and crammed them into her suitcase as tightly as she could.

'Lollie? What's going on?' Joanie ran from the living room and stood in the doorway watching her work quickly to make as fast an escape as possible. 'Woah, woah. Hey, you need to calm down and take a breath.'

Lorelai glared at Joanie through her tears. 'I can't calm down! I told you I couldn't do it, and you didn't listen. You never have and I don't think you ever will. You don't listen to me!'

Lorelai had stood there and listened as Joanie had expressed her concerns and feelings to her. Now, it was Lorelai's turn to say what she needed to say and she hoped, for once, Joanie would listen.

'I liked my life the way it was. Sure, did I wonder what it was like to be loved? To have Grayson in my life? Yes! I'll admit it. I did. But I was OK with what I had. I was getting along just fine. I had my job. I had you. I had my dreams of becoming a script writer. It was enough, but you just couldn't let it go!'

Joanie shifted her weight from foot to foot, unsure of what to do. 'Lorelai, I'm going to make us some tea and we're going to sit and talk about this.'

'No, Joanie!' Lorelai slammed her make-up bag down into her case. 'You've been right about so many things but this time ... you were wrong.' She slammed the lid of her suitcase closed and pulled it off her bed. She needed to get out of there now. 'Why couldn't you just leave well enough alone? You have no idea what it's like to be in my shoes or in my head. To see the things I see. You actively encouraged me to see the death of the person I'm falling for. You actually thought that was a good idea and now… now I don't know if I can get over this. That's something I will never unsee and his death, *Grayson's* death, I'll have to relive that every day for the rest of my life and it's because of *you*. You talked me into it and… I need to leave. I can't be around you right now because I don't know what I'll do or say if I don't get away. From you. From here. From everything.'

Joanie was sobbing now but Lorelai was blinded by her own pain. And it was making her cold. Grayson's death was on a loop in her mind and each time she witnessed it, it touched her soul and made her more numb. One day, perhaps she'd feel nothing at all.

'Lorelai, please don't go,' Joanie whispered.

'I have to.' Lorelai pushed past her, and walked down the corridor, towards the front door.

'When will you be back?' Joanie called after her, desperate now.

She didn't answer and pulled the door shut behind her. Joanie didn't follow her, but Lorelai felt her body fall against the door and the sound of her sobs echoed after her, as she ran out of the building, onto the street, and left her friend behind, for how long she didn't know.

PART THREE

The
Happy
End

◆

'Hi. Lorelai. It's… it's Grayson. I don't know what happened back there. You've disappeared on me twice now and I just… I don't get it. Or you. I don't understand why you keep running away from me. But I've got this feeling that you want to tell me why, but something is stopping you. What is it, Lorelai? Because, if I'm being honest, you don't seem very happy. And you should be. Happy, I mean. Look, I like you and I'm here for you, but I don't deserve to be treated like this. I haven't done anything to hurt you, so I don't understand what's going on. But you can trust me, I promise. So, if you want to call me, then I'm all ears, but please, Lorelai, only call if you're going to explain what's going on with you. I don't think I can take any more of your unexplained exits. If I don't hear from you then that's… that's fine. I mean, it's not. That would make me sad and I'll probably wonder for the rest of my life what the hell all this was about but I'll respect your privacy and I won't call again. I'm going out of the country in two weeks so… your move, Lorelai.'

◆

Twenty-Two

Lorelai had spent a lot of her life making sure that only the smallest number of people had got close to her, which meant in times of crisis, Lorelai had very few people she could turn to. Joanie had been her rock, but now it was Joanie, and Grayson, who she was running from, which meant the only place she had left to go was to her parents' house. She'd spent the last few hours in a daze. She couldn't remember purchasing her train ticket, nor choosing a seat as the last train out of London left the station, and she had arrived at her destination in what felt like the blink of an eye. It was only as the taxi pulled up in front of her childhood home that the driver informed her the card machine was broken and she had realised she had no cash on her. Lorelai also hadn't called ahead, hoping to sneak in with the spare key unnoticed and explain everything in the morning. No such luck. Instead, she was forced to knock on the front door with a trembling hand. It was after one in the morning.

'Please wake up, please, please, please,' she whispered, shivering in her coat, and tucking her face into her scarf to keep warm. She saw the hallway light come on through the frosted glass, and her father opened the door.

'Lorelai? What on earth are you doing here? Is everything OK? Get inside quickly and warm up!' He gave Lorelai no time to reply in between questions and pulled her inside by her icy fingers.

'Ahem!' The cab driver gave a pointed cough.

'I'm so sorry, Dad.' Lorelai's bottom lip began to wobble but her dad was already elbow deep in the pockets of his coat that was hanging on the hook, searching for his wallet.

'David? Who is it?' Lila's sleepy voice drifted down the stairs.

'It's me, Mum,' Lorelai called.

'Lorelai? What's wrong? What's happened?'

Lila flew down the stairs and pulled her daughter towards her. She exchanged a concerned glance with her husband. David shook his head slightly, paid the now curious-looking taxi driver, and then gently shut the door.

Lorelai hadn't given any thought to how she would explain her unannounced arrival to her parents. She looked at their worried faces, and all her words left her. Instead, she crumpled, giving into the onslaught of tears that she'd been holding back since she had boarded the train out of London. Her mother and father simply scooped her up and put her to bed, tucking her in and stroking her hair as though she was a child again. Lorelai had fallen into a deep and troubled sleep, and she hadn't said much about it all to either of them since. That had been a week ago.

'Fresh countryside air. That's all you needed!' Lila chirruped as she strode on with all the energy of a Jack Russell.

Lorelai's mother walked at least five miles every day and, up until now, Lorelai had staved off her nagging that she should be doing the same. Lila was insistent that a strenuous two-hour hike would do Lorelai good and something about the mossy greens, muddy browns and clear blues had called out to Lorelai that day. A nightmare, worse than any other before it, had hit her hard in the middle of the night and she'd not been able to fall back to sleep. So, to her mother's surprise, Lorelai had met her at the front door, bright and early that morning, ready to join her on her walk.

'Mum, can we slow down a bit? I'm not as used to dodging rabbit holes as you are.' Lorelai's boots had already given her huge blisters that made every step infinitely more painful than the last. Not to mention she was dragging a huge weight in her heart that made her breath catch every few steps. Each time an image from the plane fire resurfaced, every muscle in her body braced itself for impact, and her bruised heart ached.

Lorelai had never interfered with anyone's death prior to James – and that had only been because of what happened when her visions of Riggs had changed. She hardly knew anything about her... *power*. It was so much bigger than her. She wasn't special and she was certain that she hadn't been specifically chosen to be the bearer of this curse. If anything, she felt as though she'd been accidentally tangled up in this mess. That she was a stowaway on a ship but had no idea where it was heading. Someone had mistakenly given her a giant red button and even though she desperately wanted to know what it did, Lorelai truly believed it was not her job to push it any further than she had already.

Even so, Lorelai couldn't see how she could stop the plane Grayson would board sometime in the future from going up in flames. Because of course she had thought about it. She had attempted to change James's death out of a selfish desperation to learn more about herself so she could be with Grayson and she had learned her lesson. If you played with fire, the people you love will get burned. Besides, stealing a bike was all it took to change James's death, but stopping a huge explosion? Lorelai didn't know how she'd ever be able to pull off something like that, even though she very much wanted to. Lorelai also couldn't stop wondering if saving Grayson would have a ripple effect and change someone else's fate. For all she knew, meddling in James's death had meant someone else was now going to collide with that car on the day James was originally meant to. How could she play God like that? Who was she to say that one life was worth more than another? If Lorelai intervened she might be responsible for the death of someone else in Grayson's place and she wasn't sure she could live with that. Lorelai felt heavy with the weight of all these thoughts and questions. The only solace she could find was that Grayson hadn't mentioned that he was travelling anywhere anytime soon and so she had time to think everything through properly before deciding what to do.

'Absolutely not! Let's get your blood pumping and your heart racing!'

Lila's voice pulled Lorelai back to the present. She shook her head slightly to clear her mind and looked at her mother. Lorelai wondered if Lila had been a fitness instructor in a past life and, if she had been, she wished she would leave it very much in the past. Despite her internal grumblings, though, Lorelai had to admit that the crisp autumn air and beautiful countryside was helping take her mind off Grayson, even if only for a second here and there. It also kept her mind off Joanie. Joanie had texted at least twice every day in the week she'd been away. Never letting

Lorelai forget that she was still there for her. That she was still her friend, and not the enemy, but Lorelai couldn't bring herself to talk to her just yet. She didn't know when she would. In her heart, she knew it wasn't Joanie's fault and that she owed her an apology, but her whole being hurt so much that she didn't yet feel strong enough for that conversation.

She took a long, deep breath. Her mother was right. The country air was doing her some good. As was her mother's rustic cooking and the sound of her dad noodling on his acoustic guitar by the fire every evening. She may still be hurting but a calmness was slowly beginning to settle around her.

Lorelai had never come home to visit like this. She'd spent most Christmases with her parents but she never stayed for longer than a couple of days and she was always desperate to get back to London. She had never visited just because she had missed them. She did miss them, of course, but she'd created a distance between herself and them that meant it had been easy for her to stay away and focus on her life in London. She'd spent more time with her mother and father over the last few days than she had in several years. Cosied up in their cottage, with no one around for miles, and three cats to cuddle, Lorelai realised what she had been missing out on and shards of regret pierced her heart. It was something else she had denied herself. And what good had it done her?

'Sorry I've not visited more, Mum,' Lorelai said, hoping the howl of the wind didn't carry her voice away.

'I'm going to stop you right there. No need to be sorry for living your life. You've always followed your own path. I'm so proud of you for that, and a million other things.' Lila's voice was warm, but it didn't take away the sting of Lorelai's guilt.

'I know you are but that doesn't mean I couldn't also spend time with you. I… shut you out. And Dad. I'm sorry.'

'You know, sweetheart,' Lila began slowly, 'if you ever wanted to talk, have a proper mother/daughter heart to heart, then we could do that.' She tucked a strand of hair behind Lorelai's ear. 'There's so much going on in that head of yours. Why not let a little of it out?'

Lorelai wondered where she would even begin. Pulling on one strand of her life would unravel the whole messy lot of it. She couldn't explain to her mother that part of the reason she'd fallen out with Joanie was to do with her biggest secret – a secret that only Joanie knew about. A secret that had kept her from kissing anyone in a very long time. And she couldn't explain why kissing Grayson had led to her turning up in the middle of the night, unless she was honest about watching him die horrifically right before her eyes, in a vision. There was so much to unpack, Lorelai didn't know where to start.

'I know, Mum. I will. I just… not right now. It's all still a bit messy in my head and I want to make sense of it first before I talk it out.'

Lila nodded. 'OK. I understand. But sometimes talking things out while they're still a mess helps to untangle it all a little quicker.'

'Mum…' Lorelai warned.

'OK. Backing off.' Lila literally took two steps away from her daughter with her hands raised. It was meant to lighten the mood, but Lorelai suddenly wondered if this was how her mother would react, if or when she found out her secret. Backing away from her as if she was a rabid animal.

'I think I need a task while I'm here,' Lorelai said, changing the subject. 'Have you got anything I can do? Something repetitive and boring to let my brain mull things over without me really noticing. The more I actively think, the more I just want to drink gin and cry.'

'We've got plenty of gin if that's what you want to do. I keep it in the cupboard under the stairs to stop your dad drinking my fancy, expensive stuff.'

'You're my mum! You're meant to encourage me to take up knitting or quilting. Not day-drinking.'

'Sorry. You've just grown up so much. Sometimes I forget you're the same little girl who used to play with dolls and draw all over my wallpaper in permanent marker. And chase the neighbour's cat when you were small enough to think you could ride it like a pony. Do you remember that?' Lila laughed, delighted at the memory.

It was then that Lorelai realised just how beautiful her mother was. There was *life* in her face. Lila looked like someone who was well-loved, and who loved well. Like a book with dog-eared pages, its spine cracked and cover wrinkled. Those were the most prized books on Lorelai's shelves. They were the most loved, because they were the ones Lorelai returned to time and time again. Their wear and tear were born out of love. Why did no one ever say that about people? Lila's wrinkles and creases were also born out of love, from years' worth of tears and laughter. The deeper wrinkles in her brow must be from all the times she frowned or thought hard, and her greying hair the result of all the stress and excitement life had brought her. Lorelai suddenly saw the beauty in it all.

'I love you, Mum.'

It fell out of her mouth without a single thought or a moment's hesitation. It shocked her more than it shocked her mother. Lorelai had given herself the tiniest amount of permission to feel this love for her mother, and it hit her in a sudden, strong burst. It felt... good. And safe. Is this what love was? Opening that door wasn't one way. She was beginning to let her mother in, but she was also beginning to let herself out.

'I know you do.' Lila smiled a little sadly. 'I always know because I can always feel it. Even when you're far away and busy being brilliant. But it's lovely to hear all the same.' She quickly wrapped her arms around her daughter so that she didn't see the tears forming in her eyes. 'Right, so you need a distraction? Well, I've got some boxes in the loft that need sorting through. Some of your grandma's stuff. I've not had the strength to go through it all nor the heart to let any of it go but I think it's time. It'll be long, dull, dusty. Up for it?'

Lorelai took her mother's arm, and squeezed into her side as they began the walk home. It felt like the most natural thing in the world, as though this spot was meant just for her.

'That sounds like exactly the sort of thing I need right now.'

◆

'Hi, Lollie. Can I still call you that? Anyway, it's me. Again. For the millionth time. I'm sorry. I'm so sorry. I'm more sorry than I've ever been in my whole entire life and I hate that this is where we are. I promise from now on I will listen to you when you say enough is enough. When you tell me I'm pushing too hard I will hear you. I swear. So… I'm going to stop calling because you clearly need space. But I'm here when you're ready. I love you like a sister but we're better than sisters because we *chose* each other. And I still choose you. I'll always choose you.'

◆

Twenty-Three

Lorelai woke, screaming. She fumbled around, desperately searching for her lamp's switch. Only when the warm light flooded her bedroom did her breathing begin to slow. Her nightmares had been becoming more frequent, but this one had been the worst yet.

She and Grayson had been in the diner. He was smiling at her like she was the only person in the world. She looked down at their intertwined fingers but gradually his fingers became hotter and hotter until they were burning her hands, her skin blistering at his touch, but she couldn't let go of him. When she looked up at him, his face was engulfed in flames, but she could still see his big smile through the fire. Orange flames licked at his hair and his clothes until he became ash. Then he was in Trafalgar Square, and then the theatre, and then Charlatans, and each time the flames took him over, consuming him until he was no more.

There was a gentle tap on her door. 'Lorelai?' her father called. He opened the door and peered inside. 'Are you OK? I heard a noise.'

'I'm fine, Dad,' Lorelai said, trying to keep her voice steady. 'It was nothing.'

He frowned. 'You're sure? It sounded like you were scream-ing.'

Lorelai's laugh sounded hollow to her ears. 'No, no, it wasn't me. Honestly, Dad, I'm fine. Go back to sleep. Goodnight.' She settled back onto her pillows and hoped her father would take the hint.

David hesitated and gave her a long look. 'Night, night, sweetheart,' he said eventually. He closed the door gently, the frown still on his face.

Lorelai rubbed her eyes. She had wanted nothing more than her father's comfort, but it was too much too soon. The idea, though, that seeking solace in her parents was something within her reach gave her a glimmer of hope. She had heard people say they were going 'home, home', before but she'd never truly understood what it meant to return home, *home*. Before now, Lorelai had never had a desire to return home. Ever since she had discovered what she could do all those years ago, she'd pushed her parents away. Every time her mother had showed an interest in getting closer to her and being part of her life, Lorelai had created even more distance between them, to keep them from getting too close to her horrible truth.

She now suspected that her mother would be heartbroken if she found out how long she had been keeping such a huge secret, that she had slowly been collapsing under the burden. Joanie might not have been on the money with everything she'd said but she had been right about trying to talk to her parents more. Lorelai had started feeling better since she'd been spending more time with her mother and father. She wasn't dancing in the street, but she was beginning to snatch a few seconds of peace every now and again. It was a small step, but a step in the right direction, nonetheless.

She had always felt like a ticking time bomb when she was with her parents. The more time she spent with them, the more she feared she might explode and reveal her secret. She'd always thought it for the best if she saw and spoke to them as little as possible but, in doing so, she had denied them all a meaningful relationship with one another. All because she had been scared. Could this be the relationship that one day might be strong enough to withstand her curse? She had decided after the walk with her mother that it wasn't too late. While she wasn't ready to let them into the depths of her darkness right away, which was why she was keeping her nightmares to herself, she could begin opening up about other aspects of her life. Like her job, her life in London, Joanie. Coming home, *home* had been her only option when she'd been at her lowest, and now it felt like the thing that might just save her.

For the first couple of days after her surprise arrival, Lorelai had stayed tucked away in her room. She called Wesley and cashed in all the holiday she had left, which amounted to three weeks' worth. He wasn't thrilled about it but was understanding that she was going through a hard time and agreed to her request, given the way she had helped Riggs. She'd also had to miss the first movie screening of her Page to Screen club. Initially, she had wanted to cancel or at least postpone, but everyone had been so excited about it that Lorelai had agreed, via Wesley, to let Joanie host it in her place. Her parents only disturbed her to let her know dinner was ready and for the occasional cup of tea. Slowly but surely, though, her perimeter expanded to include the kitchen. She'd stand at the top of the stairs, listening out to make sure no one was moving, and she would dart back to her room if she so much as heard a floorboard creak. Her parents knew not to push her, and she'd always be grateful to them for that. She had come to them in her own time and that felt better than forcing a confrontation.

The thing that finally drew her downstairs in the end were the cats. Three glorious cats that liked to be held and cuddled and kissed and fussed over. One day, her parents had popped out to the shops, and Lorelai had lost track of time as she'd played with Huey, Dewey and Louie. So much so that she had still been running around after them when her parents had returned. Lorelai couldn't flee back upstairs without looking horribly rude, so she'd endured the small talk and tentative questions, and to her surprise she'd enjoyed the evening. The next day she had gone on the walk with her mother, and that had been the final leap.

In the days that followed, she had found more opportunities to be in their company. She'd come to see how much they loved her, and each other. The walls Lorelai had built up were starting to crumble, and although she was terrified of what her parents might say, she wondered if she could show them who she truly was. With that thought, she rolled over, and closed her eyes, hoping that her sleep would be without nightmares.

✦

The loft hadn't been touched since Lorelai's grandmother had died. Sylvia had kept albums stuffed full of photographs, one for each year of their lives and so the boxes were never-ending.

There were knick-knacks and trinkets whose sentimental value had died with Sylvia, but they still held her grandmother's essence somehow. Lorelai wasn't sure where to begin, nor how her mother expected them to get rid of any of it. The photographs held too many memories to be thrown away. There was no way Lorelai could bring herself to do such a thing. She understood why her mother had let everything gather dust for six years. That was infinitely easier than the pain of feeling her grandma so close and not being able to see, hear or hold her. Lorelai began sifting through a box of her grandmother's old Christmas decorations and thought about her own collection of accumulated tat and where it would land if she kicked the bucket. She almost laughed at the idea of Joanie looking into a cardboard box of cheap rubbish that Lorelai deemed utterly worthless, but deciding to hold onto it because Joanie would feel awful tipping it into a bin. Lorelai was sure her grandmother was laughing at *her* now, from wherever she was, and suddenly getting rid of a few of her bits and pieces felt manageable. Not the photographs though. Lorelai would have to find somewhere special for the photo albums.

'She sure liked a disposable camera, didn't she?' Lila said, popping her head up through the loft hatch. 'Tea?' She held out a bright-yellow mug with daisies on it. The loft was so cold Lorelai could see the steam rising up from the tea, curling around her mother's face.

'Please!' She leaned over and took the mug from her mother. 'How many photographs do you think are here, altogether?'

'Thousands and thousands,' Lila grunted, heaving herself up through the hatch and perching on the edge. The house creaked beneath her and they both paused for a moment, wide-eyed, until they were certain she wasn't about to crash through the ceiling.

'What are we going to do with them?' Lorelai picked up an album and settled it onto her lap. She opened it carefully, revealing photographs of her grandparents in their thirties, she guessed, standing in front of the distant Eiffel Tower holding ice creams, the sunshine creating glares on the image.

'Ah, it looks worse than it is. There's maybe two or three albums in each box and then a lot of other junk. We'll get rid of the junk and box up the albums and then see where we're at.'

Lila beckoned for a box and together they began to sort the treasure from the trash. After far too much silence, Lorelai opened her Spotify app and settled on a playlist entitled 'Chill'. It was calm and relaxing, the perfect soundtrack as they worked. Occasionally they'd share a cute photo or try to guess what some obscure item was that made no sense to either of them, but mostly mother and daughter were in their own worlds, lost in their individual memories of Sylvia. Lorelai wanted to talk about them, to bring her grandmother to life in this dusty attic, but when she looked over at Lila, hoping to strike up a conversation, her mother was completely absorbed in her task, a faraway and sad look on her face. Lorelai wanted to reach out to her, to offer her a little support, but she didn't feel that she had the right to. Not yet, anyway. The quiet began to weigh heavily on Lorelai as she struggled to find the right way to comfort her mother, but any kind of closeness was new to her and she was completely out of her depth.

'More tea?' Lila asked suddenly.

'That would be great,' Lorelai said too brightly. 'Would you mind?'

'Back in a tick.'

Lorelai wanted to weep. She'd been so grateful for that moment of connection she'd felt on their walk, but now she realised there was so much more work to be done to close the distance and mend their relationship. Lorelai wanted to sit with her mother in companiable silence, and not feel desperate to fill the void. And she wanted to know how to give her mother a hug when she was sad without it feeling like the most difficult thing in the world. She hated that the moment her mother climbed back down the steps, she felt relieved that she didn't have to try to make her feel better. *Is this really what we've become? This is what I've let us become.* She shook her head and wiped her tears away, reaching for another photo album. This one was burgundy and there was a picture of a baby on the front. On the inside, she saw her own name written in gold ink in her grandmother's handwriting. Lorelai quickly flipped the book shut once more to look at the photograph again. The baby was *her.*

'Huh,' she said to herself.

Lorelai peered closely at her baby photo but she couldn't recognise herself in the photo at all. She looked like every other baby, and the only thing she could think was that she may have looked like any other baby, but her life hadn't turn out as simply. She thought of everything that little baby had in store for her and she suddenly found herself wishing away the part of her she was ashamed of. The part of her that made the easy parts of life complicated and the hard parts unbearable.

She wanted to be kissed. To be able to kiss someone without

the pain and heartache it came with for her. Lorelai threw the photo album down, pulled her knees to her chest, wrapped her arms around herself and let the tears flow. She let herself feel all the things she'd tried so hard to stop herself from feeling. Finally, she stopped fighting them and the force of her feelings hit her full in the chest. How attached she had become to Grayson, how much she wanted to kiss him without seeing him die. She wanted to be loved, to feel that love and be free to give her love to him with wild and reckless abandon. No one had been worth the risk before but he had made her change her mind. Why him? Maybe she *did* need to face up to the idea of it being fate and predestined. Maybe her pull towards Grayson was more than simple human attraction. Maybe their souls were intertwined in some way. Maybe their destinies were merged and he was always meant to walk into her book club that day. Lorelai couldn't believe she was thinking these things, but there had to be a reason all of her usual defences had failed her and she'd fallen for Grayson. He was part of her now, forever tied together. Lorelai saw no way of freeing herself from these feelings and the weight of that truth was crushing.

Defeated, she gave the photo album an extra kick. Something dislodged from inside its pages, and the corner of an envelope poked out. Lorelai saw the letters 'lai' on the paper. Lore*lai*. She gently pulled the envelope from the album and held it up to where the light was better. *Read me, Lorelai,* was scrawled across it, her grandmother's shaky handwriting instantly recognisable.

Lorelai's heart jumped and her breathing grew heavy. She snatched up the yellowed envelope and held it to her chest. Her sudden movement stirred the air around her and she caught a whiff of the rose-scented perfume her grandmother always used to wear. She held the envelope up to her face and inhaled, imagining Sylvia spraying the perfume onto the letter, and sealing it in the pages of that album, preserving the smell of her hugs until Lorelai found it. *A letter from my grandma,* she thought. *A letter that no one knew about.*

'Everything alright, dear?'

Lila's voice startled Lorelai so much that she jumped and disturbed a box next to her, making the knick-knacks inside knock together with an unpleasant clash of ceramic. Lorelai's jump startled Lila in turn and the cup of tea she was holding wobbled, and the liquid made a satisfying splat as it hit the floor below the ladder. Lila was momentarily distracted by the spilled tea and then caught the look on her daughter's face.

'Sweetheart. What's wrong? You look so sad, darling.' Lila perched on edge of the loft hatch. 'Tell me what's wrong. Please. I think it's time for you to talk to me, Lorelai.'

Lorelai could no longer hold it in. She could no longer cope with this burden on her own. It was too much, keeping her secret all these years, and then Grayson, her fight with Joanie, and now this letter from her grandmother. It was too much. She needed someone, and here was her own mother, who she had all but ignored for years, still wanting to be that person for her.

'Yes,' Lorelai said, 'I think it is.'

◆

Sylvia almost couldn't wait for her granddaughter's dark hair to swish out of sight before she opened the letter. The edges were wrinkled from the sweat of Lorelai's nervous hands. Sylvia's fingers were stiff as they tore at the envelope's seal, but her heart was thudding. Lorelai's handwriting was large and shaky, as though her hand hadn't been able to move fast enough to capture the words pouring from her mind onto the paper. It was a letter written by someone who'd been keeping a secret for far too long.

Dear Grandma,

You were right. I _have_ been keeping something hidden and it _has_ been eating me alive. I'm telling you this because I know you'll take my secret to the grave... is that insensitive? Sorry. You know what I mean. I know you'll love me regardless. Even though I've always seen myself as a monster. Because the truth is, Grandma, I am a monster. I can see death. Not all the time, just when I kiss people on the lips. I've only seen it twice but both times I saw it, it was when I was mid-kiss. My last kiss was when I was eighteen, and I've not kissed anyone else since. I've vowed not to kiss anyone ever again. How can I when each time I've

246

ended up screaming in the poor person's face and having nightmares for weeks on end? And what if I'm causing their deaths with my kiss? Have you ever heard of anything like this, Grandma? Am I entirely alone? I feel alone. I hope you don't think I'm crazy and I swear this isn't a joke. I'm desperate now because I'm scared this is my life now. I'm scared that my life is already over when it's hardly even begun.

Please help me. If you can.
I love you, always.
Lorelai
X

Sylvia didn't weep with sorrow or gasp in shock, nor did she feel angry that Lorelai hadn't told her sooner. Instead, she tipped her head back and laughed. The noise alerted a nearby nurse who poked his head through the door and raised an eyebrow.

'Everything alright in here?'

'More than alright.' Sylvia grinned. 'I don't suppose you could fetch me some paper and a pen, could you? I have a letter to write.'

The nurse nodded and disappeared. Sylvia read Lorelai's letter once more and then held it to her heart, feeling a little less alone for the first time in her whole life.

◆

Twenty-Four

Lorelai sat on the edge of her bed and turned her grandmother's letter over in her hands. She had told her mother that she needed a lie down, and she'd promised that they would talk later – and she meant it. Something had shifted since Lorelai had come home. Home, *home*. She felt the power in that second 'home' now. It was time to talk to her mother, of that she felt sure, and time to close the gap that had grown between them. Maybe meeting Grayson had opened her up more than she realised, or maybe it was simply the right moment, but she knew she had to read the letter from her grandmother before that conversation with her mother happened, and she knew she had to read it alone. The letter was meant for her eyes only and she didn't want an audience while she uncovered whatever was inside.

Opening an envelope was such a simple act and yet one so terrifying to Lorelai that she felt nauseous. She sensed that this was important, and that things wouldn't be the same once she read the letter. It was a fork in the road, and Lorelai had a choice to make. To read, or not to read. What would happen if she didn't open the letter? Ignorance was bliss, after all. Once she read the letter, there would be no turning back. She couldn't unread it. The letter could be filled with her grandmother's advice, Sylvia passing on her wisdom from beyond the grave… or it could be a brownie recipe. But if it was something like that, then why had Sylvia written Lorelai a letter and tucked it away in a photo album, without telling anyone about it? What if Lorelai had never found it? It was Sylvia's secrecy that made Lorelai nervous.

Lorelai shook herself. *Enough.* Before she could overthink it any longer, she slipped her thumb under the envelope's seal and quickly tore it open. She pulled the sheet of paper out, unfolded it, and smoothed it onto her lap. The page was filled with her grandmother's wobbly scrawl, black ink covering front and back. Tears sprang to Lorelai's eyes as the familiarity of her grandmother's handwriting hit her. She missed her so much. She wished she was here. She closed her eyes, steadied herself, and then began to read.

Dear Lorelai,

Firstly, I love you. You know that. And I want you to know that I read your letter, and that that love is still there. It has not changed. I love you now and I will continue to love you from the great beyond. Even death won't put a stop to my love for you. I knew something was troubling you, sweetheart, and I'm honoured you trusted me with your secret. But here's something you don't know. The reason I sensed something wasn't right was because you reminded me of me, of how I behaved when I was keeping my secret. It took me years to open up to someone too. If you're anything like me (which for many reasons, I hope you're not!), you will keep this thing a closely guarded secret, only entrusting it to those closest to you. The secret being… we see death.

Lorelai's hand flew to her mouth, and she choked back a sob. 'Oh my god,' Lorelai breathed, tears falling hot and fast. 'She read my letter.' The letter she had pressed into her grandmother's hands the last time she had seen her. The letter she was certain her grandmother hadn't had the chance to read. But she had, and she had penned a reply, probably sensing her end was near, and now that letter was finally in Lorelai's hands.

She laughed in disbelief. She wasn't crying out of sadness or grief for her deceased grandmother. It was sheer relief in its purest form. Lorelai was not alone. She had hoped to alleviate the feeling of loneliness by confessing her secret to her grandmother, but she had no idea her grandmother *shared* her secret, too. Had Sylvia felt as lonely as Lorelai did? Lorelai couldn't grasp that she was not the only person who had felt what she was feeling. There was someone else who had known exactly what she was going through. A wave of sadness hit her, then. *I should have told her sooner.* Did that mean there were more people out there like her? What were the chances it was just her and her grandmother? Was it a family curse? Did it skip a generation, seeing as her mother seemed blissfully unaffected? Questions buzzed around Lorelai's mind. She turned her attention back to the letter in the hope her clever grandmother would have some of the answers.

I discovered this when I was in my teens and I retreated into my shell much like you did. Oh, Lorelai you were such a happy little child and then you vanished. Right before our eyes you disappeared and I was so desperate to talk to you. To tell you everything but I wanted it to come from you. I knew if you were anything like me, poking and probing was

*only going to force you further back into your shell. I wanted you to start
the conversation on your own terms... and now you have.*

*Thank you for your letter. I know how hard that must have been
to write but you did it, Lorelai. Your secret is no longer a secret you
need to bear alone, and I hope that that weight has been lifted from
your shoulders a little. I can feel the end is coming for me, and before
I go I want to say that there are people in this world, who may not
share our secret, but they are worthy of your trust. They are few and far
between, but you'll spot them immediately. They'll glimmer and shine,
and you'll feel that they are your forever people. When you find them,
don't let them go.*

Lorelai thought of Joanie. Joanie and her shiny smile and bright,
happy eyes. The way her whole presence sparkled. Lorelai had
been so angry at Joanie but as she read her grandmother's words,
that anger dissolved and disappeared in a puff of smoke. She
missed Joanie; she was her sister, her family, and she loved her.
She loved her so fiercely and the days of ignoring her, of not
knowing what to say, were over. She would call her tonight.

*Which brings me onto the very important matter of love. What we can
do, Lorelai, is hard. It brings sadness and complications that most of
the people you come to know won't understand. You need to do what's
right for you, but you also need to know what is possible. I married the
love of my life, Lorelai, and we really did live happily ever after. Your
grandfather was one of those shiny people and from the moment I met
him I knew I was headed down a rabbit hole I would never emerge from.
The first time I kissed him I saw how he was going to die, and it was
painful. I was in pieces, but then I realised I could intervene and stop*

it from happening. In my vision I had seen him die on the day of the King's Cross fire and I'd seen the date on the front of the newspaper he was reading. He would have been caught up right in the middle of it if I hadn't convinced him to call in sick that day and stay at home with me. We are all meant to die one day, and your grandfather was no exception, but the truth was I simply wasn't prepared to lose him that day and so he died a lot later in life thanks to my meddling. You might wonder, like I did, if there are rules. If you save someone's life when they should have died, does something unthinkable happen. The truth is, I don't know. I don't know if by saving your grandfather someone else had to take his place to maintain balance in the world. Someone may well have died in his place that day and I'll have no way of knowing. But I'm not sorry. I don't know what sort of person that makes me, but I will never apologise for the life we ended up having.

Lorelai had never paid much attention to their relationship when she'd seen her grandparents together but now that she really thought about it, she remembered how they used to look at each other. Lorelai had been too young to understand what was behind those looks, but she could see it now, the love in their eyes. Now she remembered the way their hands were always intertwined and how whenever her grandmother spoke of her grandfather after he passed, her eyes still lit up as if he'd just walked in the room. Her grandmother had found love and had built a life with that man, a life that had produced a child and a grandchild. Lorelai covered her mouth with the sleeve of her jumper, which was already soaked through with tears and she let out another great sob. Was it truly possible that she could have a real relationship? That she didn't have to be alone? Her grandmother had made it work, and Lorelai had had no idea of the secrets she had kept. Might there be a chance for her, after all, for her... and Grayson? A little flame of hope ignited within her. It was small and dim, but it was better than no hope at all.

I never met anyone else out there like me, but I met people I suspected of keeping secrets that may not have been identical to mine, but could have shared similarities. I just can't bring myself to believe you and I are alone in all this. I'm sorry we never talked about this more. I was scared that pushing you to talk about it when you weren't ready would only push you away, but I hope this letter brings you a little comfort. You're still so young, darling, don't close yourself off from the world.

If I can leave you with anything to help get you through this, it's these three simple rules.

Never tell someone how they're going to die. No one wants to be burdened with that information. Even if they say they do.

Never dwell on what might or might not have been. Spider-Man was wrong. Not all great power comes with great responsibility. It is not your job to save everyone. People come and people go. That is life. You and I are not gods. Just like everyone else, we are merely spectators. We just have a slightly wider view.

The final piece of advice to you, dearest Lorelai, is this... live. Live the life you want to live despite this secret of ours. Don't let it hold you back. I spent too long not living how I wanted to live and waiting in vain for something to change, for things to get easier but they didn't. At least not until I decided that this secret wouldn't stop me from living my life. It is what it is. We either must learn how to deal with it and get on with life or live a life that's not worth living. I decided that wasn't what I wanted for myself and it's not what I want for you either.

I don't regret a single second of knowing the ending to my great love story. Your grandfather and I loved each other and when he died, we simply parted for a brief time. It won't be long now until I'm in his arms again. That's all death is, Lorelai. It's not the ending. It's the beginning of a life somewhere new. Never fear it and, more importantly, never fear yourself; remember, you are never alone.

Love from your doting grandmother who will be waiting for you when it's your time to end one story and begin another.

Sylvia x

Lorelai re-read the letter a hundred times. Each time she felt like she could hear her grandmother gently whispering the words in her ear. Maybe she was. If her power had taught her anything, it was to never rule out any idea, no matter how crazy it sounded. Maybe her grandmother really was with her and had guided her to the letter just when Lorelai had needed it the most. Somehow Sylvia had known that Lorelai was in so over her head she no longer knew which way was up, and had led her to the letter. Until her dying day, Lorelai would believe that that was how she came to be in her parents' dusty old loft during her time of crisis.

With trembling hands, Lorelai clung to the letter like a life raft and let it carry her downstairs, where she fell into her mother's arms.

Twenty-Five

Lila didn't say a word. She simply stood in the middle of the kitchen and let Lorelai wrap her arms around her until her breathing was no longer wracked with sobs. Lila held her daughter tight, her own chest rising and falling in time with Lorelai's. In time, Lorelai became still and quiet, but she didn't pull away. She remained in her mother's embrace and Lila wasn't going to be the one to break the moment. Eventually, Lorelai sighed and stepped away, her head bowed so her hair fell over her red eyes and mottled cheeks.

'Tea?' her mother said gently. Lorelai nodded, wordlessly.

She sat down at the kitchen island and watched her mother clinking and stirring and humming her way around the kitchen. *You are not alone.* Her grandmother's words came back to her. If that were true, then it was time to tell her mother everything. Lorelai tried to find the right configuration of the right words to make the most sense. What would scare her mother the least, and what might make her accept Lorelai the most? Lorelai had had years to prepare for this moment, but she had been so sure it was a moment that would never come, she was floundering.

Now she was faced with the terrifying reality of telling her mother she had given birth to a monster. A monster who carried death with her wherever she went. Where Lorelai was meant to find warmth, she found that the icy cold fingers of death had beaten her to it. The places in life where Lorelai was meant to find acceptance, love, compassion, and the people… the person… with whom she wanted to share her life, she'd had to push away. She tried to pull some comfort from Sylvia's letter, but those words were fighting against a lifetime of Lorelai pushing people away. Once Lorelai told her mother, she would also have to tell her about Grayson, and that seeing him die was the reason she had run away from London. She hadn't been strong enough to see that. There was so much hurt and heartbreak intertwined with the secret itself, it was suffocating. When it was Lorelai's alone, it was heavy, but it grew in strength when it was shared. In her case, a problem shared was a problem doubled. Her mother sat at the kitchen island opposite her, her hands wrapped around her mug.

'Mum, I have something I need to tell you.'

'You're pregnant.' Lila exhaled with a knowing smile, her head bobbing gently. She didn't even skip a beat.

'What? Absolutely not!' Lorelai was incredulous.

'Really? Oh…'

'Did you actually think I was up the duff?'

'Oh, don't be so crass!'

'Well, did you?' Lorelai exclaimed.

'You've been so subdued. I just assumed. Wrongly, obviously. Ignore me. Carry on.'

Lila chuckled but the knot in Lorelai's stomach only tightened. Children. There was another hole that her secret's claws would puncture into her parents' world. Did it also mean no children? It hit Lorelai suddenly. No *biological* children at least. What if this was passed on genetically? It had clearly skipped a generation with her, considering her mother suspected that Lorelai's biggest secret was pregnancy (oh how she wished that was her biggest secret!), so she might have a child that didn't share her secret, but what of any future grandchildren? Lorelai couldn't risk passing this on; she would never knowingly put someone else through it. It was another thing to add to the 'Not for Lorelai' list.

But then… Lorelai's mind drifted back to the albums upon albums of photographs, and the boxes full of her grandmother's treasures. It was all sentimental fodder from a full life, well lived. A happy life. Lorelai had never known her grandmother to be anything other than seemingly fulfilled. Could that be her one day? Could she have the same carefree attitude her grandmother had had? Could she love as freely as she had? Grayson filled her thoughts again. Meeting him had changed everything. Maybe they could even get married one day, have children and feel happy? *Slow down*, Lorelai chided herself. *You ran away from him, and now you're thinking about marriage and babies?! Focus.* This wasn't a question for now. Now was about finding the right words to tell her mother the long-overdue truth. She started mulling over all the different scenarios, when her mother's voice cut into her thoughts.

'Lorelai, you know whatever it is you can tell me, don't you?'

Lorelai glanced up at her mother's face, realising she'd been caught inside her head again. She was on a loop of all the ways she could say what she needed to say, and how her mother might react. Lila's expression was kind and Lorelai could feel she meant what she'd said. It was plain as day on her gentle face.

'I know. I'm just trying to find the right words.'

'You don't have to. I get the feeling that whatever's in your head right now is all a bit of a mess. So let it come out in a jumble. I'm your mother. You don't have to be perfect in front of me. It's my job to help you turn whatever is in there—' Lila leaned across and tapped the centre of Lorelai's creased forehead with the warm pad of her index finger '—into something that makes some sort of sense.'

Lorelai felt her eyes beginning to sting. *If I cry again, I'll never get through this so… here goes nothing.*

'Mum,' she said, and her voice wobbled. She cleared her throat and tried again. 'Mum. Did Grandma ever tell you anything about what happened when she kissed people?'

Lila's cheeks tinged pink ever so slightly. 'Erm… no, darling. I don't think that's a conversation we ever had,' she said slowly, clearly uncomfortable and unsure of where this conversation was going.

'It's a conversation she had with me. Well… she told me in this letter. That I just found. Upstairs.' Lorelai pulled the yellowed letter out of her back pocket and placed it on the table between them. Her grandmother's writing glaring up at them both.

'Why would she write to you about… kissing?' Lila gave a little uncertain laugh but everything in Lorelai's body was too tense to laugh. Even the sound of her mother's light, breathy giggle set her nerves on edge.

'Because I wrote her a letter about something and gave it to her the day before she died,' Lorelai explained carefully and slowly, making sure she didn't miss a single detail. The last thing she wanted to do was rehash this story again.

'OK…' Lila said, just as slowly.

'It seems that Grandma and I have… had… something in common.'

'Right.' Lila nodded along to show she was receiving and processing the information as it came to her.

'Something I didn't know we had in common until I found this letter. She must have written it to me before she died, and it got mixed up in her things when we brought them home.'

'Can I read it?' Lila reached over but Lorelai pulled the letter back towards her.

'In a minute. I promise. But I need to be the one to explain.'

Lila's face creased in concern, and she nodded, encouraging her daughter to continue. This was the moment everything was going to change. Lorelai looked down into her tea and squeezed her eyes shut.

'I can see the way people are going to die when I kiss them. And Grandma could too. That's what she told me in the letter,' she said quickly. It came out in a rush, and the silence that followed was deafening. She so wanted her mother's approval. Her acceptance. She wanted a warm hand on hers and for her to say, 'It's going to be OK.'

Instead, she heard a short, sharp, muffled sniff. Lorelai opened one eye and looked up at her mother warily. Lila was staring at her in shock, her hand over her mouth and her eyes wide. Tears were pooling in the bottom of her eyelids. She looked devastated. *Oh no, no, no!* Lorelai's head began to thump. *She thinks I'm crazy. This was a mistake.* Deep down she had known her mother would never understand. How could she? But Lorelai now realised that a part of her, the small part where a smidgen of hope remained, had expected her mother to be there for her anyway, no matter how far-fetched her words sounded to her. Now, as she took in her mother's appalled expression, the reality she was facing was more crushing than she could have imagined.

'You don't believe me, do you? You think I'm mad. I'm so sorry, Mum. I should never have come here, I should—'

Lila waved her hand for Lorelai to stop, swallowing back her emotion so that she could talk. 'It's not that...' She gulped in between sniffs and swiped her tears away. Her expression cleared. 'It's just that... that... well...' Lila put a hand to her chest and said two little words that changed everything, '...me too.'

There was silence. Of all the ways Lorelai had imagined this conversation would go, never in a million years did she expect those two words to come out of her mother's mouth.

'What do you mean?' Lorelai whispered, her voice catching. She had expected to explain, to have to answer a million questions, to spend hours trying to convince her mum she was perfectly sane. She was wrongfooted now, and no plan for what might come next. Lila used her sleeve to wipe away the rest of her tears.

'I'm saying you and your grandmother aren't the only ones who can... do that.' She laughed a laugh that Lorelai recognised as relief. She could feel it too.

'And you and Grandma never talked about it?'

Lila shook her head and burst into tears once more.

'I think you need to read this.' Lorelai slid the letter over to her mother and waited patiently for her to read it as many times as she had to before she felt ready to talk. It didn't take her long.

'I can't believe it,' she breathed.

'*You* can't believe it? I had no idea I came from an apparently very long line of Grim Reapers!'

'I'm so sorry you've suffered in silence for so long. And I can't believe I didn't put two and two together. I assumed it would have been more obvious and I would have figured it out if you were the same.' Lila reached over the table and took her daughter's hand. Lorelai squeezed back and laughed.

'I thought I was being super obvious but then again I thought the same about you, too, that if you had the same power, I would have spotted it a mile off. Maybe that's part of the curse. It makes you feel so isolated that you don't see how you could all be in it together. That we could have helped each other through it, if we'd just looked past the end of our own noses.'

'Well, not anymore,' Lila said, squeezing her daughter's hand even harder. For the first time in Lorelai's life she felt like she could accept her mother's love and affection. Her fears had evaporated entirely. Lila couldn't reject her because they were one and the same. Peas in a pod. An apple fallen from a very nearby tree.

'Why did you never say anything? To Grandma?' Lorelai's brain was itching with questions.

'Me?' Lila squeezed Lorelai's hand then opened it and began to trace the lines on her palm with her finger. 'Why didn't she say anything to me?'

'For the same reason you didn't say anything to me, and I never said anything to you!' Lorelai would have felt frustrated if the relief washing through her wasn't so soothing.

'This explains so much.'

Lila sat back in her chair, her gaze drifting away from her

daughter. Lorelai knew what she was doing, because she was doing the same – Lila was reliving all those moments with her own mother that must have left Lila feeling confused, and all the times her mother got too close to the truth so Lila had pushed her away.

Lorelai ached for her mother. She was still here, Lorelai could talk to her mother about this now, but Lila's mother was gone. How must it feel to find out they had this hugely important thing in common now, when it was too late to talk to Sylvia about it? Lorelai was so grateful that she could have this conversation now so she could begin to mend what had been so broken for so many years.

Lila snapped out of her daze with a sad sigh.

'We are all stubborn. We learned it from one another, I suppose. Three stubborn women who would never ask for help and would refuse it if someone offered. I think we need to learn from this. You especially, sweetheart. You've still got your whole life ahead of you.'

'So…' Lorelai dropped her voice to a whisper, 'you know how Dad's going to die?'

Lila's eyes moved to the doorway. She pressed a finger to her lips and nodded.

'He doesn't know about you?' Lorelai mouthed and Lila shook her head.

'And you're OK? With knowing?' Lorelai said quietly.

'I have to be. Life *without* your dad is far worse than being *with* him and knowing. Besides, I already know. I can't un-see what I saw so I might as well keep him around as a salve to my wounded heart.' Lila put the back of her hand against her head as if she were a damsel in distress, but Lorelai saw her for what she really was: the strongest women she knew. Her grandmother, too.

Lorelai sighed. 'I've got so many questions. I don't know where to start.'

'Well, go ahead.' Lila stood and put the kettle on boil again. 'What?'

'Ask them.' Lila smiled.

'Oh... right. Yeah.' A grin spread across her face. 'This is so strange. I'm not used to talking so freely about all this with someone. Any time I've ever had questions I've just had to... ignore them really. Accept that I'll just never know. Or make up my own answers and hope I'm not too far off the mark.'

'Well, no more of that.' Lila finished making their tea refills and sat back down. 'Right. Ask me anything.' Lorelai flipped through her many questions, trying to decide which was the best place to start.

'When did you find out you could do what you can?'

'It took a while for me to figure it all out, but I had my first kiss when I was fourteen. We were playing spin the bottle at a sleepover and when it was my turn, it landed on Tommy Waldon. He was so handsome, and I was so excited. Everyone there was whooping, you know, the way teenagers get so caught up in everything, but as soon as our lips touched it was the worst pain I've ever felt. Like a thousand volts of electricity were running through my veins. I didn't see Tommy or exactly what had happened, I just saw the sparks and a man's face looking terrified through the sparks. I didn't know who the man was until later that evening when Tommy's dad came to pick him up. It was his face I'd seen. I didn't understand what I'd seen or why I'd seen Tommy's dad's face. It was years later when I was piecing together more of a puzzle that I figured it out. Tommy's dad was an electrician, and Tommy died by electric shock when learning the trade from his father. His dad was there when it happened, which is why I saw his face – he'd watched his son die.'

'Did it come true?'

Lila's expression saddened. 'Yes, but I didn't know until years after it happened. I couldn't do a quick internet search like you can now. I had to hear it through the grapevine.'

'That's awful.' Lorelai stood and gave her mother a hug. 'That must have been so confusing, and not knowing what you'd seen or why... I'm sorry, Mum.'

'Thank you, that means a lot because I know you know how it feels. At the time though, I was less concerned about what I had seen and more preoccupied with how I'd seen it. I was kissing the most gorgeous boy in school and the next thing I knew I was waking up in the middle of the circle having wet myself! I lost a lot of friends that day. I'd seen how someone was going to die but fourteen-year-old me was more concerned about her street cred.' Lila laughed, despite her sad story.

'Oh, Mum.' Lorelai was mortified on behalf of her mother.

'Don't worry so much—' Lila reached over and smoothed the worry lines from Lorelai's forehead '—that was forever ago. I'm over it by now. But, if I'm being honest, at the time I ran for the hills. I pushed everyone away from that point onwards. I kissed a few more people but it was horrible each time, and the trauma of seeing all that death, it was, well... you know how difficult it is. So I avoided romance and relationships as best I could. Then I met your father. He changed everything.' Lila took a sip from her mug and smiled.

Lorelai let that sink in. Her mother had done exactly what she had been doing – they had both come to a similar conclusion about relationships and drawn up almost identical life plans. Swearing off romance and relationships was the obvious solution, but Lorelai couldn't imagine her mother without her father. As a couple they were tender and romantic. Lorelai had loved it as a child, but once she knew about her ability, it had grown hard to witness the kind of relationship she could never have. But she and her mother shared the same ability, and her mother had opened herself up to love. The idea of her mother without her father was unthinkable, that they might never have had what they did have all these years was unfathomable. Did that mean Lorelai could have it too, that she didn't have to push everyone away to stay safe? Lorelai's mind was whirring with questions and new possibilities.

'So, what was it about Dad that made things change for you?'

'In all honesty… I couldn't tell you.' Lila smiled. 'I met your father and I don't know what it was about him that made me feel the way I felt, I just knew something was different. It was like something had awakened within me. I used to have these nightmares, full of death and despair, and they started to get worse around the time I met your father. Then when I finally kissed your father it was like…'

'…all the stars had aligned,' Lorelai said quietly.

Lila nodded and tilted her head. 'So, Lorelai, my brave girl—' Lila leaned forward and took both of her daughter's hands in hers '—now that an enormous weight has been lifted off us both, I think it's time you told me everything.'

'Everything?' Lorelai's smile began small, barely even visible. Then it grew until the muscles in her face strained to contain it.

'Yes, darling. I want to know everything.'

Twenty-Six

Lila and Lorelai talked for hours. Lila even managed to shed some light on the nightmares she'd been having.

'Have they been getting worse?' Lila asked with a knowing smile.

'Yeah... Why is that?'

'I remember my nightmares getting so monumental. They'd leave me with headaches that lasted for days and then I said yes to being with your father. As soon as that decision was made, I've not had another nightmare since. Not a single one. I don't think I even dream anymore, come to think of it.'

'So what does that mean exactly?'

'I've got my theories but it's hard to know when you've never known anyone like yourself before. Now, I don't believe in all this "other half" nonsense. I don't believe you're only half of a person until you meet someone and you create a whole. However, I do believe in soulmates. I believe that there are people in this world, multiple people, be it friends, family or partners, whose souls are made of the same stuff as yours. Like you're all cut from the same fabric of the universe and when you find each other, something clicks into place and things make more sense than they used to.'

'So you think you were having nightmares because…'

'Because something big and life-changing was about to happen and I think my little superpower was letting me know in the only way it knew how.' Lila shrugged. 'I could be wrong, there's no way to know really, but if the same thing is happening to you, I wouldn't be surprised if I'm right. Met anyone special lately?' Lila raised an eyebrow knowingly and Lorelai blushed, quickly brushing away the question.

Eventually Lorelai's father came to join them when their laughter became too loud for him to hear his own guitar playing. Lorelai quickly put the letter in her pocket and from then on, they had to quash the talk about their new-found solidarity, but by then they had got most of it out of their system. Instead, they shared knowing looks and small stifled smiles. Lorelai felt a warmth she'd never felt before. It burned from her centre, from the inside out, and she could feel it pouring off her in waves and it settled on her parents – towards her mother gently sipping tea, and her father drumming his restless musical fingers on the kitchen table. *This must be how Grayson felt when he talked about his family.* The thought was instant and so intrusive Lila noticed Lorelai's face change immediately.

'Everything alright?' she asked in concern.

Lorelai's lip wobbled and she simply shook her head. She thought of her mother and her father, her grandmother and her grandfather, and then of herself and Grayson. Lorelai had had no manual that told her how to navigate through life, doing what she could do. She'd had to make it up as she went along. Now here she was with two shining examples of women who had led not only happy lives, but had had happy marriages, too.

They had chosen to stay close to the people they loved because it was less painful than living without them. Lila turned to her husband and gave his hand a gentle pat.

'I'm going to head up to bed,' he said, taking his cue to leave. 'Love you, pickle.' He walked around to give his daughter's hair a ruffle before kissing the top of her head. He squeezed her shoulder and then left the room, humming to himself.

'So? Is there another piece of the jigsaw? You've told me about Joanie and how brilliant she is, and everything that happened with Riggs. But when I asked if you'd met anyone recently, you went as pale as Aunt Nettie from down the road.'

'Isn't she a hundred and two?'

'Exactly. So there's a *lot* more to your story, isn't there? You mentioned a Grayson earlier, but then changed the subject quickly...' Lila's voice trailed off in a question and she raised her eyebrows.

Lorelai couldn't contain it any longer. Tears poured from her eyes, and her lips curled and twisted with each heaving sob. Her mother's hands found hers, and Lorelai leaned forward and rested her forehead against them until she was back in control and could speak again.

'I pushed him away.' Lorelai spoke against the wood of the table, the words loud in her ears. 'I pushed him away because I saw how he was going to die, and it was brutal and soon. So soon.' Lorelai's head was spinning and no matter how hard she squeezed her temples it wouldn't slow down. Grayson was caught up in the whirlpool of her mind. Every word he'd ever said to her echoed around her head, his voice crystal clear in her ears. She could feel the warmth of his lips against hers and the mark they had left on her heart. With each minute Grayson drew closer to his end, the stronger the effect he had had on Lorelai, the deeper his pull, as though something inside her was willing, urging, pushing her to act.

'Is there anything you can do to stop it?' her mother said, reading her mind.

'Is… is that allowed?' Lorelai lifted her head and pushed her hair back so she could get a good look at her mother's face. Was she joking? Did she mean it?

'What do you mean is it allowed? Who do you need to give you permission?'

'I don't… I don't know. Joanie and I figured out that I *can* change people's fates, but I don't know if that is something I'm necessarily *meant* to do.'

Her mother's eyes widened. 'How did you figure that out?' Lila sipped her tea, a curious smile playing at the edge of her lips.

Lorelai had never felt closer to her. She explained what had happened when Riggs had kissed her and how that had led to her night of seeking answers.

'I kissed this guy called James. I met him at the bar that night. He wasn't a… a boyfriend or anything. And I saw him die on his bike. But then I wanted to see if my theory was correct, so I asked Joanie to do something to his bike to stop him riding it that night. I meant for her to let the air out of his tyres or something, but she only went and stole it.' Lorelai smiled as her mother's eyes creased with laughter. 'And when I kissed him again, he died in a different way. And he was much older. But that was a one-off. I've never tried to interfere at all before then or since, because what if I'm changing more than just that one person's fate? I don't

269

know anything about the bigger consequences, and… well, isn't it…' Lorelai swallowed down what she already knew was a stupid question, but it slipped back up her throat before she could stop it. She had to know. 'Isn't it like time travel?'

'You've spent far too much time at the cinema,' her mother said kindly.

'I know it sounds ridiculous, but there could be repercussions from stopping someone's death. I thought that I would throw the whole universe off kilter if I changed how someone was going to die. Whenever time travel is involved in films there are rules. Don't change the past or it'll change the future. If I stopped someone from dying does that mean someone else has to die in their place? Or the time they gain back in life gets taken away from someone else to restore the balance? You know, that sort of thing.'

'Sweetheart, I don't have the answers, but I have to believe that we can see what we see for a reason. Otherwise, why do we go through this pain? What's the *point* of it, if we can't help the people we love? I know seeing Grayson die was awful but I truly believe you can stop it, that you can change his fate. Your grandmother saved your grandfather after all, and nothing bad happened to them.'

'What about Dad?' Lorelai asked, suddenly panicked. Would her father die when she wasn't prepared?

Lila waved her panic away. 'Your dad is going to be fine. He has lived a safe life and his death very much follows suit. He's not about to die in a boating accident or by parachute failure, is he?' Lila tutted and rolled her eyes affectionately. 'Luckily, I never had much to worry about on that front. He's always had a long life ahead of him.'

'Always? Has his death ever changed?'

'It has but only because I got him to quit smoking, eat better and drink less! But the end of his life has always been far away and unextraordinary. It's peaceful. Just how I like it. And it hasn't changed for a very long time. I never had to intervene because what I saw, well, it was OK... But, darling, you're overthinking this. If you can save Grayson, why shouldn't you?'

'He's not mine to save,' Lorelai said sadly.

Lila pursed her lips. 'Of course he is! You love him. Surely that means you want him to live, whether you end up with him or not?'

'Of course I want him to live! I'm just saying that... what if he's not meant to? What if him dying is part of some bigger plan that we don't know? If I saved him, does that mean I'm sentencing someone else to the fate he was meant to have?'

'Sweetheart, breathe. If I had all the answers, I would tell you. Unfortunately, I don't. And we can't see the whole future. We see a tiny sliver of it. Who knows what might happen?' Lila swirled the remains of her tea, staring into the bottom of her mug. 'Look, I just don't believe there are rules or regulations. There's no governing body for what we can do. You're not going to go to a supernatural jail for helping someone in need and we don't know for certain if someone else would have to take his place. So maybe it shouldn't be your responsibility to worry about that? Maybe you should just focus on the good you can do with your gift, with the knowledge you do have, instead of the bad?' Lila reached out and smoothed Lorelai's hair out of her eyes, tucking it behind her ear.

Lorelai felt a swell of hope rise within her. Could she really help someone without there being a price to pay? If that was the case, Lorelai could be the hero Joanie had always told her she could be. If that were the case…

'I can't stop the plane from going up in flames but… oh my god… I can stop Grayson from getting on that plane in the first place. Oh my god, oh my GOD!' Lorelai's heart was pounding, the sound deafening in her ears. 'I can save him.' She was up from her chair in one swift moment, her entire being fizzing with energy.

'Oh, darling. He dies in a plane crash?' her mother asked.

'Yes, but he doesn't have to, does he?'

A part of her still felt that she needed permission from someone, anyone, to say that it was acceptable for her to do what she was about to do. And how wonderful that person turned out to be her own mother. She finally had someone who truly understood her, and what it felt like to be trapped in a place of dark uncertainty with no one to turn to, and no answers about what it all meant. She wasn't alone anymore.

'No, sweetheart. I don't think he does. You have the power to do something good. And even if there were rules—' Lila straightened her spine and looked her daughter in the eye, dropping her voice to a wry whisper '—as your mother I'd be encouraging you to break them anyway.'

Twenty-Seven

Lorelai raced up to her room and swiped her phone up off her bedside table. She had barely looked at it since she'd been home. She scrolled frantically until she landed on Grayson's number.

'Please pick up. Please pick up,' she pleaded as she waited for him to answer, each ring another dagger to her heart. Lorelai's eyes darted to the clock as her call rang out and went to voicemail. It was two o'clock in the morning.

'Hey, Grayson. It's Lorelai. I'm so sorry it's taken me so long to call and I know I said this before, but I mean it this time… I can explain. Please give me a chance to explain. I've been doing some deep soul-searching and… just call me. As soon as you get this. Don't wait. Please. Call me back.'

Lorelai pulled the phone away from her ear and noticed the little red bubble next to the phone icon. There were so many missed calls. She had been so desperate to call Grayson, that she hadn't noticed them until now. She swiped across. Eleven were from Grayson, most of which were from the night they had kissed. The rest were from Joanie. She swiped back again to voicemail. There was only one from Grayson. She hadn't listened to it. She'd left her phone untouched while she'd been home, insistent on shutting the world out for a while. She tapped play on Grayson's voicemail and listened to every word breathlessly.

'I'll respect your privacy and I won't call again. I'm going out of the country in two weeks so… your move, Lorelai.'

'Oh my god,' she whispered. *He's going out of the country in two weeks.* She checked the date of the voicemail. Grayson had left it a week and six days ago. 'Ohmygodohmygodohmygod.'

Grayson had looked young in her vision but it hadn't crossed her mind that his death was only two weeks away. She thought she had more time. She'd been moping around all this time, when she could have been planning how to save him. Lorelai quickly swiped back to her contacts and feverishly dialled Joanie.

'Come on, come on, come on!' she muttered, the panic beginning to reach fever pitch.

'Lollie?' Joanie's voice sounded muffled and groggy.

'JOANIE! Thank god! I need you to—'

'Oh my god, Lorelai!' Joanie exclaimed, becoming more alert. 'It's so good to hear your voice. You've been MIA for almost two weeks! I was starting to think I was never going to hear from you again.' Joanie's voice cracked and Lorelai felt a stab of guilt.

'We both knew I was always going to call. I just needed a bit of time.' Lorelai tried to keep her voice steady but she felt like she was about to explode.

'I know. I just… I worried, OK?'

Lorelai heard the rustle of Joanie's bedsheets and the click of her bedside lamp.

'I get it, I do, but I just need you to listen to me for a second—'

'No, no, let me say something.'

'But Joanie, I—'

'I'm so sorry, Lollie.'

'I know, Joanie. We can talk about this later but right now—'

'No, you have to listen to me! I've not talked to you for two weeks and I've got so much to say, to apologise for, and—'

'GRAYSON IS GOING TO DIE TOMORROW!' Lorelai cried out. The only way to get Joanie to stop talking and listen was to shock her into it. There was silence on the other end of the line.

'Why didn't you just say that?' Joanie finally said, breathless.

'He left me a voicemail two weeks ago saying he was going away in two weeks' time and when I kissed him I—'

'You saw him die somewhere other than London?'

Lorelai stood, the nervous energy in her body forcing her to pace around her room. 'Worse. He never makes it where he's going. He's going to die on the plane.'

'Shit. Right. OK.' There was only the sound of their breathing as they both sat with this huge problem. 'What do we do?' Joanie finally said.

'You mean you'll help me?'

'Lorelai, don't ask me stupid questions,' Joanie said impatiently.

Despite the dire situation, Lorelai couldn't help but smile through her tearful eyes. She had really missed Joanie. She had been so angry at her for pushing her too hard, but she had also been distraught at seeing how Grayson would die. Lorelai could see now that Joanie had acted out of a place of love. Joanie was the most loyal friend she had ever had, and she knew now that there would be times in her life when she would need Joanie's no-nonsense, tough-love approach. And she had her mother now too. She had so much to tell Joanie, but first, Grayson.

'I've tried calling but I can't get through to him.'

'You don't think he's already on the plane, do you?' Joanie gasped.

'Maybe.' Lorelai's legs gave way beneath her. She slumped into a heap in the middle of the floor and began to sob. 'Maybe I'm too late.'

'No way. Don't think like that. He might not be going until tomorrow and he could just be asleep right now. Or he's awake and drowning his sorrows as he pines over losing you, and his phone is in another room. Yes, that's it, and in mere moments he'll call you back and profess his love for you!' Joanie's voice was triumphant, but the knot in Lorelai's stomach only grew tighter.

'He didn't lose me. I pushed him away. *I* let *him* go.' She covered her head with her arm, creating a cocoon on her bedroom floor.

'And you've changed your mind?'

'Yeah. Yeah, I have.'

'What brought that on? You seemed pretty certain when you left that you were going to be alone forever.'

'Maybe it was the unexpected discovery that not only did my grandmother have the power to see how the people she kissed were going to die, but my mother has it too.'

'Are you serious?' Joanie said slowly.

'Yup. Crazy times, Joanie. Crazy times.' Lorelai would have laughed if it wasn't all so painful. *Grayson.*

'So all this time you thought you were the only one and all it would have taken was a serious conversation with your mum to find out that was far from the truth? Bloody hell!' Joanie chuckled in disbelief.

'I know,' Lorelai groaned. 'No one knows how frustrating that is more than me. But I know now and that's all that matters. We'll make up for lost time, and I'll tell you all the details soon, but focus, Joanie. Grayson. I need to stop him from getting on that plane. My grandma and my mum managed to have happy marriages with the people they loved, so I know it's possible for me to have that too. It'll be tough but I *can* do the same.'

'I'm so pleased for you, Lollie. I was so worried before. I knew you weren't happy.'

'I *was* happy, Joanie!'

'Not as happy as you could have been, though.' Joanie had her there.

Lorelai sighed. 'Alright, I'll admit to that. But none of this means anything if I can't stop Grayson getting on that plane.'

'One sec, I'm putting you on speaker.' Lorelai heard some shuffling sounds as Joanie set her phone down on her desk. Then Joanie cracked her knuckles down the line. 'OK. I'm going to search Facebook for someone who works at the same theatre as Grayson, and hope they're online this late. I'll send them a message to see if they know anything about when he was leaving the country so we can figure out if he's already left.' The sound of Joanie bashing her fingers against her laptop keyboard echoed through the phone speaker.

'I'm fascinated and terrified by how quickly you came up with that idea.'

'Do you want my help or not?' Joanie snapped, audibly pausing her feverish typing.

'Yes. Sorry. Keep searching!'

Joanie managed to find two people who worked with Grayson

who were online. One didn't respond. The other could only tell them that he finished work on Saturday.

'It's now two a.m. on Monday morning! He could have left anytime yesterday for all we know!' Lorelai's heart pounded in her chest, and dark spots were swimming in and out of her vision.

'Or he might not leave until later this morning! Don't give up just yet, Lollie. Deep breaths!'

'Can you look up flight times? From Heathrow airport specifically?'

'Of course. What was his destination?' Joanie asked and Lorelai wracked her brain. *Did he tell even me?*

'I… I don't know! Oh god, oh god, oh god.'

Lorelai became numb. No more tears came and even though her cheeks were burning hot, an icy chill ran through her. *Is this it? Have I lost him?* And then, she heard her grandmother's voice… *Don't give up, sweetheart. Fight for him. Save him. Love him.*

Lorelai shook her head, and made herself stand up, despite her legs feeling shaky. She squeezed her hands into fists and inhaled slowly. *I will save you, Grayson.*

'OK. What's the plan? What can we do next?' Lorelai asked but Joanie only exhaled down the phone.

'I… I don't know. I don't know what else we can try.'

'No, Joanie, we can't give up! We have to find him!'

'I know! I know we do but I don't think there's much else we can do. Not right now. It's so late.'

There was no way Lorelai would sleep tonight. 'Get some sleep, Joanie, and call me when you wake up. I'm going to keep calling him and I'll see if I can get hold of anyone else online. I'll let you know if—'

Lorelai felt her phone vibrate against her face. She pulled it away and her heart jumped into her mouth. It was Grayson.

'It's him!' she shrieked. 'It's him. He's calling! I have to go. Bye, bye, bye, bye!'

Joanie was screaming good luck but Lorelai barely registered it as she ended that call, and accepted Grayson's.

'Lorelai?' Just the sound of his voice, alive and well, was enough to send her reeling.

'Hi! Yes! It's me!' she squeaked, tears spilling from her eyes in sheer relief. She held a hand to her heart to try to steady the drumming in her chest.

'Hi,' Grayson said neutrally. He sounded neither pleased nor irritated to speak to her but Lorelai couldn't worry about that now. He was alive. There was still a chance she could save him. 'Isn't it super late there?'

'It's two in the morning. Wait... what do you mean *there*? Where are you?'

'I'm in New York. I've literally just landed. You were calling just as I was turning my phone on after the flight.'

'New York. Right.' Lorelai tried to remember everything she could about the vision she'd seen. What kind of plane was he on? Which airline was it? How old had he really looked? Was his death as imminent as she had thought? With a jolt she realised Grayson would have to fly home at some point. It hadn't been the outbound flight she had seen go up in flames – it was Grayson's return flight. 'What are you doing in New York?'

'I'm here on holiday. I'm going to watch a show on Broadway, that sort of thing.'

'When's your flight home?'

'Friday. Lorelai, what is this? Why are you interrogating me?' He laughed but it was a short, sharp laugh that made her stomach flutter with panic. 'I haven't heard from you in almost two weeks, not since you ditched me for the second time in this very short... relationship? Friendship? I don't even know what you'd call it.'

'I know. I know. You think I'm crazy and you have every right to, but I can explain.' Lorelai was ready to lay it all out for him.

'You've said that before,' he muttered.

'I realise how frustrating I must seem but please, just listen for a moment. This is really important.'

'Lorelai, I just don't think this is for me,' Grayson said firmly. 'This is too confusing, and I deserve more.'

It was a punch in the stomach, but one that wasn't wholly undeserved. That made it all the worse.

'I get that.' Lorelai ignored her breaking heart. 'I really do, and you're right, but that doesn't change what I have to say.'

'I'm sorry but I don't want to hear it.' He paused to take a breath and Lorelai heard the emotion rattle through it. 'You hurt me. I know that sounds stupid because we haven't known each other for long, but I really liked you. I felt... connected to you. I thought you felt the same, but you kept running away. Literally. It was humiliating and I'm just not the sort of person who's going to waste time chasing after someone who clearly doesn't want to be chased so... goodbye, Lorelai.'

Lorelai jumped to her feet as if she could run after him. As if the urgency in her physical movements might make him stay. 'No wait! Wait! Grayson!'

But he was gone.

'No, Grayson, no!'

She collapsed onto her bed, feeling as though she was shattering into a million pieces. She had been so close. She'd had him on the phone, talking to her, and she'd failed to make him listen. Failed to save him. She should have just blurted it out. Talked over him. Yelled something that would grab his attention. If she had yelled, 'YOU'RE GOING TO DIE!' he would have had to listen to her. He wouldn't ignore something like that.

She snatched up her phone and tried calling Grayson again and again but it went straight to voicemail each time. He had turned off his phone, not wanting to hear from her anymore. Not wanting *her*. The sting of rejection cut through her, but more than that was the panic and helplessness. This was so much bigger than her hurt feelings.

There was a gentle tap on the door. When Lorelai didn't answer, her mother opened the door and walked in. She looked at her daughter, a concerned look on her face. 'What happened?' she asked gently.

Lorelai shook her head, her head hanging low.

'Come on. We don't bottle things up anymore, you and I. Spill.' Her mother sat next to her on the bed, and pulled her into her arms.

'Grayson just called. From New York.'

'He made it there? That's good news,' Lila said slowly, knowing she didn't have the full story yet. The penny dropped a second later. 'Ah. It's the way back you're worried about.'

'Exactly. But he doesn't want to continue—' Lorelai waved her hands about meaninglessly '—whatever we were. He wouldn't even listen to me. He was so hurt that he wouldn't let me talk. I didn't have the chance to tell him not to get on the plane home.

I should've tried harder. He ended it – whatever *it* was. We barely got started, so why does this feel so... horrible?'

Lorelai leaned against her mother, finding comfort in her embrace. How strange this new closeness was, but it was a good strange.

'Because you *felt* something, Lorelai. That's why it hurts. It doesn't matter if you don't have a label for what it was because he made you feel something you haven't felt before. That's worth fighting for.'

'How? How can I fight for something he's already given up on? And he won't listen to me! He's turned his phone off, so how can I tell him he's going to die on the way home?' It was all so helpless. Grayson was going to die and there was nothing she could do about it.

'You've got savings, haven't you?' her mother asked.

'Savings? Yeah, of course. Why?'

'If he won't listen to you over the phone, sweetie, you're going to have to go to him. *Make* him listen. Even if he wants nothing more to do with you, that doesn't mean you can't still help him.'

The air stilled around Lorelai, and time stopped. She pulled away from her mother so she could look her in the face.

'Are you suggesting I get on a plane and fly to New York to warn Grayson he might die? That I run around one of the busiest cities in the world to find a man who wants nothing more to do with me, and convince him I'm not just some crazy person and I actually am trying to save his life?'

Lila dropped her voice to a conspiratorial whisper. 'That is exactly what I'm suggesting.'

The television was on, but Lila couldn't focus on anything other than her protruding belly. David laughed at the screen and nudged her arm at which she smiled but nothing could take her mind off the life inside her, the baby who was due to arrive any day.

Will she be like me? she wondered. *Please don't be like me.*

Lila pressed her palms against her bump and willed her wishes to come true, hoping her daughter could feel them. Lila wasn't a religious person, but she hoped if someone was up there listening, that they would heed her prayer and protect her daughter from this monstrous curse. Lila loved her husband dearly, but she lived in constant fear of him or anyone else discovering her secret, of finding out she wasn't who she said she was. From the outside, Lila's life looked idyllic. She was happily married, with a baby on the way, and she lived a full life with her friends. On paper, it was perfect. The truth, though, was that Lila was crushed by her secret every single day, and she struggled to hide the monster she knew she was. And now she had a new fear; if her child ended up with the same curse, would Lila think her a monster too?

For her entire pregnancy, Lila had fretted over what she would feel when the baby came. During her labour, all that mattered to Lila was bringing her daughter into the world safely, but once Lorelai was born, Lila distanced herself from her new-born. David had swept Lorelai into his arms, instantly in love, assuming his wife would come around soon.

Once home, Lila cried herself to sleep each night, still not able to bring herself to look at her daughter. One night, when Lorelai was a few weeks old, Lila was awoken in the night by a peculiar feeling. She listened out but all she heard was David's soft snoring – Lorelai wasn't crying. Lila climbed out of bed and softly padded over to where her baby daughter slept. Lila leaned over the crib and saw that little Lorelai was wide awake. She was staring at the mobile of stars and clouds that dangled above her, and in the inky darkness of that night, Lila finally looked in her daughter's eyes. The wave of love that crashed down all around her almost knocked her off her feet. Suddenly, she was certain of one single thing: her daughter was not and, never would be, a monster, and she would love and protect her fiercely until her final breath.

✦

Twenty-Eight

Lorclai was a jittery mess. She had only taken one flight in her life, a family holiday to Spain when she was eleven, but it wasn't her inexperience of flying that was making her anxious. Had she *really* just boarded a flight to New York? Had she really agreed to let her parents loan her the money for the trip? The plane doors were about to close so Lorelai pulled out her phone and fired off a couple of quick messages.

To Joanie: About to take off. Can't believe I'm doing this. Pray I didn't get it wrong, and this plane doesn't crash instead.

To her mother: About to take off. Wish me luck! Thank you for EVERYTHING. I love you xx

Then she switched off her phone and she braced herself for an uneasy eight hours. Lorelai couldn't believe she was doing this. It was the most spontaneous thing she had ever done. She was used to saying, 'One day.' Only those days never came – apart from this time. With the driving force of her mother and her best friend behind her, she'd booked herself on the earliest flight the following day. Yet, even though she knew this was a bit mad, never once had she questioned whether this was the right thing to do. Was this completely hare-brained and futile? Perhaps, but she had to try.

Lorelai replayed the conversation with Grayson in her head and sifted through all the memories she had of his smile, his eyes, his voice, and the way she had felt warm when she was with him. She remembered how she had pushed him away and ruined what could have been an incredible relationship, and a wave of sadness overwhelmed her. If she had known then what she knew now, would she have made different choices? Lorelai had behaved the way she had based on her knowledge at the time, but that didn't quell the feeling of loss. She knew she would have to try to switch off her emotions when she saw Grayson. To not give in to the desire to plead with him to give her a second chance or to let her explain. He had already given her a second chance and she only had herself to blame for squandering it. This trip was about his safety, and that was that. She would have to put her feelings to one side. All that mattered now was saving Grayson.

Thanks to one of her mother's over-the-counter sleeping pills, Lorelai slept for most of the flight, and was startled awake, groggy and confused, when the wheels hit the tarmac. As she stepped off the plane, her anxiety spiked again, and she knew this journey was far from over.

◆

Lorelai spent the afternoon in the hotel. When she had arrived, she had looked out of the window and been blown away by the size of the city. The sky was a clear blue and the sun was out and trying its hardest to warm up the city but as she leaned against the glass she could feel the bite of the cold trying to get to her. Everyone that rushed past on the street below had their scarves pulled up over their noses and, despite wearing gloves, they rubbed their fingers together or shoved their hands to the bottom of their coat pockets. New York was like London on steroids. Everything was taller, wider, bigger and noisier. The people moved faster and talked louder. Lorelai found herself looking up and paying attention. She had a sense of ease in London that came from familiarity and knowing its ins and outs. New York wasn't dissimilar to London in many ways but Lorelai didn't know this city the way she knew London so it felt like a completely different world. Almost fairy-tale-like. She had only seen New York in TV shows and movies but it had always felt as fantastical to her as Wonderland or Oz. She marvelled at the sheer scale of it all. She never for one second thought she would get to see it first-hand but now that she was there in such strange and depressing circumstances, she felt guilty for enjoying it. She wasn't here to sightsee.

She closed her curtains, had a shower and sat on the bed, wearing the hotel's bathrobe, flicking through channels on the television, until it edged closer to Broadway's showtime. She dressed simply in jeans, T-shirt, a jumper and a coat to shield her against the New York cold. Lorelai knew nothing about Grayson's New York plans other than he planned to see a show on Broadway. She had no idea where he was staying and the only part of his itinerary Joanie had managed to glean from his sporadic posts was that he was seeing this show on this night. Her plan was to walk around Broadway, and try to spot him in the crowds as he left the theatre. Someone would be smiling down on her and she would find Grayson, tell him what she needed to tell him and then come back to the hotel, and most likely weep. It wasn't a great plan. In truth, it was an awful one but it was the only one she had. She couldn't imagine Grayson being thrilled to see her after their last conversation, and she fully expected him to freak out about her following him to New York. That was stalker behaviour, she knew that, but what choice had she had if Grayson was ignoring her calls? Let him die? That wasn't an option.

Lorelai left the hotel and the city rolled past her as she walked along in the bitter evening air. She mumbled her speech for Grayson to herself, knowing full well it would all fly straight out of her head as soon as she saw him. As soon as her heart started to race and she forgot how to breathe she would forget everything she had rehearsed and she would make yet another hash of things. But the bottom line was that she had to at least try to stop him from getting on that plane home.

By the time she reached the theatre, people were already starting to leave. Even though it was dark and getting late, the lights of the theatre were so bright they lit up the whole street. Lorelai had to squint against them in order to see the faces of the people leaving below them. From her spot across the street, everyone was a silhouette against the backdrop of glitz and glamour. A hundred people passed her before she could scan their faces and a bubble of panic rose up into her throat at the prospect of coming this far just to see Grayson and having already missed him. She suddenly realised with a sickening jolt that this was quite literally her one shot. Her one and only chance to stop his death. Frantically she darted across the road, was almost clipped by a yellow taxi and began to pace up and down the front of the theatre, moving through the bodies and looking through the doors to see if she could see him. There was no sign of him. She checked Joanie's text message and made sure she definitely had the correct theatre, the right show and the right time. It all matched but he could have decided not to come. As Lorelai had begun to learn, one small decision could alter the rest of your life. If Grayson had decided not to come tonight because he wanted to go somewhere nice for dinner instead or if he simply decided to buy tickets for a different show, it was game over.

Dark spots began to appear in her vision and no matter how many times she tried to take a deep breath, her lungs just didn't fill. Not enough air was getting in. She had blown it. And now Grayson was going to die.

Grayson is going to die.

Grayson is going to die.

Grayson is going to die.

Grayson is going—

'Erm… excuse me, ma'am? Are you OK?'

Lorelai could hear the voice next to her but she couldn't look up to see who was asking the question. The lights were too bright. She felt a hand on her shoulder.

'Yes, I'm fine. Fine. I'm fine,' she stuttered.

Lorelai pushed herself away from the crowd, staggering back across the road. As the noise of the audience dissolved a little, she felt her chest loosen slightly. She leaned against a cold brick wall and turned her face so that it pressed against one of her burning cheeks.

'Damn it,' she whimpered.

Lorelai was exhausted to the very core of her being. All of

the worrying and the stress of trying to find Grayson, combined with what would happen if she didn't, hit her all at once. She stood like that, leaning against the wall, cold and alone, for a long time, the words running through her mind on repeat. *Grayson is going to die.* Eventually she managed to get her breathing under control and her vision cleared but her legs still felt shaky underneath her. The theatre was almost empty by the time she found the courage to look again but she knew it would be. She had had a panic attack and had blown it when it mattered the most. Without thinking, she dragged her feet in the direction of Times Square. She would figure out what to do and where to go from there. She was too far away from her hotel, and she needed to find somewhere to sit and regroup now.

The crowd was heavy in Times Square, all the theatregoers rubbing shoulder to shoulder, moving like cattle towards the nearest bars. She found a solitary empty seat opposite a row of food trucks. She was sure she would be moved along when someone saw she wasn't eating but she hoped by then she would have had enough time to figure out her plan of action. She sat down and dropped her head into her hands. She was freezing but her face was still hot, and there was a deep thumping building behind her eyes.

'The show is so different in London!' She heard the English accent before she had registered what it was saying. 'Yeah, I honestly think I prefer it back at home. Mmm. Maybe that's just because I'm used to it but I don't know. It was good to experience it somewhere new.'

It couldn't be…

Lorelai stood from her seat and whipped her head around,

scanning Times Square in a feverish panic. Because that had been Grayson's voice. She knew it. Lorelai knew his voice. Not only had she replayed his voicemail over and over again but every single conversation they had ever had was on a loop in her mind. She had been clinging on to every part of him, committing it to memory. There was no mistaking that voice. Lorelai stepped this way and that, thinking she could hear his voice again, but it drifted into nothingness each time.

Then, he appeared.

Grayson.

He was standing at the front of a queue of people by one of the food trucks. Each time the queue moved he would disappear for a moment, before reappearing again. He had his coat collar pulled up around his face and his phone tucked between his cheek and his shoulder as he reached over the counter for his order. Lorelai couldn't move. She was rooted to the spot, just watching him. The way he behaved when he didn't know someone was watching. The way he moved when he wasn't on his best behaviour. This was who he was when he was alone – Grayson being Grayson. Not for the first time, she was struck by the beauty of him, the way he smiled kindly at strangers, and the confidence with which he moved. The world wasn't ready to lose someone like Grayson. Lorelai wasn't ready to lose Grayson. She was desperate to keep him alive, and even if it was over between them, Grayson deserved to live a long and happy life. Alive and apart was better than dead and gone.

Before Lorelai could figure out the best way to approach him, he began to walk in her direction. She could hear his conversation more clearly the closer he got, and his glorious face came further into focus and then... there it was. The moment he saw her. There was an unmistakable breathlessness, a singular second of happiness after the recognition before it turned to confusion. Grayson could have walked away, he could have turned on his heel and been swallowed up by the city, but instead, he walked right up to her.

'Aden, I'm gonna have to call you back. Love you too. Bye.'

He slipped his phone into his pocket. Lorelai could see the rise and fall of his chest quicken. He blinked at her in disbelief and for the briefest of moments, a nanosecond that she would have missed had she not been looking at them, his lips lifted into a smile. And then it was gone. Lorelai knew one of them was going to have to say something but for just a moment she wanted to pretend that life was simple. As simple as meeting someone special, falling in love and living out a happily ever after. And death was a worry for long in the future when they were old and grey. For just the smallest amount of time she wanted to believe that the fairy tales and the movies she had held onto all her life could come true for her.

'What are you—'

'Please don't say anything,' Lorelai heard herself say.

She thought she would be terrified. She was so certain she would lose her nerve and fumble her way through what she needed to say. However, some hidden confidence, a dormant conviction about what she had to do, awakened within her and soothed and silenced her emotions.

'I don't need you to say anything. You've said what you needed to say and that's enough. I understand. The reason I'm here isn't to do with me. It's to do with you.' Lorelai paused. As predicted, her carefully rehearsed speech had deserted her. Before she could think it through properly, she blurted out, 'You're going to die. On your flight home to London something tragic is going to happen and you're not going to survive. If you're wondering how I know...' *No turning back now*, 'it's because when you kissed me for the first time back home, I saw it. It's a power I have. I see how people are going to die when I kiss them. It's a gift of sorts. Although I suppose it's only a gift if you listen to me and it saves your life. So please let it be a gift, Grayson. Don't get on that plane. Take a boat, hitch-hike, swim home for all I care. It doesn't matter how you get home just... *get home*. To Aden, to your mum, your dad, your aunt. They need you.'

Her shoulders dropped and the weight she had been carrying since her very first kiss all those years ago slipped from them and shattered at her feet. A friend, a mother and a love all now knew her secret. It was the holy trinity she didn't know she needed. Tears began to flow but she didn't turn her face away. Somewhere along the way she had decided to stop hiding. This was who she was and this was how she felt, and she no longer felt afraid of letting people know it.

'Lorelai, I... What? I don't...' Grayson was at a loss. He stared at her, opening and closing his mouth like a fish.

Lorelai wiped her face and managed to compose herself. 'Don't get on the plane, Grayson. This isn't a plea for you to give me a second chance. Or a third chance. I know I screwed up every chance you gave me, and I wouldn't give me another chance, either. Even though I'd love just one more because... well...' She smiled and said the truest thing she had ever said, 'because the truth is I love *you*, Grayson. I know it's mad to say that when we barely even got started but I've spent so long running from my feelings and I ended up running right into you. That has to mean something. I *know* it means something. But this isn't about me anymore. If I'm not the one for you then I want you to live to find the person who is. I want someone to feel as lucky as I felt… still feel that I got to spend even just a small amount of time with you. So don't get on that plane, Grayson.' She wanted to reach out and hug him, kiss his cheek, squeeze his shoulder but she knew that was no longer her place.

Grayson opened his mouth but when he couldn't find the right words, he closed it again. So many emotions flashed across his face. Confusion about what she was trying to tell him, hurt by how she'd treated him and now she was saying she loved him, frustrated that none of it made any sense. In the end he said, 'I just don't understand, Lorelai.' He squeezed the bridge of his nose between his gloved fingers. 'What you're saying… it's… it's madness. It makes no sense. And I can't just make other plans and arrangements based off… off…' He couldn't bring himself to say it aloud.

Lorelai's heart sank. He didn't believe her. But she had to try one more time. 'I know. *I know.* Don't you think I hear how this sounds? But I couldn't not try. I couldn't let you…' Lorelai trailed off, not knowing what more she could say. 'I know I've given you very little reason to but… if you want to live, you have to trust me. Please.'

Grayson stared at her, rendered speechless. When he didn't say anything for a long time, Lorelai knew there was nothing else she could do now. He needed to make the choice to believe her by himself. Lorelai took one last look at his confused, beautiful face and turned away from him. As she walked back in the direction of her hotel, she didn't look over her shoulder. She had no need to. Lorelai had done what she came to do. Now she just had to pray that he had listened.

Twenty-Nine

The thought of staying in New York, in the same city as Grayson and not being with him in the way she wanted, made Lorelai feel wretched. She had never longed for her mother in this way before and, despite Lila being over three thousand miles away, Lorelai missed her with a fierceness that shocked her, and it was that closeness that kept her afloat in this period of darkness. As soon as she made it back to the hotel, numb from more than just the cold, she began to pack.

'Hello darling, how did it go?'

Lorelai had made the call to her mother, not the other way around, and yet as soon as she heard Lila's kind voice, Lorelai wasn't able to speak.

'Hello? Lorelai? I think it might be a bad line?'

She tried to speak through her tears but ended up squeaking as she tried to take a breath.

'Oh sweetheart. Get your breath back and then tell me what he said.' Lila waited patiently as she swallowed back her emotion. Lorelai didn't take the phone away from her ear all the while, for the first time finding strength in having her mother close.

'He didn't say anything really.'

'What do you mean? Nothing at all?'

'Well, he said he didn't understand but that was to be expected.'

'You told him he was going to die!' Her mother shrieked down the phone so loudly Lorelai had to pull her ear away from the speaker.

'I know, but if you didn't have the power you have, would you believe someone who came up to you and told you how you were going to die? You'd think they'd lost the plot.'

'Possibly,' her mother said stubbornly, 'but I think I'd be a little wary from then on, just to be safe.'

'That's the best we can hope for now. I did walk away from him quite quickly once I realised he was struggling with what I was saying. But then again he didn't stop me either,' she added.

'Then he doesn't deserve you, Lorelai.' Lila's voice had hardened, her tone clipped.

'Mum...' Lorelai almost laughed. She'd never given her mother an opportunity to be protective. Despite the ache from her interaction with Grayson, the squeeze of love in her chest for her mum made her feel safe.

'No, listen to me, darling. Power or no power, no man deserves you at your best if he can't handle you at your worst. Regardless of what your worst may be. If you two were meant to be together, he would have stopped you from leaving and would never have let you go. It's his loss and his loss alone. There is someone out there who would help you bury bodies if he had to and would feel lucky about it, too!'

Lorelai laughed and her chest loosened, her breathing coming more easily now. If she'd known she had been missing out on pep talks like this all these years, she would have opened up to her mother a long time ago. She wasn't in a place to believe what her mother was saying was true, but it felt good that someone cared enough about her to try to make her smile.

'Then I guess the search for love continues. Well... I guess the search begins really. I didn't expect to find Grayson and before him I was quite content with Joanie by my side.'

'Have you spoken to her?'

Lorelai could hear the rattle of a teaspoon in a mug as her mother stirred what she assumed was a freshly brewed cup of tea. Suddenly, she longed to be back in her parents' warm house with a cup of tea of her own. Not in cold and brutal New York where she felt desperately unwanted.

'Not since I saw Grayson. I'll call her when I get on the boat and she'll be waiting for me in Southampton.'

There was no way Lorelai was getting on a plane for obvious reasons, so she had spent a considerable amount of her savings booking herself onto a five-day cruise across the Atlantic, which finished in Southampton where Joanie had promised to meet her. Five days alone with nothing but her thoughts and battered heart for company, but it was what she needed. Time to be alone and regroup before getting back to reality.

'Well, you make sure to call me when you get back to London.'

'Actually, Mum... would you mind if I came and stayed a bit longer? I don't think I'm quite done asking questions.' It was a snap decision but relief flooded her as she said it.

'What about the cinema?' Lila asked and she was right. She had no holiday left to take, and Wesley wouldn't hold her position for her forever. But for the first time in her life, she wondered if working at the cinema was where she was really meant to be.

'Maybe… maybe this was the push I needed to quit.'

'But darling, you love working there!'

'I know. I know I do, and I would really miss but. But maybe …' Lorelai's heart pounded as she thought about what she wanted to say. She knew she had to say it out loud to someone before she scared the feeling away. 'Maybe it's time I do some dream chasing after all. Running the Page to Screen Club was a fun distraction but it just isn't quenching my thirst like I thought it would. Maybe this is the push I needed to quit my job and finally show my scripts to someone who might actually be able to make my dreams a reality. And anyway, it's not just about work. I've spent so long feeling alone when I didn't have to, and now I need my family more than ever. I need *you* more than ever.'

'Oh, darling—' Lila's voice caught '—I would love that.'

'OK, Mum. Thank you. For… all of it, you know.' Lorelai felt the sting of fresh tears and she knew she needed to hang up soon or she would never stop crying. 'Speak soon. Love you.'

'I love you, too. Don't you forget it.'

Lorelai finished packing, cried some more before taking a shower, and then she cried again. She fell asleep eventually, and when her alarm woke her there was a blissful second of innocence before *everything* came flooding back. She allowed herself one final cry before leaving the hotel. She gave her room a mournful look before she closed the door and headed to the hotel's reception.

'Hi, I'm just checking out.' Lorelai kept her puffy eyes down, hunting for her sunglasses at the bottom of her bag.

'Room number?' the woman at the desk asked.

Lorelai noted that they must be around the same age and she

longed for the same authority the other woman had. She held herself in a way Lorelai could only dream of, and she looked like an adult. An adult who had her life together. Whereas Lorelai felt decidedly *un*together, and had no idea what to do next once she returned to her life. Where did she go from here?

'Eighteen-zero-two.' Lorelai shook her head so her hair fell over her face. The woman tapped away on the computer.

'Says here that you're not due to check out until tomorrow.' The woman's perfectly tweezed eyebrows came together in puzzlement.

'I know but… family emergency,' Lorelai said.

'Oh no, I'm so sorry to hear that you'll be leaving us so soon. You have no extra charges with us so that's everything taken care of. Is there anything else I can do for you today?'

Yes, actually. Can you teach me how to be a fully functioning adult who doesn't feel like she's going to fall apart at any given moment, because you seem to have that down? Or if there's a small chance that you're actually dying inside just like I am, can you teach me to be better at hiding it? Because you and I both know I have tears in my eyes and I look like I'm about to have a nervous breakdown.

'No. Thank you,' Lorelai said instead.

The taxi ride to the Manhattan cruise terminal was excruciatingly long and lonely. Standing in the queue to board, surrounded by mainly couples who were there on honeymoons or celebrating anniversaries or simply enjoying spontaneous romantic getaways, was even lonelier. The sad little tilt of the head people gave her when she said she was a party of one was enough to bring her to tears – again. And that only prompted further gestures of pity. An elderly woman even reached out and placed a reassuring hand on her shoulder as Lorelai's eyes welled up for the thousandth time that day and said, 'Time heals everything, my sweet,' before taking her husband's hand and leading him onto the ship.

The ship itself was spectacular and she realised why tickets were the price they were. Lorelai could hardly believe she was in a floating vessel that was about to travel across the Atlantic Ocean. It was vast and grand, decked out in marble and crystal. Lorelai's gaze was drawn to the large chandelier above her. It was dripping with jewels that swayed gently in the breeze, casting rainbows of light onto the guests below. She was offered a glass of champagne as she walked into the main foyer, which she downed in one long gulp. She hid the empty glass and took another, pretending she hadn't received the first. She closed her eyes and felt the rush of the champagne go to her head and dull the pain of losing Grayson. She tried to focus on rebuilding her relationship with her mother and the fact that she would be seeing Joanie again in less than a week. While Joanie was on her mind, Lorelai pulled out her phone to give her the heads-up that she was safe and on board the ship but Joanie had beaten her to it.

Safe travels! I hear the view from the bow of the ship is spectacular. Go and get a good look at the New York skyline before you head home. You'll regret it if you don't. x Lorelai slowly made her way to the bow, taking in the opulence as she went. She had never experienced anything quite like it and although it made her feel out of place, she tried her best to appreciate the beauty. This was what she needed to do – focus on the positives. She made her way outside, and the sea air against her face cooled her rising anxiety a little. The view even more so. Joanie was spot on. It was breathtaking. The sun was disappearing behind the silhouetted buildings, the light just glinting off the highest windows. She could see the queue to board the ship on the dock and it was still as long as it was when Lorelai was in it, and although she knew Grayson wouldn't be there, she still scanned the line just in case.

She knew she would do that in every crowd she was in for the rest of her life. Search for him. For another chance to get it right. The cruelty of the situation hit her, full force – she had learned how to finally open up by pushing away the first person she had wanted to open up to. Was this yet another prank the universe had decided to play on her? She sincerely hoped the bag of tricks was now empty and the universe would leave her alone. She sighed. She would be OK on her own if that's how her life ended up. But was love a real possibility for her now? Would there ever be anyone better than Grayson?

She felt a sharp twinge in her chest. Someone better than Grayson didn't exist. He was it for her, she knew that. She recalled her conversation with Joanie before she had finally fallen asleep the previous evening.

'It only feels like someone better than Grayson doesn't exist because this is the eye of the storm,' Joanie had said to her. 'You won't be able to think rationally for a while because it's all too painful. Too raw. And maybe you only want Grayson this much because you know you can't have him. It's a classic forbidden fruit scenario! But that also means you can get over him faster. Just focus on getting yourself home and I'll take care of you.'

They had both known Joanie was only saying these things to make Lorelai feel better, so Lorelai had played along. It was better than dwelling on the truth.

'By *take care of* do you mean feed me Ben and Jerry's and margaritas until I'm severely ill?' Lorelai had asked.

Joanie had chuckled down the line by way of an answer, and Lorelai had been hit with another wave of heavy sadness. It would take more than ice cream and cocktails to make her feel better. What Lorelai had felt for Grayson hadn't been a 'forbidden fruit' situation. She had met men before who had shown an interest in her and not one of them had ever awoken the kind of feelings in her that Grayson had. Never once had that part of her raised its head in interest until Grayson had walked into the small function room and helped himself to tea in a polystyrene cup and a broken custard cream. She would never find the words to accurately describe what it was about him that made her light up, that made her feel warm from the inside out, that made her trust him when the thought of trusting someone scared her so much. It was its own kind of magic and she knew better than to try to explain something unexplainable.

'Beautiful, isn't it?'

The voice came from her left, slightly muffled by the sea breeze. Another passenger. She had wondered if she might get a few people trying to talk to the lonely girl who was travelling on her own. She had prepared a few polite phrases about enjoying the peace of being alone but she didn't expect to have to use them so soon. She dare not look at the person trying to engage her in conversation in case they took it as an invitation to continue.

'Very,' she said, hoping that was enough to satiate this stranger's need for conversation.

'Too bad you didn't get to spend longer in the city.'

'Mmm,' she agreed automatically, hoping that this chat would be over soon. It took her a few seconds to fully process what the stranger had said. The speed of her own thoughts, the noise of the people around her, and her heavy heart seemed to have dulled her senses. She knew that voice. Of course she did. Yet she still didn't dare to turn her head towards him, for fear she may be hallucinating. 'What are you doing here?' she asked softly, testing the waters.

'Well, someone told me if I got on a plane, that would be game over for me. And although I don't entirely understand what she meant or how she could possibly know, it freaked me out enough to find a different way home,' Grayson said.

'And it just happened to be this cruise at this time?'

'No… Joanie might have had something to do with that.'

'She called you?'

'No. I called her. It's not every day you meet a psychic and you left in such a hurry. I have a few more questions and needed to find you.'

Lorelai finally turned to him. There he was. She wasn't imagining it. He was standing there, and if she reached out she could touch him. 'I'm not a psychic and… I know how it sounds, Grayson.'

He was keeping the November chill at bay under a thick coat, a knitted scarf and a pair of grey fingerless gloves. She wanted nothing more to be close to him, sharing his body heat, feeling his arms around her. Maybe he would let her. He was there, in front of her, wasn't he? Asking questions, trying to understand, despite everything she had put him through. That had to count for something.

'Before these last few weeks, I had never dreamed of telling anyone. Anyone other than Joanie, that is.' Grayson raised an eyebrow. 'Yes, Joanie knows. She thinks I'm a superhero.'

Another person she'd put through hell because she wasn't willing to put the effort in to understand herself. It was easier to be a mess and let everyone else pick up the pieces than it was to do the work yourself and take responsibility, to hold yourself accountable. But she was ready now — it was time to make a change.

'She's the one person who said from the beginning I needed to trust you. To let myself feel whatever I was feeling for you and open up. She's been your biggest champion since day one. But I tried and I failed. I freaked out and fell at the first hurdle. And even though I have ruined things with you, I couldn't just sit back and let you die, Grayson. I just couldn't.'

Lorelai's voice cracked, and she started to cry for what felt like the hundredth time in twenty-four hours. Grayson took a step forward, reaching out to her. She couldn't believe he was here, now offering her comfort and her heart called out to him. She felt the pull towards him but Lorelai resisted.

'Just wait. I'm on a roll. These last few days have been the most I've ever talked about this properly and I don't want to scare this confidence away.' Grayson nodded slowly, lowered his arms and wrapped them around himself instead. 'For so long I've thought of myself as a monster. That this thing I can do is uncontrollable and so I locked myself in a cage. I didn't trust myself around anyone and I didn't trust anyone around myself. But I realise now, too late, that it's not enough to shrug and say, "This is what life is like when you're a monster." Especially when you've made no effort to discover what kind of monster you are or even if you are a monster at all. Meeting you has made me question everything, and I didn't know if I was strong enough to face up to it all, but I think I am now, and that's because of you. If I'm capable of seeing death then maybe I'm meant to be capable of... saving lives, too.' Lorelai paused to catch her breath.

'I'd really like for you to stop calling yourself a monster,' Grayson said gently, but with a determined look in his eyes. 'That's not who you are.'

'How do you know that?' Lorelai asked quietly.

'Because I just do. Because I know you. Deal with it.' Grayson's voice was matter-of-fact and Lorelai couldn't help but smile through her tears. He continued, 'And I'd say you are definitely capable of saving lives, Lorelai.' He gestured around him. 'You know, if it all turns out to be true.'

'Still not convinced?'

'I don't think you have any reason to lie, but is it wrong of me to want some kind of proof?'

'It kind of is, if that proof comes in the form of other people dying on that plane.'

'Oh god...' Grayson's eyes widened.

Lorelai reassured him quickly. 'I've called the airline. I doubt they'll believe me, but I said they needed to check the aircraft. I've asked my mother to keep calling too and say the same thing. If anyone can make sure someone double-checks something, it's my mum.'

Grayson nodded thoughtfully, his face still etched with concern. He still needed more.

'The first two boys I kissed both died the way I saw they would. If that's not proof enough I don't what is.' Lorelai shrugged.

'There's no real way to test what I can do. Not without watching someone suffer.'

'Shit. I'm sorry.'

Lorelai held up a hand and waved away his apology. 'I don't want to become some vigilante superhero. I don't want my life to become about kissing random strangers in order to save lives.' She turned to the skyline. She thought about all the people in all of those buildings. How many of them were close to death? How many of them had less time ahead of them than behind them? How many of their paths could Lorelai realistically alter with just one kiss? Was wanting a normal life selfish when she had been given such a life-changing, or a life-*giving*, power? These were the new questions she now faced.

'You don't have to,' Grayson said. 'But maybe it's time to think about… whatever it is you can do as being something other than a thing you need to be afraid of. It's part of who you are and who you are is… amazing.' His eyes brightened and Lorelai's heart leapt.

'Amazing? Really? After all this, that's how you would describe me?'

He took her hand in response, and instantly her whole body ignited at his touch, just like it had the day they'd met.

'You can be a temperamental, infuriating, pain in the neck and still be amazing. People are complex creatures, Lorelai.' Grayson drew circles on the back of her hand with his thumb.

'I think that's something I understand now. You're not either a monster or a saint. Most of the time it's…'

'It's a bit of both?' Grayson laughed nervously and inched closer to her. He was so close now, Lorelai could smell the mint on his breath.

'Yes, we're all a bit of both.'

Lorelai's hair caught the wind and a strand blew in front of her face. Grayson delicately removed it with a finger and tucked it behind her ear, lingering to caress her face.

'You know, I've only had a second kiss once.' Lorelai smiled.

'Really?' Grayson was hovering just inches from her face, waiting for her to close the distance, just as he had in Trafalgar Square. Only this time Lorelai knew she wouldn't run.

'The first kiss is usually enough to put me off kissing them again. Or kissing anyone again for that matter. But I did a bit of experimenting just after I'd met you. I know this is essentially me admitting to kissing a bunch of people who weren't you but it was all because I was preparing for... you. Someone kissed me and I saw his death change between kisses, so it made me want to know more. I needed to know I wasn't going to seal your fate and kill you off if I kissed you. I needed to know I was only watching someone die. Not causing them to die. I kissed this guy and I saw him die on his bike. So Joanie stole it and when I kissed him again the vision had changed.'

'So you're not like... the grim reaper?' He raised an eyebrow.

'No.' Lorelai winced a little but still managed a small smile, 'Thankfully not. My lips do not have the power to set someone's death in stone. It can still change whether I've kissed them or not.'

'OK,' Grayson said, a small frown on his face, 'I'm new to this but I *think* I understand. It's good to know I'm not in any danger.' He smiled, tipping her chin up to him with his finger.

'None whatsoever,' she whispered. Lorelai took hold of the lapels of his coat and pulled him to her and without leaving herself a moment to hesitate, to second-guess herself or to change her mind, she kissed Grayson with everything she had.

There was no plane. There was no fire and no screaming. Instead, there was a garden. It was so very green, lined with trees so dense that the sun had a hard time shining through. Lorelai could hear the birds chirping above them and there was a clinking sound coming from behind her, like people laying a table, getting ready to eat. Just like when she kissed Joanie, she realised quickly that she was seeing everything through the eyes of her older self. Eyes that didn't see quite as well as they used to, even though she had glasses perched on the end of her nose. A peaceful tiredness overcame her and she sank into it. It was almost overwhelming to the point of tears. She felt a hand shake hers gently. Lorelai looked down and saw Grayson's umber skin against her own wrinkled hand, his fingers entwined with hers.

'Lorelai?' His voice sounded quiet and weaker than she was used to but it was him. It was definitely him. She found it hard to raise her head to him, but when she finally saw his smile the struggle was worth it.

'Grayson.' She could barely raise her voice to more than a feeble whisper but she knew he had heard her because he squeezed her hand.

'Shh, don't speak, darling.' He rubbed his thumb against the back of her hand like he had done only moments ago on the bow of the ship. 'Thank you for saving me. In more ways than one. Thank you for giving us this life. It's been a pleasure. I love you. More than anything but now it's time to let go.' Grayson didn't sound sad. He sounded prepared. Like he knew this moment was coming. Lorelai tried to squeeze his hand, to let him know she understood but all her strength had left her. All she could manage was one last smile before everything went dark. Lorelai had seen something she'd never seen before; her own ending. Which could only mean one thing: Grayson would outlive her.

'Well?' Grayson asked a few moments after they parted, his cheeks wet from her tears.

'Sorry,' Lorelai said, wiping her tears from his face.

'I'm getting used to you crying when you kiss me. I'm trying not to take it personally.' He took the end of his scarf and gently dried her tears. She looked at this man who had her heart and for the first time in forever she felt... free.

Three people now knew her secret and not a single one of them had run from her. For years she had shut people out for fear of them discovering the real Lorelai and abandoning her. She realised now it was Lorelai who had abandoned herself. It was Lorelai who had trapped herself inside a cage, choosing a life that left her unfulfilled and in denial. Now she had a mother who not only understood her but had experienced what she was going through. She had a best friend who had always been there for her and was prepared to fight anyone who hurt her. And now a love. A person she adored who knew her secret and had still chosen to kiss her. A man she had run from on several occasions, who was still standing in front of her with his arms wide open. Now, not only had she successfully saved Grayson's life but she had given him a life longer than her own. She had given him decades that she would share with him, but so would his family. She and Grayson would be together always and she knew she would do all she could to make sure their life was a happy one, full of love and laughter and total honesty.

'So... what did you see?' Grayson asked, his eyes beginning to glisten as well.

Lorelai remembered her grandmother's note. *Never tell someone how they're going to die. No one wants to be burdened with that information. Even if they say they do.* Telling Grayson, she decided, would be a burden on him. It might stop him from living life to the full. She would take away the idea of living every day as if it were his last and where was the fun in that?

Lorelai shook her head and leaned in for another kiss as she whispered, 'Let's just wait and see, shall we?'

Thirty

Six Months Later

'You did great. You can relax now.' Joanie put her arm around Lorelai's shoulders.

Minus the initial troublemakers, every single member of the Page to Screen club had continued to attend each month. Even Riggs had decided to join. He'd got the job working at the voice-over studio but realised he'd missed the cinema too so had joined the club. Lorelai realised, too, that she had never given him enough credit. He seemed to not only be enjoying himself but also genuinely cared about being part of the discussion and had become a valued member of the group. As for Lorelai, she had had every intention of resigning, but Wesley had convinced her to drop down to part-time instead, so she now balanced life at The Duchess with pursuing her screenwriting dreams. She had never been happier.

Even though the club members had all become closer and Lorelai knew everyone better now, she still wasn't entirely com-fortable talking in front of everyone. Public speaking wasn't one of her skills but she was thankful that the club had become exactly what she had envisioned it to be. Everyone was settling into their seats in the smaller screen at The Duchess, and Lorelai and Joanie were standing at the back, surveying the crowd. The movie they were watching this month was *The Princess Bride*.

'Thanks. Oh, shhh! It's starting!' The lights dimmed and the title card of the movie appeared on the screen at which the group clapped and whooped.

'Don't shush me!' Joanie gave Lorelai a playful shove. 'Shush *him*. He's the one that's late and making a nuisance of himself.' Joanie pointed to the doorway where Grayson was holding his sopping wet umbrella at arm's length and using his already soggy coat sleeve to dry his face. He squinted through the dark, scanning the seats and the backs of heads and Lorelai couldn't help grinning. Grayson was looking for her.

'Pssst,' she whispered. His head whipped around and when he saw her, his face broke into a smile. Six months had passed since they had returned from New York. Things weren't *easy* per se but life with Grayson was more than Lorelai could have ever hoped for. At first, Grayson had found it hard to wrap his head around her ability, and he'd asked endless questions – many of which Lorelai hadn't had answers to – but the most important thing was that he believed her and he hadn't run from her. It had also taken him some time to truly trust that she wasn't going to get cold feet and run away again. She had had some making up to do but now, six months down the line, the dust had started to settle and they had begun to find their groove.

And the nightmares had stopped.

'Hello, you,' she whispered.

'Hello, *you*. Sorry I'm late. I got held up getting out of the theatre.' Grayson wrapped his arms around her and although he was damp from the rain she didn't mind. He pressed his lips to her cheek and lingered there a while. Upon learning what it meant for Lorelai to kiss someone, what it put her through, Grayson never surprised her with a kiss. He always let her come to him. Lorelai could see how unnatural that was for him as he was an affectionate person by nature but she made sure he never felt unwanted. It turned out that Lorelai liked surprising *him* with kisses, and Grayson was a fan of this set-up. He loosened his arms but, before he let go entirely, Lorelai let her lips brush against his for a moment.

She had learned a lot about herself since her initial experiments. Her vision hadn't changed over the course of their relationship, however she wasn't forced to watch it again and again when their kisses were pecks. Shorter kisses were safer kisses. She had also learned her focus played a large role. If she was able to ground herself more in the present and focus on the Grayson in her arms as opposed to the Grayson in her mind, the vision wasn't as clear or as loud and it didn't pain her as much to watch. Through every new discovery, Grayson was curious but never pushed her to talk more than she was willing, and he was understanding if not able to completely know what it was she was going through. They were finding their way through uncharted waters but they both knew that as long as they held on to each other, they wouldn't drown.

'How'd it go today?' he asked.

'I didn't throw up so...!' They gave each other a double thumbs up and leaned against each other, giggling.

'Shhhhhh!' Joanie held a finger to her lips. 'You're going to miss half the film if you keep wittering on.'

'Inconceivable!' Grayson said, quoting from the movie they were about to watch.

'You keep using that word but I don't think it means what you think it means!' Lorelai added and they burst out laughing again. Joanie rolled her eyes but was smiling happily at the pair of them.

'You two have officially become *that* couple.' Joanie moved away from them and found an empty seat. She kept throwing them looks like she was embarrassed to be seen with them, which just made them laugh harder. Grayson looped his arm around Lorelai's waist and dipped her back, playing out their own scene from the movies.

'Do I love you? My god, if your love were a grain of sand...' he began but Lorelai pressed a finger to his lips so she could finish the quote for him.

'...mine would be a universe of beaches.' There was a moment of silence between them as the movie played on. 'It might be a quote from a movie,' she said, 'but I mean it, you know. I do. Love you, I mean.'

'There's a reason I picked that quote, too.' They grinned at each other. 'That's the first time you've said that since New York.' His eyes sparkled in the light of the cinema screen, his arm still around her waist, holding her tightly, wanting to stay in the moment for just a little longer.

'I know. I didn't want to rush you into feeling something you didn't feel before now. But it doesn't mean that I haven't been feeling it,' Lorelai said, suddenly serious.

'It does seem a shame to use someone else's words for such an important declaration but I'm not sure I could come up with anything better on my own,' Grayson said, looking away from her, feeling exposed, but Lorelai took his chin in her hand and pulled his gaze back to her. She couldn't help but think of her vision. She had never told Grayson what she had seen and never would, so their long future together was her happy little secret. But it didn't stop her from dropping the odd hint every now and again.

'My love, we have a lifetime to find the perfect way to say I love you.' Grayson smiled against her palm at hearing her say those three words. 'And so for now, let's keep it simple and start with this kiss.' Lorelai closed the gap between them and kissed him like there was no tomorrow. But Lorelai knew that, in fact, they had many more tomorrows to come.

Epilogue

How often does death cross your mind? Is it once a year, when you're reminded of your own mortality? When you're scared into living every day as if it's your last? Or is it daily, when something as simple as the prospect of a kiss sends you reeling into the abyss?

The thought of a kiss used to send me reeling. To the point where I vowed never to kiss another living soul again. It was a vow of solitude that went against everything I knew in my heart to be right. I was a hopeless romantic who had promised to live a life hopelessly void of romance. And then I met someone who made me think of death not as something to be feared, but as something that can be embraced with open arms — but only if you have spent all the time leading up to it actually living. Being reminded of death doesn't have to be the burden I always thought it was. It most certainly doesn't make me a monster. It just means I've read the last page of the book. I know how the story ends. But what happens up until that final page?

Well, that's up to us.

Acknowledgements

Huge love and thanks to everyone at HQ! Mel Hayes, Grace Dent, Stephanie Heathcote, Melissa Kelly, Joanna Rose, Lucy Richardson, Rebecca Fortuin, Georgina Green, Harriet Williams, Angela Thomson, Sara Eusebi, Darren Shoffren, Kelly Webster and, of course, the wonderful Manpreet Grewal! You've all been so brilliant and patient through such trying times. Thanks for taking me on and for making this book what it's become.

Thank you to my book agent, Hannah Ferguson. Thank you for continuing to navigate through all the theatrical obstacles that make bookish life more complicated than it needs to be. Speaking of theatrics, hugs also to my team at Curtis Brown, who have to navigate my bookish obstacles which make theatrical life more complicated than it already is. I don't know where I'd be without any of you!

There's a running joke that all the women in my family are witches so Mum, Nan, Auntie Julie, Auntie Kim… if you start seeing dead people, please give me the heads up. And, of course, huge thanks to all my family: Dad, Grandad, Tom, Gi and the Gremlins, who support everything I do.

Thanks to my friends who love me at my worst. Scott Paige, Mollie Melia Redgrave, Paul Bradshaw, Matt McDonald, Matt Gillett, Celinde Schoenmaker, Alex Banks, Emma Kingston, Rob Houchen, Johnny and Lucy Vickers, Giovanni Spano and Tasha Jenkins, Louise Jones, Louise Pentland, Sophie Isaacs, Becky Lock and, of course, my bestest friend of them all, Edgar the Cat.

Finally, thank you to you for choosing to read this book. Whether you picked up this book because you've been with me from the start or whether this book was just another on your TBR pile, thank you all the same. ♥

ONE PLACE. MANY STORIES

Bold, innovative and
empowering publishing.

FOLLOW US ON:

@HQStories